CHESS

CANDACE ROBINSON

AMBER R. DUELL

FOR HAYLEY

CHAPTER ONE

CHESS
BEFORE

Everything in Ivory was so … *pristine*. White and silver and sickeningly clean. Every time Chess crossed the border from Scarlet, he was overcome with the desire to soil it, even in some small way. Now, he was sullying a set of satin sheets. The vampire riding him—*what was her name again?*—moaned as he grabbed handfuls of her tight arse.

His gaze shifted from her perky breasts to the ceiling of her home and how the plaster had been artfully molded into scallops spreading away from the simple chandelier. *Fuck.* If he was noticing the décor, he wasn't into this. Accepting the invitation into this female's bed had sounded like a good idea at the time, but he'd only just finished drinking from a donor's neck. The feeding had fueled his lust as the blood had powered his body, and the voluptuous brunette had made the offer at the precise moment.

Now, boredom stirred.

Not bored. Preoccupied, he decided as the female made slow, grinding circles on top of him. He needed to finish this so he could do the job he was tasked with. The one his mother—the Queen of Scarlet—had given him. He scowled. Best not to think about his mother at the moment unless he wanted to leave with aching balls.

Chess growled and flipped the female over, setting her on her hands and knees. She gasped, then groaned as he slammed back inside her. Holding her hips, he pumped into her over and over, harder and faster, until his release barreled through him. He squeezed his eyes shut and thrust one final time, emptying himself into her, with a low grunt.

"Already?" she asked, peering over her shoulder at him in disbelief.

He snorted. They'd been at it for over an hour, and though he could last twice as long, he was running late. "Sorry," he said, sounding every bit as insincere as he felt, but he didn't give a fuck. "Things to do, places to be."

Climbing off the bed, he gathered his clothes, stopping only long enough to step into his black trousers, before heading for the bedroom door. She huffed in irritation as he slipped into the hallway, but by the time he reached the female's front door, she was finishing herself off, if her moans were any indication. At least she hadn't bothered to ask him to stay.

Chuckling to himself, Chess made it to the street. The home was nestled between a bakery, meant for the mortal donors who either lived in or visited Wonderland, and an art studio. All of the buildings on the block were white marble, veined silver, with large frosted windows and steep roofs. In the distance, he could barely make out the peaks of the Ivory Palace. Unlike the one in Scarlet that loomed over the city from atop a cliff, Queen Ever's residence was only a short walk outside the city.

He hummed to himself as he meandered back to the place where he'd hidden his attire. The white suit and silver tie would help him blend in with the citizens of Ivory as they readied for the royal ball, and the mask he'd chosen was a silver-plated cat. Since it covered nearly half his face, no one would recognize him. Especially with his hair pulled back and brown contacts hiding his yellow eye color. Not that his mother cared if anyone knew who he was. It mattered to Chess, though, but only because it would make it easier to blend in at the palace if he looked the part. He'd always lived by the motto: *work smarter, not harder.*

The fast-paced violin notes drifted around him from streets away as he changed quickly in an alleyway, tucking his black vest and trousers behind the same planter where the costume had been. Finally, he hid the dagger he would use to take Ever's heart inside his jacket. Then Chess slipped silently back onto the empty alabaster streets. Most vampires seemed to already be at the palace given the lack of souls in his sight. Shops were shuttered and windows dark. Before, when he'd joined the female at her home, the city had been bustling with costumed bodies and laughter.

Soon, they would all be subjects of Scarlet. The Queen of Hearts had waited nearly a year for the opportunity to have Chess sneak into the enemy's lair. She'd plotted and schemed with Rav while Chess … well, his *plan* was a simple four steps.

One—*Attend the party.*
Two—*Find Ever.*
Three—*Kill Ever.*
Four—*Flee.*

He was no coward, of course, but he wasn't a fool either. Murdering the White Queen in her own palace would bring every guard down on his arse—at least the ones who hadn't turned on their queen already. Once Ever was dead, her prick of a brother could step right into the role of ruler. Rav was the next in line to rule after she was gone, which meant the hostile takeover of Ivory would have a peaceful transition. Hypothetically. Rav didn't necessarily want to sit on the throne—he just wanted Ever to shut the fuck up about human consent before they were turned.

But none of it mattered to Chess. As always, he was just along for the ride. His mother, Imogen, had disappeared when he was eight years old, only for her to drag him to Wonderland once he'd turned twenty-two. *Following* her and Rav's murder of his father, who had become King of Scarlet after abandoning Chess as a baby. Losing his shitty mortal life and his shitty life prospects wasn't a hardship. He'd never felt anchored to anyone or anything before, so he embraced the carefree lifestyle in Wonderland. Feeding, fucking, and exploring until his heart was content, all for the small price of murdering a few of his mother's enemies. His mother would rule alongside the white-haired fucker and Chess would play. It worked well for everyone.

As he finally reached the edge of the royal grounds, he paused to study the exterior for plausible escape routes. Any of the rounded first floor windows would give him easy access to run, but jumping from the second and third floors could result in minor injuries as each pane of glass was capped with tiers of carved spikes. Together, they appeared like silver vines climbing up the sides of the building. Beautiful and deadly, just how Chess preferred. The most stunning things in Wonderland had both qualities and he made it his mission to track them down. Fuck them, study them, sometimes kill them…

The most troubling obstacle he faced was the silver moat surrounding the grounds. If he didn't get back across the drawbridge in time, he would have to swim. He would never admit it, but water was the one fear he hadn't been able to overcome after turning immortal. When a bunch of older street youths had tossed him into the Thames at twelve, he'd nearly died. Sure, he'd figured out how to swim that day, but he never looked at water the same again.

Adjusting the cat mask on his face, Chess took one step onto the drawbridge, then another and another, ignoring the gleaming water on either side of him until he was finally across. The prince released a small breath and entered the bustling castle through the rounded doorway. Marble floors shone underfoot and a massive chandelier with sconces shaped like lilies dangled above. Delicate violets hung in garlands around the ceilings to add a splash of color to the otherwise monochromatic space.

It wasn't his first time inside, but when he'd visited with his mother for *negotiations*, all had been still. Now the sound of chatter, laughter, and pleasured moans joined in with the orchestra's classical tune. Masked vampires filled the entire entry, spilling into rooms on either side. There were foxes and wolves, full-faced masks and half-masks, silver and white. A female with purple hair—Maddie—skipped across the room beside her pink-haired sister, Mouse, both wearing elaborate hats in addition to their masks.

Chess ignored the Mad Hatter and her Dormouse of a sister by plucking up a goblet of warmed blood from a tray as a servant passed. He then inhaled the wonderful metallic scent. Where had Ever come up with enough fresh human blood to serve so many? Not quite the humanitarian as she pretended to be. Only turning willing humans to serve them—*fah.* Immortality was a gift. It was only fair that the newly-turned had to serve the one who gave it to them. Murdering mortals, however, seemed to be acceptable. It would take fully draining at least five dozen adults to give everyone a single glass, unless they only took a small amount from hundreds of donors.

How, Chess wondered absently, *did Ivory have so many willing mortals living in a city that feasted on them?* At the Ruby Heart Palace, there was no confusion about where humans stood. They were food, not servants or friends.

Brushing away the thoughts, Chess slinked farther into the palace in search of Ever. He moved along a wall of full-length mirrors and sterling busts of former Ivory monarchs. Bodies swayed around him, knocking his goblet more than once. Blood sloshed over the sides, sliding down the backs of his fingers. He switched hands and licked the precious liquid off.

"How do you like the vintage?" came a soft, regal voice.

Chess spun to find a female smiling brightly at him from behind a silver lace mask, her eyes a deep brown. *Ever.* The queen's white hair was plaited and artfully woven with a diamond crown atop her head. Her silver gown shimmered in the candlelight, hugging her perfect curves and highlighting her assets. Chess didn't bother to hide his perusal of her body. *A damn shame he didn't have a chance to fuck her.*

"An elderly woman, if I had to guess," he mused.

"Perhaps," she answered, swirling her own goblet. The blood clung to the sides. "There were many donors." She looked him over and cocked her head. "Who are you?"

"I could tell you, but that would take all the fun out of wearing a mask," he whispered with a smirk.

A wide grin crossed her face. "Ah, so does that mean you don't know who I am?"

"Perhaps I don't," he teased, sipping at his drink. "How about you give me a tour and we can chat more? It's my first time attending one of your balls."

Ever plucked the goblet from his hand—her warm fingers brushing his, sending a heat straight to his cock—and set them both down on a nearby table. "I don't normally give tours, but for you, I suppose I will." She leaned in and murmured, her hot breath hitting his mouth, "But only because you're wearing a mask of my favorite animal."

"Does that earn me a *private* tour?" Chess purred, imitating a cat, and Ever trailed a hand down his arm, tantalizingly slow.

"Oh, indeed. A very *personal* tour." She smiled coyly and backed up three steps before turning with the unspoken order for him to follow.

Chess watched the Ivory queen sashay through the crowd, his eyes studying her bare legs as she nodded at those who caught her attention. Alas, there wouldn't be time for him to tear the gown from her body, slide his hands down her curves, explore the swells of her breasts, and fill her with his hard length. She smelled of lilies and, he was sure, would taste just as sweet. He'd wasted too much time fucking around earlier. *Ah, well.* There was plenty of hot arse back in Scarlet, and the prince had no trouble filling his bed at home.

Sliding between party-goers, he followed Ever from one white and silver room to another. Each resembled the last. Colorless, soulless. Even the room with a variety of stringed instruments was bland with its white and silver violins and cellos. They needed to add more than the splash of color the violets gave in the entry way—the palace needed paint, fabric dye, and richly stained woods. He could solve those problems once Ivory was absorbed by Scarlet and make this place less of a mausoleum.

When Ever finally opened a door near the back of the palace and disappeared into the garden, he smirked behind his mask. It seemed she found him just as attractive… Perhaps a *little* time to play first wouldn't hurt—there were countless places he could fuck Ever without being seen. Against the pillars of the gazebo, bent over one of the granite benches, on the edge of the large fountain. Shit, he would even take her on the ground amidst the blooming flowers since none of them had thorns like the rose bushes back home.

"Such a lovely garden," he murmured as they ventured to where they were alone. There were hydrangeas and hyacinths, tulips and lilies. No roses, though, and he wondered briefly if that was because Imogen was so fond of them.

"Isn't it?" Ever hopped up to sit on the edge of a low, ivy-covered wall. Flowers budded among the foliage, promising future white blossoms.

With a chuckle, Chess prowled closer, toying with her. Ever reached out and took his arms, tugging him closer, then ran her hands up to his shoulders. Her light lily scent became stronger, intoxicating, his mind clouding. Chess leaned down so she could wrap her fingers around the back of his neck. He set his palms on both sides of her hips and studied her plump lips.

"So tall," she murmured and leaned toward him. Her palms skimmed his neck and down his chest, his eyes fluttering. "And so *strong.*"

Chess licked his lips, bringing them a breath away from hers while she continued to explore his body with exquisite movements. His cock stirred as she glided her fingers lower, to the button of his trousers, then dragged them back up, teasing him.

"How about a kiss?" he asked, surprising himself. What the fuck was he doing? Kissing was usually the last thing on his mind and he never bothered to ask with words.

In answer, she pushed him back and rammed her knee into his groin.

"What the fuck?" he groaned, doubling over in pain.

Ever shoved him sideways so he tumbled to the ground, her form looming over him. With a knife in her hand. "Did you think I wouldn't learn about the assassination planned for tonight, Princeling?" She threw the knife into the air, the blade spinning, and she caught it.

He chuckled despite the ache radiating through his groin. He should've known she hadn't singled him out so quickly and gotten him alone out of lust. Ever was said to be a virgin queen, but he didn't believe that one bit. *Thinking with my cock again.*

But he wouldn't fail in his task.

Steeling himself, he pushed away the pain and leapt at her, grabbing her wrists. Fighting her so close to the palace was bound to get him caught. If the wrong guards noticed, he was fucked, so he began dragging her farther into the garden, holding her tightly so she was unable to use the knife.

Ever twirled away, ripping herself from his grip, her dress whirling around her, and brought her arm up. The blade—*a second blade*—pierced his chest. Pain flared through him, hot and sharp. *Sloppy,* he chastised himself just as the metal cut through flesh and scraped at his bones. Chess grunted and fell back into the grass. Ever glared down at him with icy brown eyes.

"Guards!" she shouted.

Fucking hell. There was a good chance the guards who had heard her would haul him off to the dungeon. He wasn't about to let himself be caught. Ripping the knife free of his chest, he took a garbled breath.

"Tell me, was this your mother's idea or my brother's?" Ever asked curiously as a flurry of movement caught his eye.

When six familiar guards surrounded them, a smug grin tugged at the corners of Chess's mouth. "Wouldn't you like to know?"

"Arrest him," Ever snapped, seemingly at the end of her patience.

Only the guards didn't move toward him. They moved toward *her*.

"Rav may be an arse," Chess said as he tucked Ever's knife into his belt, "but he has an equal claim to your throne." The bastard hadn't wanted it before, choosing Imogen over the crown, but now the couple felt no need to choose between territories. Why would they when they could have it all? "I guess you didn't know that he still has friends in Ivory."

A flash of panic crossed Ever's face and she whirled, fleeing back into the castle. Chess held up his hand to stop the guards from following her. "I never turn down a game of cat-and-mouse," he said, pulling his feline mask away from his face. She wouldn't get far and it would—dare he say it—be *fun* to chase down the proud queen. *Run, mouse. Run.*

CHAPTER TWO

EVER

PRESENT DAY

A queen didn't always wear a crown because she wanted to. Sometimes the world required it.

Ever never asked to be the White Queen of Wonderland. Never chose it. But she fulfilled the duty nonetheless because she wanted to keep humans safe. Not from her bite, or her kill, but from becoming immortal if they didn't choose it. Being a vampire wasn't a natural sort of thing, so forethought was necessary, the decision conscious, just as both she and her twin brother, Rav, had chosen. Before the Red Queen murdered the former White King and White Queen, the royals had waited until the siblings were ready to turn them. But karma came to the Red Queen when she met her own demise from a murderous beastie. *Thank you, Jabberwocky, for that glorious and vicious kill.*

Ever peered around one of Ivory's rather ridiculously large

tree trunks, her gaze settling on *him*. Chess. *Surprise, surprise, Princeling. I do believe I owe you your death.* He was hiding from the Kingdom of Scarlet after being accused of murdering his mother, Imogen, the Queen of Hearts—who'd ripped the bloody organ out of so many.

She watched as he stood in front of the glistening silver lake, the gray of the world growing darker as night descended, and peeled his black vest from his broad shoulders. He shook his head, his chestnut hair framing his chin and neck. She rolled her eyes. Who was he trying to impress with no one else around? The water? Apparently, he assumed the lake that would be running its liquid hands up his chiseled body needed to be impressed by his presence. Conceited prick.

Time to die.

Ever tiptoed in his direction until she was close, so close that her digits could easily brush his bare back before digging her fingernails in to tear off his flesh.

The wind blew past them and Chess tilted his head back, inhaling the air without turning around. "You found me."

"That I did, Princeling. I won't ask for a kiss as you did with me, I'll just get on with it instead." This time she didn't use a dagger to stab him in the chest. She thrust her hand forward, breaking through his rib cage, gripping his still-beating heart, and ripped the warm organ from its home.

Ever spun him around to face her. His lips were parted, his eyes wide as he stared at the thick crimson sliding down her arm and dripping to the ground.

"I didn't miss your heart this time," she cooed. Chess's knees buckled and his body collapsed to the dirt with a *thump*.

A rustling stirred at the edge of the forest. Ever dropped the heart and darted away from the prince's still body to duck behind a tree. Out from the tall silver and white bushes came a male, shoving his long white hair with red tips behind his shoulder. *This is the perfect day.*

Rav—her twin—stopped, hovering over Chess's dead

body, but she couldn't focus on the fact that he was her brother…

He was now her enemy, especially after turning her own guards against her in the past. Before she could surrender to her thoughts of thinking of him as family, Ever leapt out from her hiding place and slammed her feet into his back while her hands gripped the sides of his head. She used him for balance as he shouted curses at her, but his words ceased, became trapped in his mouth, after tearing his head from his body in one easy motion. Rav fell to the ground beside Chess. *Glorious.*

"Dear, deceitful brother." She grinned as blood leaked from Rav's neck wound, pooling at her feet. "Goodbye."

"You did it, Ever, but you weren't the one to rip out my heart as you'd dreamt about, were you, darling?" Imogen purred, appearing out of thin air in front of her. The dead Scarlet queen's crimson curls hung down her back, and she wore a silky red dress with a low v-cut that went past her navel, exposing her milky skin.

"Bloody hell," Ever growled, pushing away what had been a wonderful fantasy until Imogen had rudely invaded it. Couldn't she remain dead in someone else's daydreams?

Ever lifted the white queen chess piece that she always carried in her pocket for luck. She'd been toying with it for what had to have been hours while lying in bed, unable to sleep, only thinking of things she wished would come to fruition. It had been a while since she'd rested in a proper bed, not since she lived in the Ivory Palace.

Nearly four years had passed since Ever had stepped foot inside Wonderland. She had spent most of her time tucked away in the mortal world, hidden inside a safe house like a coward. Until recently, when she reconnected with an old friend and discovered the Queen of Hearts had been murdered. Come to find out, it had been Maddie who had done the marvelous deed.

There was so much Ever had missed, and if she'd known her friend Mouse had been taken, that Maddie had been banished to a cottage in Scarlet, she would've returned sooner. *Should've checked in on them.* But there was still the part of her that didn't want to face her brother because that blasted piece of her still loved the fool. Wonderland hadn't changed him. He'd changed himself. He'd never cared about ruling before, but from her old friend, she learned he was planning on joining all of Wonderland's territories since he was the only ruler left.

Ever squeezed the chess piece, to the point that if she pressed any harder, her strength would break it. She wanted revenge against Rav, but she also wanted Chess.

In the past, the prince had never once approached her. He'd always watched her when they'd been at parties, just as she'd watched him. She'd waited for him to slink up and attempt to woo her, and on the night of her masquerade ball—when he tried to retrieve her heart—was the moment she'd taken matters into her own hands. Because she'd expected betrayal from him, she was prepared to stab the prince, but then she'd been caught off guard when her staff had taken her brother's side. She should've ripped off Chess's head or tore out his heart before escaping.

Releasing a huff, Ever sat up and pressed her back against the ornate headboard. She was safe once again, and she was tired of it, tired of not doing anything. Lingering in her Wonderland safe house wasn't the answer. Her friends were safe, and she wouldn't risk them.

Ever shoved the silky sheets aside and pushed up from the bed. Most of the safe houses only had the necessities, some more, but this one was like a small palace underground.

Grasping the edges of her lacy white nightgown, Ever drew it over her head, knowing she couldn't parade across Wonderland wearing anything ivory in color. She tugged on the blue jeans from the floor, followed by her *Dracula* T-shirt—that made her smirk—and a pair of checkered Vans.

She scooped up the black wig and shoved her hair into its bothersome depths. The thing was itchy and hot and, eventually, she would set fire to it.

Ever tucked the chess piece into her pocket and lifted her backpack. As she pulled open the door, the main glistening, white room sat empty for everyone except for one immortal at the table in the middle of the area.

Ferris.

She blew out a breath, alerting him to her presence. Ferris's hand stilled on a notebook he was sketching in and he hurried to shut it. His brown gaze peered up at her and an eyebrow arched. Since she'd seen him last as a mortal, he appeared mostly the same. Some vampires inherited different hair colors, eye colors, but he'd gained neither. For her, it was her hair, which had become white as snow instead of the deep murky brown it had once been.

"You're not sleeping?" Ever asked and stepped toward him.

He ran a hand through his short, dark hair. "Nope, not today."

Earlier, Ferris had been mostly quiet, but his eyes had drifted to Mouse every so often. Always drifting to Mouse, even back at the club before Ever went into hiding. When he'd been human, after Maddie and Mouse brought her to a run-down club, Ever had drank from him with her friends. He'd had a heavenly taste, but she'd seen the truth in his blood, the pain, something only a few royals could do. After that, she didn't want to drink from him, didn't want to see his suffering again.

Ever sank down in a chair beside him and took out a pack of blood and her canteen of water. She figured she better get her strength up before leaving.

"How do you like being a vampire?" Ever asked to break up the silence.

"It's better than being human." He paused, and bit his lip, his eyes meeting hers. "You never told them what you saw?"

Ever shook her head, thinking about him at nineteen … the car wreck … his pregnant girlfriend dying. At the club, he'd seen the pity in her eyes when her gaze had unintentionally latched onto the promise ring he'd worn on a chain around his neck, the one he'd given to his dead girlfriend. He'd somehow known what she'd seen and an understanding had passed between them in that moment. "It's not my place."

Ferris let out a relieved sigh. "Thank you."

"No thank you needed." If he wanted to tell Maddie and Mouse more about his tragic past, then he could. But the past was the past. No, that was a lie. Sometimes the past did require a bit of betraying. Chess… Rav...

A low, groggy moan came from one of the bedrooms where Mouse was sleeping. "How is she?" Ever glanced back at Ferris. He'd been with Mouse at the palace for two years as Imogen's Knave, while she'd been in a cell. Ever also learned Imogen had taken him to her bed, then fucked him before turning him into her vampire servant. He'd done it all to protect Mouse, to try and help her escape. If anyone was a damn prince, it was Ferris, especially since she'd known through his blood that he'd never wanted to get close to another female again.

"She's a fighter," he said softly. "The palace wasn't good for either of us, but even with some of the shitty things I had to do there, I'm glad I was with her."

The former White King and Queen had never mistreated Ever or Rav. The twins had been made into a prince and princess after falling into Wonderland, but the royals' servants had always had a choice before becoming immortal.

"I need you to do something for me," Ever finally said.

Ferris threw his head back and rolled his eyes at the pearl chandelier hanging above them. "Bloody hell, don't tell me you're leaving already."

"Promise me you'll watch over them while I'm gone."

His gaze fell back to hers and understanding was there. "I will."

Ever finally mixed the blood and water, then drank the thick concoction down. Ferris's fingers tapped against his closed notebook, and she wondered what was inside. But she didn't ask, didn't want to know if his demons were in there like they'd been inside his head.

"Do you miss the drums?" She smiled, remembering the one image he'd held that helped him through his past before Mouse had saved him from his overdose.

Ferris nodded, giving her a curious look at the sudden change in subject. "I do."

"When I return to the Ivory Palace one day, you will come and bring a new set with you." She needed new guards anyway.

His lips tilted up at the edges. "They'll be fucking loud."

"Good. I'm sick of quiet." Ever smiled and stood from her seat to bid Mouse and Maddie goodbye before returning to the mortal world.

Ever adjusted her backpack, then left Ferris to himself. Mouse's door was still wide open and the White Queen walked in, finding her friend lying asleep in bed, her breaths even. Instead of the serene expression her face normally held in the past as she slept, a scowl sat in its place. Ever wondered what she was dreaming, or perhaps, what the nightmare was about. Her stomach tightened at the thought that she was the reason this had happened to Mouse … and to Maddie.

She stepped farther into the room toward the bed—the area was similar to where she'd slept, except the bed and wardrobe were both obsidian, while everything else was a glossy white. Mouse's pink braid rested over her shoulder, and on the bedside table, her blue and yellow caterpillar, Des, lay atop a bright green leaf, fast asleep too. Maddie had told Ever that her sister acquired the creature while a prisoner inside the

Ruby Heart Palace. A caterpillar in Wonderland wasn't destined to become a butterfly as in the mortal world. They didn't have those insects here, so instead, it would remain a beautiful wingless creature for all eternity.

"Mouse," Ever whispered, lightly shaking her friend's shoulders, and Mouse jerked forward. "I wanted to tell you goodbye, but I'll only be gone temporarily."

Mouse blinked, her violet eyes glazed, and let out a small yawn. "I can come."

"No, you will not. You still need time to heal." She didn't mean the physical wounds. In the past, Ever wouldn't have minded her coming, but not this time, not after the suffering Mouse had endured at the hands of Rav and the Queen of Hearts. She bent forward and kissed the forehead of her friend, who still smelled of gardenias like she always had.

Mouse nodded, but her lips pulled into a tight line, hesitant, as she laid back down. Des lifted her small head and peered at Mouse, as though checking to make sure she returned to sleep all right. Mouse's breaths were already even so Ever padded to the next room, then knocked lightly on the door. It only took a moment for Maddie to answer dramatically.

When Ever arrived earlier to the safe house, her friend had appeared just the same as the day the White Queen escaped the palace—purple curls, the tilt of her hat, her attire. They'd been friends for over two hundred years. She'd found her in Wonderland, lost, starving. Ever had pretended to be a normal female since she'd been acclimated to vampires using her because of her title. And when she'd revealed herself to be a queen, Maddie had treated her the same, never differently, always honest. Then she'd brought her sister, Mouse, to the palace, and like that, Ever had found true family again.

"You're leaving already?" Maddie asked, pressing a hand on her hip, her honey-colored eyes meeting Ever's. Her usual violet attire was replaced with a long black shirt that must've belonged to Noah—the human Maddie had turned immortal due to a wretched incident where he'd almost died at the hands of Imogen's friend, Osanna. Ever hated that bitch.

"Rav's heart awaits my stake," Ever said with a smile.

"That bastard deserves two stakes," Maddie sang. Her expression turned serious as she cocked her head. "Let me come with you."

"We discussed this earlier, and you agreed to wait. We can't show all our cards at once, so it will be only me for now. However, if I don't return in a month, then that means something's wrong. You can't stay in hiding forever or as long as I did … like a coward." Ever gritted her teeth at how long she'd been gone, how much time had been wasted.

"You're not a coward. If something does happen to you, we will murder your brother with all the hatpins in Wonderland." Maddie wrapped her arms around Ever and held her tight, her comforting cherry scent enveloping them. "Now, let me at least walk you to the door."

"I wouldn't mind that at all." Ever released Maddie and headed toward the stairs. Ferris was already gone from the table and must've silently slipped back into Mouse's room to watch over her.

They walked up the glistening white steps together in silence, and when Ever grasped the door handle, she glanced back at Maddie. "You know this, but don't open the door for anyone unless you hear my knock. Even then, remember to aim your gun at the heart."

"Or my sewing needles." Maddie grinned and patted Ever's shoulder. "Now, go kill that bastard and reclaim your kingdom. But if you need us, we shall be ready."

They were all wanted. Mouse for escaping, Maddie for hiding her, Ferris for fleeing with Noah's sister. She assumed Noah might also be since she'd recently learned Rav knew he'd been turned by Maddie. It wouldn't be hard for Rav to put two and two together. However, Rav didn't seem to know that it was Noah and Maddie who'd helped Mouse escape.

Ever smiled and gave Maddie a small wave as she ventured out into the night, knowing exactly where her first stop would be.

CHAPTER THREE

CHESS

The inside of the London cab smelled like old cigarettes and peppermint, nearly blinding Chess to the scent of the driver's blood. He was wrinkled, bald, and at his age, probably full of prescription drugs to keep him alive, so he wouldn't be on the menu anyway. Chess enjoyed the occasional drug-riddled human, but the sort who would give him an enjoyable high— not thin blood or lower cholesterol. They made the blood taste downright atrocious.

Brick buildings flickered by the window. Hedgerows, street lights, and all the *cozy* trappings of a mortal life. He hated it. All of it. The flower boxes, the warmly lit rooms in the homes. Perfect family cohabitation. It was much better when everyone lived their own lives, did their own thing, and relied on themselves. Like him. Imogen was his mother and he had loved her, but they hadn't truly *needed* each other. The image of her heart in his hand flashed through his mind, and he shoved it away as he always did before an unwanted emotion could swallow him whole.

"Turn here," Chess instructed.

"Have a destination yet?" the man asked in a raspy voice, taking the turn.

Chess had flagged him down near a train station and simply told him to drive when he climbed into the backseat an hour ago. There was nowhere to go—at least nowhere he felt safe. Every club he knew in London played host to vampires from Scarlet and they would undoubtedly turn him into Rav. It was bad enough he was slumming in the basement of an abandoned home outside the city, but he needed to feed. There hadn't been time to gather supplies when he'd fled Wonderland and the bleeding bastard who currently ruled Scarlet, so he'd had no powdered blood to sustain himself. He hadn't dared return to Wonderland either.

"No," he replied, weariness settling into his bones. "Just keep going."

The driver shrugged and continued on while Chess turned his attention to the streets. They passed people in groups of two or more but none alone. How was he to lure someone into an alley for a bite this way? He could compel an entire group, but it took more energy than he had. He could manage two humans at most tonight, and one of them needed to be his driver because shockingly enough, he had no money. He scowled, knowing there were hundreds of pounds sitting in his dresser back at the Ruby Heart Palace in case he wanted to play with mortals without compulsion. Buy their drinks, buy them dinner, play the long con... He sighed. The only ones getting conned now were the vampires and mortals in Scarlet.

Everyone would believe Rav when he claimed Chess murdered their queen. It wouldn't even be that shocking, given how ruthless Scarlet could be. Yet, as callous as Chess was, she was still his mother. Sure, she had abandoned him when he was eight years old. But his father had left them both when he was only a baby to become Scarlet's king, meaning his upbringing was less than ideal, sleeping on the streets, pick-pocketing, or worse—whatever he'd needed to do to eat. To survive. But that was in the past. Imogen had killed the father he'd never met and come back to give Chess the best gift of all: eternal life. He'd forgiven her easily after that. She'd loved him enough to come back for him, after all, but he'd had no desire to wear her crown.

Maddie didn't seem the type to want it either, though, and she'd slaughtered his mother. Granted it was likely to save her sister… If he hadn't left to track down Ever, he might've been there to stop it from happening. He'd trusted the Mad Hatter. Trusted that, in exchange for allowing her to save Mouse from the dungeons, that she would give up Ever's true location. He'd traveled for days, searching up-and-down the Red Queen's territory for this elusive safe house, only to return empty handed … to find Imogen dead. He hadn't told Rav because he was the one who wanted to find Maddie, and he hadn't wanted the bastard to discover that he was partly the cause by allowing the Hatter to retrieve her sister. Guilt twisted in his chest, and he rubbed the sensation away.

First, he needed to deal with the back-stabbing arse. Then he would take care of that purple-haired twat.

No—first he needed to feed.

Rolling the sleeves of his white dress shirt, Chess sighed a second time. "Take me to the closest club outside of London."

"You got it," the driver said, sounding relieved to have an end to this trip.

Chess settled into the backseat and stared at the cab's roof. What was Rav's game? Did he *really* think Chess had killed Imogen? After centuries together, even while barely tolerating the other, the accusation felt like a betrayal. Surely, he knew Chess better than that? And if he *did* know the prince hadn't murdered his own mother, what was his motive? Even if Rav was desperate for a crown, he had one waiting for him in Ivory once Ever ran from her kingdom. Right after she'd stabbed

Chess... He rubbed at his chest, thinking about the old wound, that night, her face... Since then, he'd wanted to find her *desperately*.

"Like sister, like brother," he grumbled to himself.

Ever had at least had the decency to stab him in the chest with a real blade. He had to respect her for that anyway. Before he fled, he'd thought she was a coward for hiding, but he understood now. It wasn't about being a coward, it was about being strategic. There was no path to achieve revenge if one was dead. And, before he met his final end, Chess had every intention of burning Rav alive.

"Here we are," the driver said, pulling the prince from his thoughts.

Chess leaned forward and met the man's eyes in the rearview mirror. "Thank you for the ride," he cooed, infusing his voice with his vampiric influence, letting the power smooth his tone. "I've had a rough night, so you won't charge me for the trip."

"No, I won't," the mortal agreed jovially, as if it were his idea. "You have a good night."

"You too," Chess said with a smirk and slipped out of the cab. He stood in front of a large gray building with darkened windows. The loud, thumping music from inside promised a bloody good time, so he approached the line of humans standing outside. The hunger growing in him was a stark reminder that there was no time to waste waiting alongside them. He cracked his neck and with a quick burst of speed, entered the club, unbeknownst to the muscular bouncer.

Dozens of humans packed the dance floor. Smoke swirled around their ankles while neon lights flashed overhead in time with the bass. A woman with two twisted knots atop her head stood on a raised platform, headphones pressed to one ear, tweaking the music on her turntables. Chess inhaled, closing his eyes for a moment to revel in the sweet scent of her blood, though faint since it was still in the vein. It only made his mouth water more. *Fuck*, he was hungry.

He opened his eyes and met the piercing blue gaze of a man across the room. The way the blond mortal sucked on the straw in his drink sent a rush of heat straight to Chess's cock… It had been way too long since he'd sank his fangs into someone's soft flesh. Chess grinned and prowled straight for his conquest, avoiding the sea of dancing bodies.

"Hey there." He reached the area near the bar, resting an elbow on a tall table, and stood in front of the delectable mortal. Smudged glitter shone across both of his cheekbones under the flickering lights. "You alone tonight?"

"Not anymore." The man stood a little straighter and scanned Chess up and down. "What's your name?"

"Charles," Chess lied.

"Alec," he said and stepped closer, sliding a calloused hand up Chess's arm. "Want to dance?"

Chess plucked the drink from Alec's hand and set it on one of the high-top tables along the wall, then flicked a glance at his lips. "I have a much better plan."

The twinkle in the mortal's eyes told the prince that he understood exactly what he meant. Chess leaned in and inhaled Alec's scent across his neck, the delicious blood lingering beneath his flesh. Playfully nudging the man backward, Chess soon had him up against a wall where he slowly ran his tongue up Alec's skin, tasting the salty sweetness. The mortal was practically begging to become Chess's personal drink. The prince kissed his way up the mortal's throat to his shapely lips. His fangs threatened to make an appearance as he tasted him further, twisting their tongues together. He held himself back, warming Alec up so the influence would be easier to apply. Not that it was a hardship. The human was an expert with his tongue, slipping it between Chess's lips, sliding and sucking. When he felt the bulge in Alec's trousers press against his leg, his fangs dropped of their own accord.

Heat coursed through Chess, as he was starved for more than blood…

Chess grabbed the back of Alec's neck to steady himself and to keep him from pulling away as the prince trailed his lips across the mortal's cheek to reach his ear. "Let me feed," he said, using the last bit of influence that his strength allowed. If anyone at the bar or on the dance floor noticed, they would never know what he was *really* doing.

Then he sank his fangs into the human's soft flesh—hot, metallic liquid burst over his tongue. Chess moaned, his eyes fluttering as the warm crimson glided down his throat. Mouthful after mouthful of utter bliss. The prince's cock grew painfully hard when Alec groaned, not in pain, but in pleasure. Drinking a final gulp, Chess flicked his tongue over his bite marks and retracted his fangs, power coursing through him.

"Thanks," he whispered while grinning.

"Shit," Alec breathed. "I don't know what that was, but it was fucking hot."

"Oh?" Chess quirked a brow. What sort of club was this exactly? He turned to take a second look at the clientele, but Alec tugged him, spinning him so his back was against the wall. The desperate look of *need* on his face sent a thrill through Chess. "*Oh?*"

Alec lunged forward and captured Chess's lips again, this time with more force. Chess would let the mortal have his fun, believing he was stronger, more dominant. If things continued, he could show him just who the alpha was later—*in private.* Alec's hands roamed the prince's chest, and soon, his mouth ventured to explore more of him as well. Nibbling Chess's ear, unbuttoning his shirt as he licked down his neck…

Chess's glazed expression drifted to the dance floor. The masses moved against each other, grinding, swaying. It hypnotized the prince as Alec sucked at his neck. *Damn,* he needed this. They were going to have to find an empty bathroom or dark alley soon so they could please each other properly.

A figure entered the dance floor. Two figures. One with obsidian hair and a short, black lacy dress, showcasing long legs, and the other, a dark-skinned male with his braids tied back. The couple danced along with the crowd yet there was *something* that caught his attention about them. The graceful movements, perhaps. But the hair on his arms now stood on end.

Vampires.

Fuckity-fuck. He had been so preoccupied by blood, so damn hungry, that he hadn't bothered to do a sweep of the club. They didn't seem to notice him, or, if they had, they didn't care. Still, it was better if he got out of there, just in case.

"Sorry," he said, extracting himself from Alec. "It's been fun."

Alec said something in protest, but Chess was already making his way toward the door. If the couple hadn't recognized him yet, he didn't want to tempt fate. Sparing them a last look before reaching the door, he froze. He squinted, his gaze stilling on the female's features. That heart-shaped face, those deep brown eyes, that pouty mouth he had asked to kiss, had wanted to kiss before taking her heart…

No.

It couldn't be … could it? Almost four years had passed since he'd seen the White Queen, but he'd seen her twin nearly every day for centuries. It was *Ever*. He didn't recognize the male with her, but who the fuck cared about him? He'd been searching her out for *years* and now he just *happened* to run into her? It wasn't like him to look a gift horse in the mouth.

"The enemy of my enemy…" he said to himself. With a grin, he buttoned his shirt as he backtracked to the bar, sitting on the stool to watch and wait. To plot how best to use this opportunity to his advantage.

CHAPTER FOUR

EVER

Silver trees with ivory leaves surrounded Ever, and the branches rustled violently, creating an interesting melody. It wasn't only her friends she'd missed over the years, but Ivory, more than she could've imagined.

After trudging through the forest for a long while, the grass rippled as the wind picked up even harder. Sharp rain fell from the dark sky, where the moon sat full and the stars shone brightly.

"Of course, it would storm at this moment," Ever grumbled, shaking her fist at whatever vampire gods might've been looking down on her.

Ivory's trees thinned, giving way to Scarlet's red and black ones. She picked up speed, traveling a good distance before her ability lagged, requiring her to stop. *Damn.* She wished the speed would've lasted longer so she could've gotten to her first destination quicker. The wildlife stayed hidden among the trees, peering at her as she passed. She caught sight of a crow, studying her, seeming as though it wanted to peck her eyes out. If she drew too close, the little bastard would try, but she would be faster.

"Yes, it's a lovely day, isn't it? Even though I'm a soggy mess." She couldn't help grinning at a bald squirrel baring its sharp teeth at her in a smile.

As Ever entered the kingdom of Scarlet, screams filled the air of the city. She didn't know whether it was a brawl, lovers role playing, or someone getting slaughtered. It was the usual dark melody of Scarlet accompanied by the scent of blood and decay. Tall black and red glossy stone buildings surrounded her, and ruby lanterns led her way to the specific house where she needed to stop for a moment. A three-story building with gargoyles perched at each corner of the slate roof and crimson curtains hanging from the large arching windows.

Bringing the tendrils of her dark wig forward to cover her face, she ascended the six steps, then lifted her hand to use the hideous snarling wolf knocker. Ever schooled her features but mentally rolled her eyes at the décor. It took a few moments before the unlatching of the lock sounded. The door swung open to a tall female staring at her with a pristinely arched green brow. Her long emerald hair matched that pompous brow perfectly, and her golden dress with a popped collar brushing her cheekbones made her look even more haughty.

"What do you want?" Osanna asked in a bored tone, barely scanning the White Queen over.

"So, you haven't found new help yet?" With a bit of grace, Ever moved the locks of her wig aside and lunged forward just as Osanna's eyes widened in recognition. Her hands easily grasped the vampire's head, and she ripped it off in one swift motion, a loud crunching sound echoing delightfully. Blood spilled down the throat of the headless body, the scent of metal filling the air, as it slumped to the ground with a perfect thump. Smiling, Ever tossed the head beside the cunning bitch, brushed her hands together, patted her lucky chess piece in her pocket, and whirled around before continuing through the city.

That was for Maddie and her new lover, Noah. Osanna had nearly killed him, leaving Maddie no other choice but to save him. Of course, there had been another choice … to let him die. Which was what Ever would've done by allowing nature to take its course, but perhaps, this once, she could agree that Maddie made the best decision she could in the situation, especially since the Hatter hadn't had the White Queen to confide in.

The rain slowed to a light mist, but Ever kept her head down as she passed several vampires carrying ice chests. Another vampire was fighting with a male over a mortal female. His hand shot forward, tearing open the male's chest while the woman screamed. Ever really needed to fix this calamity of a city. Things could be bloody without being so damn violent. Her wet hair hung in her face until she arrived at a portal leading to the mortal world. She would meet with her spy soon.

Beneath a gnarled, bat-infested scarlet tree, was a completely exposed dirt hole. In the mortal world, the portals were always hidden. She remembered the day she'd stumbled upon the one with her brother centuries ago. It had been in the woods behind their parents' home, and she'd slipped through while Rav had hurried to stop her from falling. However, they'd both fallen.

Most of this was her fault. If Rav had never gone down the hole with her, he would've never hurt Maddie—she wouldn't have been taunted by him all these years. But Maddie was happy, content, with Noah now, and Ever would hold onto that.

As she dropped to her knees and crawled through the dirt, a tingling sensation coursed through her. Bright green and red beetles scurried around her, their scuffing noises echoing.

At the end of the tunnel, bushes blocked her exit, and she pushed them back as she crawled the remainder of the way out into the night. Ever hoisted herself up to stand in a park surrounded by trees and a playground that looked as though it hadn't been used in quite some time. Brushing off her hands, she ran the short distance through the trees to her safe house near a lake.

A hidden door was buried at the base of a walnut tree farther away from where Londoners routinely ventured. Ever shoved her key in the lock of the camouflaged door and lifted the lid, letting the earthy smell caress her nose. She scurried inside and locked the latch, then trotted down the few steps to her small space. There wasn't much besides a mattress, pouches of dried blood, her viola, solo games, stacks of clothing and wigs, and a few other necessities. The past few years, she'd played solitaire so many times that she'd lost count, plucked the strings of her instrument just to hear any other noise besides her thoughts, breathing, and the mortal world's creatures above.

But tonight, there wasn't much time if she wanted to meet her spy. Pulling off her wet clothing, she rushed to get dressed for her mission: to begin taking back what was long overdue.

Ever adjusted her tight, sleeveless black dress and ran a hand through the dark locks of one of the new wigs from her stash. The other one was practically rubbish after the rain so she'd tossed it into a bin along the way to the club. It was easy to get things from the mortals—just influence them and they would give a vampire anything. But she tried only to take what was necessary, which had been more so lately.

Outside the gray, windowless building, loud beats from the music drifted on the breeze. Over the years, she tried and failed to appreciate most modern sounds. She preferred violas, violins, and the piano. Anything classical. Bach, Beethoven, Mozart. However, she did like the way Yo-Yo Ma ran his bow across his cello strings. It had been decades since she last went to one of his concerts.

Ever passed several women who appeared tipsy as they stumbled from the club. She entered the stone building, sweat and alcohol hitting her senses, along with something even more delicious. *Blood.* And *plenty* of the heavenly liquid. It had been years since smoking was allowed in establishments, and that was a good change because the odor had always wreaked havoc on her.

Ever's gaze locked with the bald bouncer's, and she used her influence to avoid paying and to gain access into the spacious room ahead of those waiting in line. He didn't hesitate as he let her pass, a distinct huff echoing from behind her. Neon lights flashed around the dark room, which was filled with warm bodies. So many mortals, the blood pumping in their veins, made her mouth water. Even though she'd drank plenty earlier, she wanted more, just one taste. But there wasn't time for it. She searched around the room, her gaze falling to a busy bar with a female bartender wearing a black bow tie, then to a male toying with the sound system as Ever looked for her vampire spy.

"Hello, beautiful," a deep voice said from behind her, wrapping his strong arm around her waist, "care to dance?"

"Sure." Ever smiled and turned around, finding a broad male in front of her with beaming dark brown eyes. His long braids were wrapped in a bun at his nape, and he wore tight trousers with a sleeveless shirt that showed off his ebony skin and bulging muscles.

March. Her spy and friend.

"Did you find what you were looking for?" March asked as he took her hand and led her into the middle of the club where people were drinking, grinding, kissing, and touching in secret places. She trusted March because she'd sired him long ago and knew his heart from what she'd seen in his blood. He was loyal to her, always had been. And she'd wished that he'd still been a servant in the palace when her guards had turned on her. Yet he'd left Wonderland years ago to live in the mortal world, and she hadn't reconnected with him until recently, when he'd told her about Imogen's death, Mouse being held prisoner, Chess accused of his mother's demise, and Rav's new plans for Wonderland.

"It took me a while, but I did," Ever said, biting her lip.

He brushed a lock of her wig over her shoulder. "I was about to come searching for you."

"Don't ever do that."

March used to attend the tea parties that Maddie and Mouse hosted at the Ivory Palace. He'd always yearned for more from Ever, but she couldn't give him what he wanted. They'd given each other oral pleasure a time or two, but even then, Ever refused to give herself to anyone fully. It wasn't that she didn't want to have sex with someone—it was that she couldn't trust most individuals. Not after having numerous vampires sent to her to get information, whether it had been from the Red Queen, the Queen of Hearts, her own damn brother, or just random vampires who'd wanted her kingdom for their own. But with March, she didn't want to hurt him by not feeling the same way, even though she had considered giving her body to him at least once.

"I discovered something new." He paused, drawing her close, his hand caressing her lower back. "Something you may find interesting."

"What do you know?" she asked, swaying side to side with him to the beats of the music.

March leaned in so his mouth was just below her ear, his lips brushing her neck. "He's using humans as servants now."

Rav. Ever inhaled sharply, her eyes widening. "What do you mean?"

"He's not changing them as he did before, but keeping

them influenced instead."

What the hell? Ever pulled back and took a deep swallow. "Like actual slaves?" Rav had all the guards and servants in the world, had *her* guards. Or not, since March had told her he'd murdered every single one of his guards and servants in Scarlet after Imogen died. But for some unknown reason, Rav had gotten her guards to turn on her.

March spun her in a circle. "Yep. He's not taken his beloved's death well, it seems."

Could her brother be any more of a bastard? Before, the vampires he and Imogen sired were given no choice physically, but at least they weren't slaves mentally. Just when Ever didn't believe things could get worse, they sure as bloody hell did.

"Anything else?" she asked.

"There might be something, but I need more time to figure it out." He bit his lip. "I just need to do this once more with you." His lips crashed to hers in a fierce kiss. She didn't hesitate as she kissed him back, her tongue dancing with his, her tugging him closer by his waistband so she could feel his hard length against her. Sparks didn't course through her veins from it, or vibrate through her heart, but it felt good nonetheless.

"I'll meet you again soon," Ever whispered near his ear— no mortal would be able to hear it, but a vampire's senses were far more superior. "In three days."

March gave her one last kiss before walking away, his arms flexing as he ventured through the crowd and out of the main room. She wished she could make herself feel something more for him because he was a good male, but she just … couldn't. She didn't think she would ever feel love for anyone. Not how Maddie practically glowed when she'd discussed Noah. But it didn't matter. She had herself and Wonderland to focus on, and that was good enough.

She allowed the music to fill her ears, let her body move

to the intense beats. For once, she truly absorbed the sounds and didn't compare it to the music she preferred to hear, somehow finding it not as tedious. But that might have been because of the intoxicating scent of the blood around her, enveloping her, getting her high from the enticing odor.

With a smile, she brought her gaze down from the ceiling and focused on the bar across the room, her gaze connecting with a lithe male sitting on a stool. She stilled, her lungs frozen.

The prince of Scarlet.

Chess wore attire that he never would've donned before— a white dress shirt with the sleeves rolled up, his chestnut locks pulled into a low ponytail, several layers loose and framing his face. He stared straight at her, his arms folded over his chest, and a smirk on his villainous face.

CHAPTER FIVE

CHESS

The color drained from Ever's face the moment she recognized Chess, and his grin grew wider. There she was, finally noticing him. Even though she was dressed in all-black attire, she was still as beautiful as a white rose. When he'd seen her last, she had been confident as she led him through her masquerade ball, into the garden. Confident as she kneed him in the groin and stabbed him in the chest. But then, her expression had shattered as the guards turned on her. It was good to see she hadn't forgotten him or the threat he'd brought—even if he was no longer working on his mother's orders.

The memory of his mother's body flashed through his mind. Her blood pooling across the marble floor, her chest gaping open, broken. The feel of her heart in his hand. Warm. Heavy. How her eyes had stared, lifeless and dull, up at the ceiling. The scene played out in his mind over and over ever since he'd walked in to find her dead, his body frozen in shock for the briefest of moments. A flood of grief threatened to swallow him. He shook off the memories—they would do him no good at the moment.

Seconds stretched between Chess and Ever, each feeling longer than the last. The impulse to tackle her right there in the crowded club and drag her home warred with the urge to let this play out. Bringing her back to Wonderland could potentially clear his name—*prove* he was still loyal to Scarlet and hadn't desired his mother's death. If he gave Rav everything he had planned to give his mother, perhaps he wouldn't try to frame Chess for her murder. If that was, in fact, what Rav was doing. If Chess knew whether the arse really believed he was responsible, things would be a lot easier to sort out. But, if Rav wanted the prince dead, he might spin the situation so it looked like Chess was working with Ever to murder Imogen.

Fucking bastard.

He needed to make a decision and make it quickly. Attacking Ever in the middle of a public, mortal space wasn't an option, but he knew she would never leave with him willingly. He sat on the bar stool and studied her every little movement. He ran his thumb across the seam of his mouth as he took in her lips, still parted in surprise, and the few strands of white hair sneaking out from beneath the dark wig.

Beside him, people called out drink orders. Liquid sloshed into glasses and ice clinked behind the bar, each tiny sound putting him more on edge. Ever had to be running through different escape options at the moment so he needed to act. Now—before she slipped through his fingers … *again.* He didn't have another four years to waste searching for her.

He sauntered toward her, the music booming around him, yet he heard every breath escaping her pretty mouth. Panic swirled in her eyes for the briefest moment before her expression smoothed. At least she wasn't bolting…

"Your Highness," he said with a small bow.

Ever straightened, pulling her shoulders back, her creamy skin flawless, the swells of her breasts begging to be touched. "Princeling," she replied through gritted teeth.

"I've been searching for you," Chess purred, skimming his index finger across his lower lip.

Her eyes narrowed. "I'm sure you have."

"My mother would love to have a chat with you," he said, testing her knowledge of recent events. Imogen wouldn't have wanted to talk to Ever and they both knew it. Given the chance, she would've attacked the White Queen so fast that she didn't see it coming.

"Mmm, yes, I'm sure she would have…" She paused and raised a brow as she inched closer to him. "If she were still alive."

"There are little birds singing in your ear then, eh?" He figured as much. There had been a vampire dancing with her—he could've very well been the one to have told her. Most of her own guards had turned on her, but that didn't mean Ever had no friends in Wonderland after Rav killed those still loyal to her. The crazy Hatter was long suspected of being a spy and, after she killed Imogen, Chess had little reason to doubt it despite Maddie's insistence that she didn't know where Ever was. *Liars and sneaks.*

A man in a mesh T-shirt stumbled into Ever, spilling his beer and knocking her into Chess. He caught her by the waist and they both stiffened, her breasts pressed firmly against his chest. The White Queen's lily scent drifted to his nostrils and, before he could draw the smell in further, she shoved him away. With lightning-fast reflexes, he latched onto her arm, taking her back three steps with him.

"Well, that wasn't very nice," Chess chided, his gaze locking onto her brown eyes.

"Let me go," she hissed.

Chess tightened his grip on her arm. "After nearly four years, I think you owe me a conversation at least. You did stab me, remember?"

"I owe you *nothing*. You deserved it." She fisted the front of his shirt and paused, seeming to remember they were in a mortal club, surrounded by humans. "And you took my throne."

Chess chuckled. "Did *I* take your throne?" He leaned down, his nose brushing the tip of hers. "As I recall, it was your brother who stole the allegiance of your guards. Whether or not my mother asked me to take your heart the night of the ball, your time as queen was over. You chose to flee that night instead of fighting to keep your crown, so don't push the blame onto me."

Ever was rather pretty when she was angry, despite the hideous wig. Color filled her cheeks and her eyes sparkled under the flashing white lights. It was much more attractive than her false seduction at the ball—just before she kneed his family jewels. As a betting male, he was willing to guess she was a spitfire in bed when she was upset. Under different circumstances, he might've even offered a good hate-fuck.

Alas, he was wanted in Wonderland, his mother was dead, and he had three scores to settle. If he played his cards right, Ever could lead him straight to Maddie, then help him destroy Rav. Followed, finally, by Ever's destruction. He owed it to his mother for failing to stop her death. Without any living monarchs in Wonderland, war would eventually break out, but what the fuck did he care? Chess had always enjoyed traveling through Wonderland and doing his own thing instead of playing at politics. Let the courts implode.

Ever opened her mouth to reply when the burly, tattooed bouncer from outside the door stepped up to them. "Everything okay here?"

"Yes," Chess and Ever answered in unison. Nosy mortal. Everything would be perfect once he convinced her to help him get revenge.

The bouncer looked between them for a moment. "You

better take the argument elsewhere."

"We're finished," Ever assured him, twisting her arm from Chess's grip as she released his shirt. She shot him a scathing look and stalked toward the door.

"Wait, darling," he called, flashing the bouncer a smile. "I have the keys to the flat."

Without wasting another second, he darted after her. He would be damned if she vanished again after all this time. Stepping to her side, he hooked his arm through hers and held tight as they exited the club. The line of humans waiting to get inside nearly wrapped around the side of the building now and a new bouncer had replaced the one who had interrupted them inside. Ever's features tightened, her teeth grinding as they passed beneath a softly lit street light. He felt her arm muscles flexing with the desire to rip him off her, but there were still too many humans.

"We need to talk," he said in her ear. "No fangs, no fights."

"Just words?" she snapped, keeping her gaze straight ahead to a narrow, dark alleyway across the street.

"Exactly." The violence would come later … after she helped him accomplish what he wanted. He didn't fail at the tasks his mother assigned him, and just because she was dead didn't mean he wasn't going to fulfill her wish to see Ever killed.

They stepped from the pavement, and she tightened her arm around his, her fingernails digging in to his flesh. "Like I would ever believe a word out of your mouth, Princeling."

He chuckled. Of course she wouldn't—just as he wouldn't believe her—but that didn't matter. They could tell each other beautiful lies all the way back to Wonderland for all he cared. Perhaps a hate-fuck could be in the cards after all.

Speeding up their pace, Chess practically dragged Ever into the shadows between two shops. Rotten food and piss permeated his senses, but it offered the privacy they needed. He hauled her to the other side of the industrial bin before releasing her. She took a step back and let out a loud breath.

"We can help each other," he offered without preamble. He would keep the fact he was wanted for matricide to himself. If Ever already knew, she would've rubbed the information in his face, and it would work to his advantage if she thought he still had the full privileges of being a prince.

Ever laughed, the sound incredulous. "Us? Help each other?" She shoved him again, both hands slapping his chest. "Be serious, Chess. The only help I will be giving you is to the grave."

Fuck this. She wasn't going to believe him. He didn't even blame her for it because he would've had the same reaction. Letting her race back into hiding was *not* an option, however. "Don't say I didn't try to do this the nice way," he said with a sigh.

And lunged.

Chess didn't want to have to do it, but she'd left him no choice. His hands wrapped around her neck, squeezing. Once she passed out, he would take her back to his basement where she would eventually wake as good as new. She would be just as trapped as him when the sun rose, leaving them with ample time to come to terms. Ever kicked at him while he lifted her off the street by the neck, pressing her against the brick building. He shifted to take each blow to the legs instead of his groin. Once was enough.

Ever's fangs lowered and she took a gasping breath—*tried to*—as she reached out to claw at his face. Couldn't she just pass out already? Chess slammed his eyes shut to avoid getting them scratched and took those blows too. He would heal before the night was over. All he had to do was get—

Palms landed on either side of his head. *Ever's palms.* Chess's eyes flew open and he met her defiant gaze. A grin spread across her lips as she tightened her grip on his head and then—

Crack!

CHAPTER SIX

EVER

*C*ocky prick.

Who the hell did the bastard think he was? Chess was no prince of anyone's heart. Ever was easily able to wound him again—this time making him unconscious, his lying words trapped away. She should rip his heart out right there, relish in spilling his blood.

Not yet, the tiny voice of reason murmured in the back of her mind.

"Fine," Ever huffed. Chess was the one who had lived in the palace the longest. He knew Rav best. Better than her. Ever only knew the old Rav before they'd come to Wonderland, or the one who she'd lived with inside the Ivory Palace's walls. Even then, he'd always been full of lies and secrets. It had been centuries since he'd truly been her brother. Chess had been right under his mother's wing, performing deeds for her and Rav. No one else still alive had been that close. According to March, all of Rav's other guards and servants were dead. Too bad it couldn't have been the Ivory guards who'd betrayed her. It would've served those bastards right.

She peered down at Chess as she stood above him. After she'd twisted his head, breaking his precious little neck, he'd tumbled to the ground in a heap. It was nothing less than what he was trying to do to her—she had just used a more expedient method to render him unconscious. The Princeling wanted a chat? She supposed he would get one. But it would be her way. Not his.

Heavy footsteps sounded behind her, and she whirled around to find a short man wearing tight trousers and a silky plaid shirt.

"Shit, sorry," the mortal mumbled when he discovered Ever and ran his hand through his shaggy red hair. "Just needed to take a piss. That line isn't moving at—" His eyes widened when they landed on Chess. "Is he all right?"

"He's fine." Ever waved her hand nonchalantly in the air. "Just passed out drunk as usual. I really can't bring him anywhere."

The man blew out a breath, hesitantly approaching her. "I know it's not my business, but sometimes it's best to leave people like that. They need to want to help themselves first."

"Oh, I know." She shrugged. "We won't be together for much longer." Before the mortal offered to help or waste more time, Ever thought of the perfect plan. Her gaze met his and she focused on him, swaying him with her influence. "You will drive us back to my home."

The mortal's dark irises glazed over as he nodded. Ever could easily scoop Chess up and carry him to her safe house, but it wasn't every day a female toted a male around in the mortal world. With a closer look from prying, immortal eyes, even with her disguise, she would be recognizable, and Chess even more so.

"First, help me take my boyfriend to your car," Ever instructed, unable to contain her smirk at what she was about to do.

Without a word, the man lifted Chess on one side while Ever held him on the other, the prince's feet dragging across the pavement as they walked the short distance. The vehicle was an older model with chipped green paint and a dent on the passenger side door. Above them, the full moon shone brightly while most of the stars were hidden from the light pollution. Back in Wonderland, the werewolves would be in human form on this night, but it was rare they would slip out in the mortal world. However, she still kept a gun with silver bullets in her safe house just in case.

The man unlocked the door, and they propped Chess in the backseat, his head leaning against the window. He shouldn't wake any time soon, but if he did, she needed to have the advantage, which she wouldn't have if she slipped into the front, so she slid in beside him. No one had seemed to pay them any mind since it wasn't unusual to see someone drunk or passed out from the club. This was positively perfect.

The mortal remained quiet as he sank down into the driver's seat and started the engine. He stayed focused on the road after she gave him the instructions on how to get to the old park.

"Put it on a classical station please," Ever said, needing a bit of calm after this tedious night.

A harder melody with fast bow movements across cellos came through the car stereo and she relaxed in her seat. She peered up at the ceiling with a smile while moving her index finger side to side as though performing her own symphony to the music. Imogen was dead. Ever had Chess in her clutches. And her brother would come soon enough. It was like the notes of a song, falling splendidly into place.

After about ten minutes, the car stopped in the crumbling parking lot of their destination. Not a soul was inside the park and only a few cars passed down the dimly lit street.

Ever leaned forward as she spoke to the mortal in an even

tone. "After we shut the door, return to the club, and if you were planning on meeting someone, tell them you're late because you forgot something at home." She then opened the door and wrapped her arms around Chess's waist, yanking him from the vehicle, before hoisting him over her shoulder. With a grunt, she adjusted his lithe body and shut the door using her foot. A pleasant aroma of pine and rain radiated from him, and she held her nose, brushing the smell away for a second.

"Come on, Princeling," she whispered as the mortal drove away. "You get to come to my home sweet home."

A light breeze with the scent of earth blew around her. An owl hooted in the distance, and the branches of the trees rustled. Ever walked past the dilapidated playground, then used her speed to hurry through the trees to the safe house— she didn't want to hold Chess a moment longer.

The gnarled walnut tree came into view, and Ever fished out the key from her small cross-body purse. She held onto Chess's legs as she knelt to the ground, pressing the key into the small lock. If it weren't for her vampire sight and knowing the precise location of the keyhole, she would never have been able to find it. After lifting the door, she carried Chess down the ladder.

As her feet hit the bottom, she scanned the small space and thought about where she should rest her new *guest*. The mattress or the floor? *The floor it is.* Ever dropped Chess's body on the wood with a thump and retrieved a few items from a crate in the corner. Rolling the prince to his stomach, she drew his arms behind his back and circled them with a heavy metal chain, then used another to tightly bind his ankles. He wouldn't easily escape those since he would have to be a magician to tear through the metal.

Smiling, Ever stood and brushed her hands together, silently thanking her lucky chess piece for this. She then removed her heels and picked up her viola and bow. With a satisfied sigh, she sat atop her mattress, running her bow across the strings of her instrument as she waited for the villainous prince to wake.

"Mmm," Chess groaned, rolling to his side, facing her.

Ever stopped playing her viola and perked up, finding the prince's eyes still shut. She arched her brow when he let out another deep groan, the edges of his lips pulling back into what looked to be a smile. It didn't sound like a painful awakening as she'd expected, or wished for, but as though he was having a *pleasureful* dream. She gripped her viola in one hand and her bow in the other, then stood from the mattress in front of him.

Chess's spine arched while he tossed his head back. "Right there," he whispered. "Fuck. You're so good at this. Keep sucking. Harder, faster."

She snickered to herself. "What a fool."

"Don't think you aren't getting a turn, sweetness," he purred. "Let me taste you now, Ever."

Her eyes widened. What the fuck? He was dreaming about *her*? About *tasting* her?

"Damn, you taste like sweet nectar."

Ever cleared her throat and kicked him in the ribs with her foot, not wanting to think about *where* he was performing this act with his mouth. "That's quite enough of that."

Chess's eyes jerked open, his yellow gaze meeting hers. He blinked while staring at her, as though he couldn't believe she was standing before him.

"What were you dreaming about?" Ever cooed, holding up her viola and running the bow across its strings to play a melody.

The prince lifted his head and shook his arms behind his back when he seemed to finally come to a realization. "What the fuck is this?" He jerked his chains, writhing like an insufferable snake. However, his movements did go along well with her music as she continued to play, like a cobra being mesmerized by a charmer performing a song on a pungi. "Stop playing the damn violin!"

She cocked her head, her movements pausing. "It's a *viola*."

"What the fuck ever." He clenched his jaw, still rattling the chains on his ankles as he pushed himself up to a sitting position. "Release me."

"I don't think so, *Princeling*. You're lucky I didn't kill you." She knelt in front of him so her nose was incredibly close to brushing his. "You wanted a chat? Well, here we are. We do it *my* way. Not yours. You're the one who betrayed me in the first place. Trying to play the role of the Huntsman in *Snow White*. You know what happened at the end of that story? She won. The Evil Queen died." Ever clucked her tongue—the dig was specifically about his wretch of a mother. "Refresh my memory … what happened to the Huntsman?"

Chess narrowed his eyes, his nostrils flaring. Her gaze unintentionally drifted down to his pouty lips that had been tasting her in his pathetic dream. But the little voice at the back of her mind wondered briefly what that would feel like, those plump lips between her thighs, flicking his devilish tongue slowly up her center. *No. No. Bloody hell, no.*

"Unbind me and I'll be a good little boy," he purred. Her gaze slid back up to his, thankfully clearing her horrendous thoughts.

She sat across from him, slowly plucking a string on her viola. "Name the song I was playing and perhaps I will."

"Simple." He grinned, his lips spreading wide so each of his perfect teeth were on display, his fangs bared. "'Fur Elise.'"

Damn. She should've chosen a harder song. "I'm still not untying you, Princeling."

"We can work together," he said, confidence lacing his words. "We both want the same thing."

What could they possibly both want that was ever the same? They had nothing in common besides liking the taste of blood. "And what is that?"

"Your brother dead."

Ever held her gaze steady, keeping her features neutral. She knew Rav wanted him for the murder of Imogen. But she'd believed before that, they were the perfect devious trio. After all, he was the only father Chess had ever known. "And why does it matter to you if he's dead?" she slowly asked. "Aren't you Scarlet's new king? You can do with him as you wish. Send him back to Ivory. I can then return to my home, reclaim my throne, and kill him myself." She arched her brow, seeing if she could get him to admit his lie or not.

He gritted his teeth. "I can't."

"And why ever not?" She smiled, waiting for him to admit that he was wanted in Scarlet for the murder of his mother.

"Because Rav is the king at the moment."

Ever laughed then, the heaviness of the sound spilling out from her throat, so much her eyes watered. "Of course he is. Did you really think my brother would hand over Scarlet to you, even though you're the rightful heir? Look what he did to me, his own sister." She paused. "My contact did say Rav seems to have narrowed his search for Imogen's murderer, but we still don't know who ripped out her heart."

"Who's your *contact*?" Chess asked, his voice suspicious.

She bet everything on it that he was thinking her contact was Maddie, but he couldn't know she'd recently met up with her. "He's here in London. I haven't been back in Wonderland since I ran from the ball. I only recently emerged from this *fabulous* home of mine and reconnected with an old friend."

Chess leaned toward her, his heavenly scent caressing her nose. "Your *lover*?"

"That's none of your business," she spat.

"Help me become king and I'll help you return to being queen." His gaze focused on her hair. "And take off that wig. It looks like shit."

"What a way to entice me into working with you," Ever said dryly but drew off her wig, letting her long white locks fall down her back.

Chess's eyes widened for a short moment before returning to their normally cocky stare. "Ah, there's the White Queen in all her glory. I don't think I've ever seen you with your hair down." He ran his tongue across his lower lip. "If you unbind my wrists, I promise to play fair."

He was such a lovely liar. But she was too. "Perhaps another day." She lifted her bow and returned to playing a song, just for him, on her viola while he seethed.

CHAPTER SEVEN

CHESS

Chess had never needed the luxuries that palace life offered, but he sure as hell appreciated them. Especially now that he was lying, tightly bound, on the floor of Ever's...

He wasn't sure it could be called a *home*. It was a literal hole in the ground with added creature comforts. It was no bloody wonder he struggled to find her safe houses in Wonderland all these years. If they were as well hidden as this one was, it was going to be nearly impossible, and Maddie was undoubtedly locked away in one of them right now.

He'd just have to smoke the Hatter bitch out. Right after he took care of Rav and cleared his name because, otherwise, searching Wonderland would be a nuisance.

Turning his attention to Ever, he studied her face. She'd fallen asleep on her mattress hours ago with the viola tucked under her arm. The worry had drained from her features as she slumbered, making her appear younger. Her lips were parted, her breaths soft. The wig she'd worn the night before and the fancy up-dos he'd seen her wear previously didn't do her justice. Her white hair looked softer than his sheets back in the Ruby Heart Palace. Sheets he would do nearly anything to fuck her on if the situation was different…

"Oi," Chess called to Ever. He couldn't get distracted right now. Despite his many, *many* attempts to free himself, he was still just as confined as when he'd first awoken and he was over it. "Oi, Queenie. You going to sleep all day?"

Ever's eyes cracked open and she smiled with a yawn. "What else should I be doing, *Princeling*? Entertaining you?"

"Oh, I would like that very much. I'm sure you know all sorts of ways to keep a male *entertained*," he said with a coy smirk. "But unchaining me would be a good start."

"Hmm, let me think about that…" She closed her eyes again, her smile widening. "No."

"No?" Chess threw himself up into a sitting position and scooted up to the mattress, chains clinking. "I can make this very uncomfortable for you as well, you know. Unless you plan on murdering me every day?"

"Perhaps I do," she mumbled.

Chess held back a growl. He had no intention of staying like this any longer—he was no one's prisoner. Getting caught was his fault. He'd been too sure of himself in the alley outside the club, but he should've known the queen of Ivory wouldn't go quietly. Temporarily killing her was the only way he was going to get her back to his basement. Going straight for a pseudo-death was much faster and more efficient than dragging her off while awake, though a raging headache did accompany it after.

Not quite as uncomfortable, hm? Chess would need to play a little dirty, he supposed. With a smile, he dropped his fangs and slinked forward. Ever's arm hung off the mattress, her lily scent caressing his nostrils. She didn't even open her eyes as he neared, then he drove his teeth into the exposed flesh of Ever's forearm as hard as he could. Her blood burst in his mouth and he lost all sense as her flavor—the richest he'd ever tasted—sent a wave of ecstasy through him.

Ever screeched and, grabbing a handful of his hair, ripped him off her. "What the hell are you doing?"

Chess grinned as a trickle of her warm blood flowed down his chin. "Tit for tat."

"I never bit you," she snarled, throwing him away from her.

He fell on his side with a *thunk*, unable to use his limbs to stop himself. "Unchain me and maybe I'll let you."

Ever stood over him, wrinkling her nose. Blood trailed down her arm from his bite, dripping off her fingertips, but the puncture wounds were already healing. "Don't flatter yourself. I'd rather drink from a dead man."

She moved to step around him, and he raised his chained legs into the air to block the path between himself and the mattress. "We both know that would kill you."

"And yet"—she stared at his legs hovering before her—"I stand by my statement."

"Such a brutal white rose, you are." He chuckled. "I could make you feel more alive than any feeding could. Would you like me to prove it?"

She picked up her viola from the mattress behind her and ran a bow across the strings. She tilted her head as if listening for something. "Mmm, the notes seem to say *no*." Ever kicked him in the ribs, forcing him to lower his legs as he curled in on himself just long enough for her to get past him. Silently, she picked through a pile of neatly-folded clothes and selected a long-sleeved jumper with three old musician faces across the front with the words *I listen to dead people* above them. *Dead composers*, he thought, but had no idea which. Then she slipped inside a side door and the sound of water sloshing in a bucket filled the room. A few moments passed before she came out again smelling of soap, dressed in her fresh jumper, and her white hair was tucked beneath a curly brunette wig.

"I'm going out," she announced.

"What?" Chess rolled to his stomach, pushed onto his knees, and managed to stand. Fuck his hurt pride, the indignity, the embarrassment of being captured. She was so sure he wouldn't get out of this place that she was prepared to leave him alone? Without talking things out first? What if she was caught by someone else tonight? What if she— His anger immediately deflated as fear coursed through him instead. What if she was going to tell her spy she'd caught him? What if she learned the truth that he was a wanted male and turned him over to Rav in exchange for Ivory?

"Afraid of being alone?" Ever asked sarcastically.

"We need to talk," he said, serious.

The tone of his voice must've gotten through to her because her body stilled, her eyes narrowed in thought. He was seldom outwardly serious—even she had to know that. His reputation always preceded him as the untroubled prince.

"About what?" She angled her head to the side. "I'm not releasing you."

"Why not? You don't think you could snap my neck a second time?" He almost winced, knowing the jab might curb her willingness to listen. "I can help you get your throne back."

"And why the hell would you do that?" She crossed her arms over her chest. "It's your fault I lost it."

"It's Rav's and my mother's fault technically, and as you said, she's dead." Pain scratched at his insides as he said the words, but he knew they were necessary to prove his point. "I don't give a flying fuck who rules Ivory or Scarlet, and I never did."

"It sounds like you care now," Ever drawled, her lips curving into a smile.

Chess opened his mouth to deny it and paused. Did he care now? Not about Ivory, no, but was he going to let Rav rule Scarlet? It was rightfully his—Imogen never crowned Rav. If she had wanted him to rule when she was gone, surely she would have made him king? Did that mean his mother *wanted* Chess to rule? He didn't have any interest in wearing the crown but Rav had just set the entirety of Wonderland against him. Betrayal colored his vision red for a moment. Chess *would* rule Scarlet, as was his birthright. To keep Wonderland the playground he knew it to be, yes, but also to spite Rav.

"I care slightly more than before," he finally admitted, shrugging one shoulder, the chains digging in. "If you need your brother's head, I certainly wouldn't mind giving it to you."

Ever laughed. "How kind of you. And what would you be getting out of this arrangement?"

Maddie, dead. But he couldn't admit that to Ever when the two females were such good friends. Chess needed to play the game with the White Queen. Make her trust him. Eventually, the murderous Hatter would appear. As an immortal, all Chess had was time. He could be patient if he had to.

"I suppose you've got me there," he said with a smirk. "Rav was never made king, which means the title belongs, rightfully, to me. I've never been good at sharing. Unless of course it's in bed. If you'd ever like to introduce me to your lover from the club, I'm sure we could work something out."

Ever's fingers rapped a rhythm on her arms as she studied him. He wished he could read every thought flickering through her head. While her face remained passive, the conflict flashed through her eyes. Belief. Disbelief. Back and forth between the two.

"Prove your usefulness to me first," she said, completely ignoring his invitation to a threesome.

That might be tricky if it included waltzing back into Scarlet. "How?"

"Tell me everything Rav's been doing." She lifted her chin in challenge. "Starting with the day of my masquerade ball."

Chess grinned. "Done. But first," he purred, "unchain me."

Ever scowled. "I'll unchain your legs but not your arms."

"I'm losing feeling in my fingers. They'll be no good to you if they shrivel and fall off," he said, winking.

"Everything you say only makes me want to leave you bound. Take the offer or leave it, Princeling." She shrugged.

"You drive a hard bargain, but I suppose you leave me little choice. I am at your mercy, oh majestic queen." He would get his arms free soon enough because he couldn't run like this if a situation arose where he needed to flee.

Ever dropped to her knees in front of him and pulled a key to the padlock from her back pocket. When she looked up at him from beneath her lashes, those pouty lips parted, a bolt of desire stormed through him.

Fuck me, that was a sight. Now if only his hard cock were between those full lips—sucking, licking, tasting—as it had been in his dream. His fingers threading through her ivory hair while he groaned. Ever's delicate hands working him instead of the metal lock near his feet. Her gaze shifted to the growing bulge in his trousers and she inhaled sharply before turning her attention back to the chains.

When the lock was finally removed, she unwound the chains from his legs, the links clanking together, echoing, as she gathered more of it into her hands. It only took her a minute to complete, but by the time she was done, the air practically crackled between them.

"There." She sighed, sounding slightly breathless, and stood. Their bodies pressed close, only an armful of chains between them.

Chess could've sworn her body shook slightly when their eyes met, and his cock throbbed painfully, wanting nothing more than to make her scream his name. "Thanks," he said in a husky voice. What would she do if he drew her close, claimed that pretty mouth with his? He'd asked last time in her garden and received a resounding *no* with her knee to his groin, but she didn't seem to loathe the idea so much now with her hooded eyes.

Stepping back, Ever tossed the chains into a corner. "Don't make me regret it."

"Of course not," he promised. Not yet, at least. He stretched his legs, shaking the feeling back into them, before lazily sinking down on the edge of Ever's mattress. He peered up at her with a wide grin. "So, your brother…"

Two nights passed as the White Queen questioned every aspect of Rav's life. Chess shifted uncomfortably where he sat on the floor, his arms still chained, as Ever lifted a bottle of mixed powdered blood to his lips. The weak solution scratched at his throat, and he released a small cough. Ever lowered the bottle without glancing at him, instead plucking absently at the strings of her viola.

"How did you know I liked my meals half-dissolved?" he asked.

"A wild guess," she mumbled.

When she flicked a glance at him to raise the bottle again, she gave a small sigh. She set the instrument aside and Chess drank in her bare legs as her dress slid up. Every curve was visible beneath her tight black dress, the skirt barely covering her firm arse. Not that he'd felt it himself but he'd gripped enough in his lifetime to know just by glancing. She looked so good in the damn scrap of fabric that he almost didn't mind being her prisoner. *Almost.*

The backs of Ever's cool fingers grazed the corner of his lips where a trickle of blood escaped. He felt her touch all the way to his cock when she wiped it away, but she gave no indication that she wanted him. No increased heart rate, no catch of her breath…

Infuriating, honestly.

When had he ever spent so much time with a female and *not* had them want him? He'd never talked this much either. Ever knew everything about her brother now. His feeding habits, his relationship with Imogen, their political policies. Everything Chess knew, she now knew. Except, of course, that Rav had ordered for Chess to be thrown in the dungeons.

"I need to meet with someone," Ever said, pacing the room. She'd been plaiting and unplaiting her dark wig. "You'll have to come with me."

He *had* to? Interesting. She'd been fine with the idea of leaving him alone before, when his legs were chained. "I promise to be your perfect guard." He winked, though he wasn't sure if that was the truth. They had a tentative truce, but the flight response still lingered inside him. He could trust her just as much as she could trust him.

"No." She cast a glance at the chains in the corner. "I could chain you again, but you've held your end of the bargain. If we're to take down my brother together, we need to try having a little faith in each other."

Chess scanned her over, his brow furrowing. "Who are you and what have you done with Ever?"

She snorted, unamused, and took another key from her pocket. "Turn around."

Chess turned slowly, half expecting her to bash him over the head, but she quickly unlocked his chains and peeled them away. He groaned as blood rushed back into his fingers. Rolling his shoulders, stretching the muscles, his bones *cracking*, felt painfully good. "Bloody hell." He moaned deeply to himself and looked over his shoulder at Ever.

At the sight of her dilated pupils, he swallowed a sarcastic comment he wanted to make about not letting her tie him up again in the future. In fact, he would probably beg her to do just that if it got them to share a bed. Or a table. Or literally any surface. Her riding him. Him fucking her with maddening, lustful thrusts.

"Do you like it when I moan?" he said with a smirk.

Her gaze snapped to his, losing the lustful stare. "Excuse me?"

"If you want to hear it again, I know just how you can accomplish that." He rolled his shoulders once more and turned to face her fully. "A variety of ways, in fact."

"You're absolutely incorrigible," she huffed. "Maybe I *should* leave you here."

Chess laughed at her annoyance, but he had no real desire to stay behind in her safe house. Leaving with her would be safe enough. While he didn't trust the White Queen, she'd avoided being seen for nearly four years, so he knew their destination would be clandestine. That only made him want to go more.

"I'll be on my best behavior," he vowed, placing a hand over his chest. "Prince's honor."

After hesitating for a long moment, she headed up the ladder. His gaze fixed on her arse and he cursed at how stretchy the fabric seemed, hiding any glimpse of what was beneath. He suspected she knew as much or she wouldn't have climbed the ladder first. They both knew he was too much of a scoundrel not to look.

Just before pushing up on the hatch that would lead them outside, Ever arched a brow at him. "Princeling, you should understand this: you need to *have* honor in order to swear on it."

CHAPTER EIGHT

EVER

The prince's cock had hardened at Ever's touch, the bare brush of her fingers had ignited something within him while unlocking the chains near his ankles. But that shouldn't be difficult to believe since he was known to fuck anything that walked. She wouldn't be surprised if he'd been with a werewolf in his past—while the creature was in beastly form. Perhaps he wouldn't go *that* far, but still.

Though what made Ever pause for a second, a *very* brief one, was that an extremely small, *foolish*, part of her wanted to see what hid beneath those tight trousers of his, see what had everyone so eager about it in her world. Wondered how it would compare to the others she'd stroked, had in between her lips.

Ever! she scolded herself. *This is what you get for remaining a damn virgin for centuries.* Queen Elizabeth was known as The Virgin Queen back in her day, but everyone knew she was no such thing and took lovers into her bed. Ever should've coupled with March at some point in the past, but again, she knew that wouldn't have been fair to him. And she wouldn't be selfish just to lose her maidenhead.

She and Chess walked from the park to the pavement, the wind barely blowing, the moon only a sliver of yellow resting in the night sky.

"So," Chess drawled, rolling up the sleeve of his dress shirt. "Who are we meeting this fine evening? Your lover from the club?"

"Yes." Ever pushed the braid of her dark wig over her shoulder as several cars passed them on the street. Tonight, she'd chosen to wear another short black dress but with a pair of knee-high leather boots instead of the heels. In truth, as mundane as it was, she would've rather worn her checkered Vans, jeans, and another T-shirt since she couldn't very well parade around in her white attire.

"How long have you two been fucking?" Chess smirked. "Since before or after you left Ivory? I don't remember anyone by your side at the masquerade ball."

"It's none of your business." Ever lifted her chin, still thinking about when he sank his teeth into her arm. It had been a snaky move but something she would've done. She looked him over, and he'd readjusted his short ponytail. The front locks hung deliciously at his chin. *Pathetically*, she'd meant. "What I do remember from that day at the ball was you trying to murder me."

"Are we going to rehash this every time we speak?" Chess asked, his long fingers toying with his hair. "I'm sorry."

Ever knew that was a downright lie. "For?"

"Trying to take your heart." He placed a hand over his chest and sighed. "Your turn."

"What?"

He circled her as though she were his prey before coming to a stop in front of her. "Say you're sorry for kneeing me in the groin and stabbing me."

What a spoiled prince he was. Did he think she would bow down and apologize after everything he'd done, especially in light of his own flimsy apology? "Are you serious? You're insufferable. And I don't accept your insincere apology."

He didn't deny he'd been false about the sentiment, yet the past was the past. That didn't mean she trusted him though. He would betray her in an instant if a better opportunity arose—and vice versa—but for now, this was the best resource she had for taking down her brother.

Ever spotted a black taxi, waved her hand, and the car slowed to a stop in front of them. They were headed to the same club from a few days ago where she would meet up with March. Sometimes he was early and sometimes he was late, but he was always there.

Chess opened the door to the taxi and motioned her inside. "My lady."

Ever released a very unladylike snort and slipped into the car, sliding over to the window. The taxi reeked of old food and possibly sex. Chess took a seat beside her, a little too close, and shut the door.

"To Serenity nightclub," Ever said, using her influence on the young mortal driver. He barely looked old enough to drive, his head shaved and pale skin covered in acne. "First, put it on the classical station, please."

"Of course," the boy said, changing the radio station until violins and flutes filled the car before driving down the low-lit street.

"You're really into this stuff, huh?" Chess asked. "At the ball, I thought the music was just for the occasion."

"Well," Ever said slowly, "if you had gotten to know me instead of trying to *kill* me, then maybe you would have learned some things."

"You wound me with that response." His fingers seductively tiptoed across the seat toward her but not daring to touch her. "So why the viola? Why not the violin?"

Ever thought back to when she was younger, when she'd still lived with her parents and brother. When Rav had simply been Ravon. Her twin who'd followed her everywhere, even fallen with her into Wonderland. In truth, she'd wanted to play the violin at first. The instruments hadn't been around the mortal world that long, but when her uncle from Italy brought them as gifts for Ever and her brother, she'd laid eyes on Rav's viola and had to have it once she'd heard its sounds. Rav wanted the violin just as much so they'd traded.

"I like the lower notes and its larger size," Ever informed him.

"You like larger, huh?" Chess grinned, biting his lower lip.

"*Very* large," Ever said slowly, "and I'm certain it's not something you would know much about."

Chess chuckled. "You can find out any time you like." He then paused, locking his yellow gaze with hers. "You play well." His voice seemed sincere for once.

"Do you play anything?" she asked, unable to stop herself. But she was always curious about those who could play music.

"No, my father left for Wonderland when I was a baby, and my mother was too busy trying to provide for us. Then she abandoned me, too, and I was left to myself at eight years old. Years later, my mother came back and turned me, then brought me to Scarlet. By that point, I didn't care to learn about anything that didn't involve my new world."

Ever's stomach sank at his words and she didn't understand why. She shouldn't have felt sorry for anything he'd said. But he'd raised himself, then his mother had shaped him into what he was today. "A pity Rav didn't teach you," Ever said, wondering if he had ever played again. Once they'd fallen into Wonderland, he'd stopped.

"Rav was preoccupied with fucking my mother and being an arse. So, I found my own entertainment."

"By turning mortals unwillingly?" Her eyes narrowed.

Chess frowned for a minute, thinking. "Only in my

younger years, when my mother wanted me to learn how the process worked."

Ever didn't understand how he could worship the ground his mother had walked on, especially knowing that she'd murdered his father even though he'd been a good male. But Ever wasn't going to discuss more family matters with him now. He'd told her plenty of information about her brother, how he often slinked to the mortal world to bring a new human home to toy with, how he and Imogen fed from them, turned them, enslaved them. Then, most of the time, they killed them shortly after when they displeased Imogen in even the slightest way.

The car slowed to a stop, and Ever leaned forward. "Forget you drove us to the club and go where you were planning to before." They then stepped out of the taxi and headed for their destination.

Outside the building, cars lined the street, more than the previous night. Mortals strutted toward the entrance, some with plenty of skin on display. One woman wore a long vinyl jacket over fishnets, while others had on black lingerie, miniskirts, tight leather trousers, and harness bondage.

"Seems we're underdressed for the occasion." Chess leaned in and whispered, "Or should I say, *overdressed*?"

Ever blew out a breath and rolled her eyes as he brushed his hands down the front of his button-up shirt and dark trousers. The line outside the club was much shorter than last time, and she assumed most of the people were already inside.

"What's going on tonight?" Ever asked when they approached the bouncer. It was the same man as a few nights ago, his shirt tight across his bulging muscles.

"It's Kinky Tuesday," he answered, his expression serious.

"Let us in," Chess said silkily. The bouncer's eyes instantly glazed over, and the man gestured for them to go inside.

They walked down the narrow hall to the main space

where the music blasted through the speakers. Heavy, techno beats drifted to Ever's ears and heavier white smoke surrounded the mortals dancing in the room under the flashing bright lights.

"I know what we're doing tonight." Chess's voice came out playful.

Ever followed his gaze across the room, her brows lifting. A man wearing strips of leather over his lean body cracked a whip as a female in a thong and bra wrapped rope around a woman in a tight pink corset.

In another corner, couples, ball gags in their mouths, thrust against each other in several large metal cages. Everything about this night was sinful as partners grinded, arousal filling their eyes.

Ever had seen her fair share of couples seducing one another, but she couldn't help being in awe of their movements, the atmosphere.

The scent of lust, blood, and sweat enveloped her, and she peered at Chess, who swiped the tip of his tongue across his lower lip. And she knew he was feeling it too. She could control it, but she was still fighting the urge to tear throats apart and drink as thirst stormed through her.

Ever peered around, searching for March's braids, his tall frame. But she didn't spot him anywhere. At the bar, several people who looked as though they were trying to be vampires, with light contacts and fake fangs, flirted while sipping on beers.

Glancing up toward the large rectangular window above them, she tugged on Chess's sleeve. "Let's try upstairs." Sometimes March waited for her at one of the tables there.

Chess nodded and they broke through the crowd, past sweaty bodies. She let the prince lead her up the metal stairs. They may be on the same side for now, but that didn't mean she trusted him enough to allow him to walk behind her in this place.

Pictures of what looked to be old musicians hung across the red-painted walls. At the top of the stairs, the room opened up to a large space cluttered with pleather sofas against the walls, black tables and chairs in the middle, and several dancing couples.

She glanced at faces and found a male with braids sitting at a table, but it wasn't March. Her gaze flicked toward the bar across the room and she scanned the seats, then froze.

White hair, red tips.

Her brother faced the bartender, chatting with him. Four other female vampires stood beside him, wearing tight, short crimson dresses. Long red locks cascaded down one's back, another orange, and the other two with dark braids. Even from behind, she would notice the bastard anywhere—that hair, his build, the relaxed way he stood. Chess, the fool, didn't seem to notice as he started to walk in the direction of the bar.

Just as Rav turned, Ever shoved Chess onto a sofa beside them and climbed into his lap, straddling his narrow hips while blocking his face. Chess's mouth parted and his eyebrows rose before his normal cocky expression fell back into place. When he opened his mouth to speak, she muffled his voice by crashing her lips to his. Her mouth skated across his—he didn't hesitate, thoroughly returning the kiss, his fingers digging into her hips. She plunged her tongue into his mouth, caressing, tasting his damn luscious flavor, finding herself *liking* it. Gripping his hair tight, she rolled her hips forward. He let out a low groan as she did it again and again, knowing she should stop but not wanting to. It wasn't even him doing this—it was all *her*. His length hardened against her softness and instead of this being a distraction from Rav, it was turning into something else. Something that she didn't want to end. She yearned to tell herself that she didn't know who she was grinding against, wanted to pretend it was someone else, but she knew exactly who she was riding. In that moment she didn't care.

Chess's hands left her hips, trailed her thighs, then reached up her dress to grasp her buttocks.

His lips drew from hers, leaving her hungry for his taste. "Do you want me to take you right here or somewhere more private?" he rasped in her ear. "I'll do whatever the fuck you want."

"I-I…" Ever couldn't formulate words as she inhaled his pine scent. And she was *liking* who she was doing this with? As his hand cupped her breast, she halted her movements, grasping what she needed to say. "My brother is at the bar with four females. I didn't want him to see us. Slowly look up and tell me what he's doing now."

Chess's jaw clenched at her confession, his eyes hardening. He leaned forward, his breath hot at her ear, tickling her neck. "He's not here."

Ever jerked her head up and flicked her gaze toward the bar. Rav wasn't there. She jumped from Chess's lap and peered around the room. He was nowhere in sight and neither were the females he'd been with.

"Downstairs. Now." She grasped his hand and tugged him with her so they could avoid Rav until they formulated a proper plan. They were five against two. She didn't feel up to her full strength and she was sure Chess wasn't either after sitting underground for days while not having enough blood to drink.

The room was foggier than before, and even with her vampire senses, she could barely make out anything besides the outline of bodies, their intoxicating odor.

"This way." Chess clasped her hand and pulled her through the crowd, the smoke thinning. The prince then drew her to a sudden stop. "Dance with me." He pressed his fingers to her lips before she called him a fool. "To the door."

Instead of fighting him, she gave into his touch once more. But she told herself it was all for show because she truly hated him and they needed to get the hell out of here.

Yet she couldn't stop feeling his earlier hardness beneath her, the way her body had molded to his.

CHAPTER NINE

CHESS

Even in a room full of alluring blood, Ever's lily scent consumed Chess. The only thing keeping him from taking her into the bathroom, locking the door, and ravaging her until she screamed his name was the looming threat. Rav was somewhere in this club and that wasn't something he could lose sight of—even if he hadn't laid eyes on the male himself.

"I'll make sure he doesn't spot you," Chess whispered in her ear. He gripped Ever's hips, nuzzling her neck as they moved slowly toward the door. Too slowly, but they had to keep from being noticed. Running straight for the exit would undoubtedly draw attention, even if they did it quickly enough not to be seen by the other dancers. It was too crowded to avoid running into them all and Rav would know what a trail of humans, seemingly fallen over themselves, meant. It wasn't necessarily Chess and Ever who had fled, but it was evidence that *someone* had.

So Chess swayed to the beat, Ever against him.

Tantalizingly close. Now that he knew her lips tasted of wild berries and her blood blissfully rich, it was all he could do to focus on the faces visible through the manufactured fog.

Where is the fucking git?

Ever had said four females were with Rav at the bar, but they seemed to have vanished too. Dividing and conquering...

Ever grabbed onto the sides of his already-wrinkled shirt, shifting him slightly to peek over his shoulder. Chess's attention snapped to her. "Are you all right, Queenie?"

"Positively lovely," she hissed. "I adore playing a game of spy the arsehole."

"Does that mean you like my help?" he purred.

She snorted.

He couldn't help thinking about their moment upstairs. Her riding his cock over his trousers, the scent of her arousal. It carried similar notes to the light lily coming from her skin and the boldness of her blood mixed with a sweetness he would do almost anything to taste. His mouth watered at the idea of running his tongue through her desire.

Rav. Not fucking. Focus on Rav. "I don't see them anywhere," he said, doing his best to sound unaffected.

"Perhaps he found another poor soul to fuck and enslave." She wrinkled her nose in distaste, then released her grip on his shirt and flattened her hands on his sides instead, poised to push him away.

It was entirely possible that was why Rav had come, but this club was out of the way, farther from the entrance to Wonderland than most vampires traveled. Not to mention that he usually hunted alone. He wound an arm around Ever's lower back and tugged her tightly to him. "It may be safer to take you back upstairs. I wouldn't mind having you in that position again."

She inhaled sharply and Chess was sure she was about to tear out of his arms when a figure appeared beside them. Chess's grip tightened, his body tensing. "Who the fu—"

"March!" Ever breathed in relief, pushing away from Chess. She latched onto the male's arm and leaned into his touch. "I was starting to worry about you. Rav is here and he's not alone."

Chess realized he'd seen him before—it was the same male she'd been dancing with the last time they were here. Her lover, most likely, since they had also kissed. His lips pressed into a hard line.

"I know," March said quietly. "They're scouting outside. I barely made it past them—" The male's eyes narrowed as he focused in on Chess. "You're with the *fucking prince of Scarlet*?"

"Do you think they know I'm here?" Ever tugged March's arm, ignoring his comment about Chess, and they drifted away from the prince. She didn't even gift him a glance over her shoulder.

I don't think so.

Chess started after them as they wove through the moving bodies. Was she really walking away from him? Didn't she know there was nothing stopping him from running outside and telling Rav that Ever was inside? Well, other than the fact that Rav probably wanted Chess *more* than his own sister at the moment, but she wasn't aware of that. Yet.

He jerked into motion, following Ever and March. If the male tried to tell her about Chess's predicament, the prince would be forced to act. *Fuck.* What was he going to do? He couldn't kill Ever's acquaintance in the club while blending in *and* keeping her as an ally.

"Woah now," Chess said, slipping up to Ever's other side. "Who's this handsome piece?"

The male flared his nostrils as his eyes locked on Chess. "What are you doing with him, Ever?"

"It's a long"—she cast a withering stare at Chess—"*long* story."

"The Scarlet Prince, though?" March stepped sideways,

putting space between her and Chess. "You know what he tried to do to you."

"March," she snapped, peering over her shoulder as she steered them toward the bathrooms. "Sorry, but they could come back inside at any moment."

March looked between Chess and Ever with wide, disbelieving eyes. "Make this make sense," he said in a stern voice.

Chess slid in front of them, walking backward, through the swinging men's bathroom door. He stood aside, gliding his arm out with a flourish so they could join him. "Leave," he told a stocky man washing his hands. The mortal's blue eyes glazed over, and he hurried back to the dance floor without turning off the tap. With the room free of mortals, Chess leaned his back against the door and folded his arms across his chest as he studied March. "It makes sense, cupcake, because I am the only one close enough to her brother to help her kill him."

March barked a laugh. "You? But you're—"

Ever elbowed March and they exchanged a wordless warning that Chess couldn't understand. Finally, March let out a long breath. "Fine," he conceded. "You're still my queen and I trust your decision."

Ever reached out and gave March's hand a squeeze. The affection between them rankled in a way he'd never experienced before. How she'd turned away from Chess toward March as if he were her savior. Sure, Chess hadn't proven himself to be a white knight in the past, but he hadn't acted as her enemy in the last few days. *Not precisely, anyway.*

"I'll explain later, but we have to leave," Ever told March. "We need a plan and our weapons before we move against my brother."

March chewed his bottom lip. "Are you sure? We're evenly matched now and—"

"Evenly matched?" Chess's brow rose. "Did your mother

never teach you to count?"

March puffed his chest and stepped forward with his hands in fists. Ever flung an arm out in front of the vampire, bringing him to an immediate halt. "Those females with Rav are nothing special," March growled.

Chess rolled his eyes. Rav didn't travel with others, but if he *were* to bring anyone with him, they would not be *nothing*. He likely plucked the strongest females from the royal guards. But why—for *who?*

"Enough," Ever demanded. "We need to feed and get out of here unseen."

"Are you out of blood again so soon?" March asked.

Ever narrowed her eyes in Chess's direction. "My house guest is a bottomless pit."

"Please." Chess snorted. "You hand-fed me every drop and you *liked* it."

Someone pushed on the door. Chess met Ever's gaze and smirked, stepping away. The man pushed a little harder and stumbled. Chess just managed to catch him by the forearm as he fell inside. "Oh look." He kicked the door shut again. The short, pale mortal was extremely unappetizing, in his opinion. Blood was blood, but he had a habit of eating with his eyes. Convenience was key at the moment though. "Dinner."

"Chess," Ever warned.

"What the fuck?" the man snapped, attempting to tug his arm from Chess's grip.

"Allow us to feed," Chess purred to the man, letting his words sway him into compliance. The man relaxed and Chess lifted the mortal's arm to his mouth. He latched on without another word, blood flooding his mouth from where his fangs punctured. Ever could complain all she wanted but he knew she didn't disagree. Humans lived amongst vampires in Ivory—they were treated with respect for the blood contributions—but that didn't mean they weren't viewed as cattle. Humans cherished chickens, would even decorate their kitchens with them, and yet, most ate them without hesitation.

Chess pulled in a few long mouthfuls, allowing the thick metallic liquid to slide down his throat, before pushing the man toward Ever. His body hummed with new energy. "Your turn."

Ever glowered. "I'd rather not take your leftovers."

"And yet, you will." Chess licked the blood from the corner of his lips, feeling March's heavy gaze on him. "You too, if you're hungry."

"I ate earlier." March gritted his teeth. Then, softer to Ever, "I hate to say it, but he's right. You need to feed to keep up your strength."

"I know." She sighed, kneeling on the floor beside the mortal as her fangs lowered. She then lifted the man's other arm, sinking her teeth into his flesh.

Chess watched her suck and swallow, her eyes filling with pleasure, and the smirk faded from his face. Damn, he wished in that moment she were sucking on something else. *And swallowing.* March cleared his throat and Chess ground his teeth together. Now was not the time for fantasizing when Rav was just outside. Waiting to drag him home and imprison him.

"All right," Ever said to the man after she took her fangs from his arm. "Go into the cubicle and stay there until we leave."

The man turned robotically and strode straight for the first cubicle, shutting the door behind him.

"Now," Chess drawled. "Let's get out of here."

"Why don't you go on ahead and distract them," March suggested. It sounded innocent enough but Chess could see the challenge in his eyes. "He's your *stepfather*, after all."

Like hell he would leave Ever alone with this asshat. Give him the chance to tell Ever that Rav wanted Chess locked in the dungeon? Fuck that shit. "Alas, I have no interest in returning to Scarlet so soon."

"If you're going to help me get Rav's head…" Ever spoke

slowly, seeming to weigh her words as she spoke them. "It might be beneficial for you to be by his side."

The prince crossed his arms over his chest. "Fine," he said reluctantly. He would distract them … but not with his own body. The stakes were much too high for that. "But I'll need help."

Ever and March both chuckled at that, then exchanged a look, sobering. "You're serious?" Ever asked.

"I am *always* serious, my prickly white rose." He cracked his neck and straightened. "Now, you"—he waved a hand in March's direction—"will take a human out back and feed. The scent of blood will draw their attention. I'll wait nearby to intercept them before they reach you and Ever will leave through the front."

"Why would I need to lure them out back?" March asked.

Chess huffed. Must he explain *everything*? Bleeding idiot. "Because we need all five of them to leave the entrance to the club unattended. Unless you'd like to chance one of them not giving a shit about my appearance. Believe it or not, if a vampire doesn't enjoy males, they won't lose sight of their mission and ogle me."

"*Wow*." March shook his head in disbelief. "Could you be more self-absorbed?"

"Confidence," Chess corrected, motioning to himself. "It's called *confidence*."

"So, March lures them to the back of the club with the scent of blood, you stop them before Rav gets to March, and I sneak out the front," Ever summarized, bringing the conversation back on track.

"Bingo." Chess bopped the air between them as if he were touching the tip of her nose. It was a decent plan considering there was no time to plan anything better, even if he wasn't going to fulfill his part of it.

March's eyes narrowed as he considered the plan. "Ever?"

"It should work," she conceded.

Should? It would. If Chess had any intention of following through on his part. March had no reason to avoid Rav and his minions. Chess had never heard his name uttered in the Ruby Heart Palace or as a suspected cohort of Ever's. He seemed smart enough to think on his feet so, when Rav approached him, it would be easy to spin a lie. An average vampire, taking a jaunt into the mortal world for dinner. And what did it matter to Chess if the lie wasn't believed? Ever wouldn't need to know he left her spy on his own.

"Of course it will work," Chess promised. "Go straight back to the safe house and I'll meet you there."

"How do I know you won't lead them back there?" she inquired. "Or run off?"

Fair question, but that was a lot of extra work. "If I wanted to hand you over to your brother, I would have. And you didn't seem concerned about my scampering off when you left me standing on the dance floor alone."

Ever hesitated then nodded and gave March a quick hug. "I'll see you again soon."

"Ever, are you *sure* this is a good idea?" The male pulled away to meet her gaze. "We can think of something else that doesn't require you leaving, by yourself, with the same male who tried to assassinate you."

"I'm not at all sure," she admitted. "But I've been alone with him for days and he hasn't tried anything."

"Well, you *did* have me chained," Chess quipped.

"You're not helping," she growled. Then, to March, "Trust me."

"Anything you say," March agreed. The tick in his jaw said otherwise, but he was apparently smart enough to know his place. "Now, hurry before they decide to come back inside the club."

Ever raced from the bathroom without giving Chess a second glance. March glared at him from across the bathroom as Chess smirked, a silent war waging between them. With stiff shoulders, narrowed eyes, fangs dropped, Chess waited for him to attack. To warn him away from Ever. Seconds ticked by. Five. Ten. Thirty. If March didn't get outside, neither Ever nor Chess would escape.

"If you hurt her—"

"You'll rake me over the coals, yes, yes." Chess waved a dismissive hand in the air. "I'm terrified."

He took two rapid breaths. "You're not *my* prince and I have no reservations about killing you."

"No one does," Chess admitted with a laugh. And it was true. He had many enemies and no close friends back in Scarlet. The only thing stopping people from trying to kill him—besides his renowned skills—was his mother's wrath.

March cursed under his breath and swung open the cubicle door. The man stood, staring at the wall with a blank gaze. Gripping his jaw, he turned the man's face so he could make eye contact and influence him. "Come with me."

The dazed human stepped out behind March. Chess slid sideways to allow the pair to exit the bathroom and took a few deep breaths. *All right, Chess. Time to do some sketchy shit.*

The prince slunk back to the dance floor just in time to see March escort the man outside through a back door. Giving the club a once-over, he saw no trace of Rav or female vampires. Only Ever. She stood near the exit, close enough to a group of girls to appear like one of their friends, and when the door opened to allow more people inside, she sniffed the air. The next moment, she slipped outside.

And, a few steps behind her, so did Chess, wearing a smug grin.

CHAPTER TEN

EVER

Even if Rav had been alone at Serenity, would Ever have sought him out and given him the death he deserved? Once her brother was dead, she swore to herself she would play a song over his body. One he would hear even from his grave. It would be a song not only for him but for her.

After Rav's death, Chess would certainly claim the throne destined to be his, even though he should've been king already. But could she separate herself from Scarlet and let him rule as king? He didn't seem to turn mortals unwillingly, yet that didn't counter the fact he'd tried to take her heart—kill her. Perhaps he wasn't as villainous now that his mother was gone and he was wanted by Rav, but she also knew he most likely wanted Maddie dead for what she'd done. And if the prince chose to pursue Maddie, Ever would easily end his life without a thought.

The coast was still clear of vampires, except for an annoying prince. Slinking farther behind her, Chess moved like a shadow. If Ever didn't already know that the prince was secretly following her from the club, she wouldn't have been attuned to it. He was quiet, nimble, yet she could feel his presence, like silk to flesh. She bet he was even gloating, grinning, thinking he'd gotten away with his lies.

He was a cocky nuisance who she would be glad to be rid of soon. Even after drinking the delicious blood from the mortal in the bathroom, she could still feel the taste of Chess's tongue on hers.

Ever hadn't gotten to discuss the prince's situation with March, but the male seemed to understand what she had wanted to tell him. Keep quiet about anything on Chess.

The night was out in full force, the lights lessening as she padded down streets and cut through trees to avoid having Rav potentially spot either one of them on the main road. Ever may have been disguised well, but Chess still looked himself. She should've made him wear a damn wig, and she would the next time they ventured out, even if it meant she had to cut one of her own to suit him.

It wasn't that late and the way home wasn't dreadfully far, but she still would've preferred taking a taxi. Ever hadn't hailed one, though, because she didn't want to distance herself from Chess too much, just in case he decided to go rogue and plot something else. Like skulking away to Rav and confessing where Ever was staying in exchange for a pardon.

The trees grew thicker around her as she entered the woods, their branches creaking with the wind. A pale moon shone through the limbs, and a few hedgehogs scampered about. She approached the tree in front of her safe house, then sank down to the ground, propping her back against the trunk. Chess's shadow lingered several trees away, but she didn't look in his direction. She waited outside to see how this charade of his played out.

After ten minutes of Ever's thoughts bouncing back and forth, hoping March was all right, Chess stepped from the trees, making his presence known with heavier footsteps. What a cocky fool.

"There you are, Princeling." She smiled, lifting her head, pretending only then to notice him. Even in the night, his yellow eyes shone like a cat's. "I thought I was going to have to hunt you down."

"Aww, were you worried about me, Queenie?" He smirked as he stopped across from her, fiddling with the edge of his shirt sleeve, rolled at his elbow. "All went well at the club. You should thank me."

Ever inwardly rolled her eyes as she stood. She reached into her dress pocket to take out the key when a leaf crunched behind Chess. Snapping to attention, she watched as a female wearing a short, skin-tight vinyl dress stepped into view. Her orange hair fell in thick curls behind her back. It was one of Rav's vampire friends from the club.

Ever's fangs lowered and she prepared to leap forward when the female spoke to Chess. "I knew that was your arse I saw leaving Serenity." The female chuckled, barely sparing Ever a glance. "I lost you for a while but finally found your booted tracks in the woods."

"Ari…" Chess offered her a flirtatious smile. Did the fool not realize the vampire had been with Rav? But then again, Chess hadn't seen Rav or the other vampires he'd been with. "What are you doing here?"

"I was with the king back at the club." She shrugged.

"With Rav?" Chess asked, arching a brow. "Since when do you frequent the mortal world with him?"

"Since he asked me to. He needed vampires he could trust to assist, so he asked me, Anna, and a few others who Imogen considered friends." She pressed closer. "He wanted to recruit Osanna to help find you, too, but found her dead. He suspects you may have had something to do with that as well."

"I'm a little busy right now." Chess's voice came out clipped.

Ever hid her smile, liking where this was headed and waiting to see what Chess would do. Then Ari's focus latched onto Ever. "Who is this?" Her brow furrowed before her eyes widened in recognition. "You did it—you finally found the bitch? I'll bring her back to the king and tell him you found her, unless you want to kill her first?"

A pity that things had to turn south so quickly. Chess and Ari seemed to be friends, so it looked as though Ever's time with Chess had to come to an end. The White Queen readied her hands, her fangs still lowered, prepared for their attack. But when Ari launched forward, Chess moved faster, gripping her head and ripping it off with one fatal yank. The female's body slumped to the ground, crimson pooling from the wound.

The prince stared at Ever, his chest heaving as he held Ari's head. Blood dripped from her severed neck to the ground.

For a moment, Ever thought he may have killed his friend to ensure her safety, though she would have easily torn out the vampire's heart. Yet she knew the true reason why he'd done it—Ari was a threat to his lies.

"She was your friend?" Ever asked.

"Not exactly, but my mother's," he said softly. "Yet she did come to my bed on several occasions."

Ari hadn't tried to drag him back to Rav so Ever believed the vampire had considered him to be more than *not exactly*. The female must've thought taking Ever to her brother would pardon Chess, perhaps even lead to them having another tumble after. She briefly wondered what it would be like to take a lover to one's bed when they weren't friends. And then an image slid forward—she shoved away the thought of her sitting in Chess's lap back at the club, on top of his cock. There had been a *reason* for that.

She needed to discuss other things, not think about her pretend tryst with the prince at Serenity. Ari had mentioned Osanna, so Scarlet knew she was dead. But Ever didn't seem to be a suspect. She needed to continue playing her part, making it seem as though she knew nothing. "Who do you think killed Osanna?"

He scowled. "I don't know, but Osanna had many enemies."

The Hatter being one. And she bet with what recently happened with Maddie's boyfriend, Noah, that Chess believed there was a strong possibility the Hatter had killed Osanna. Yet Ever couldn't tell him that it was her who murdered the twat because he wasn't supposed to know she'd returned to Wonderland.

Ever peered at the tree trunks, wondering if Rav or one of his other female vampires was going to break through the foliage. But no one came.

"We need to take the body to the nearest lake," she finally said. They couldn't leave the body there in case one of the vampires tried to track Ari down before she turned to ash in the morning.

Chess nodded and handed Ever the vampire's head, then lifted Ari's body. The lake wasn't too far away, and they used their speed to get there, easily ducking beneath low-hanging branches.

After tossing the remains in the murky water, Chess washed the blood from his arms and hands, but crimson still stained his shirt.

They then slipped into the woods, heading back to the safe house. Ever lifted the door and allowed Chess entrance before locking them both inside. The prince unbuttoned his shirt and slowly peeled the fabric from his lithe body. As he turned to face her, she averted her eyes from each taut ab. When he'd come to the Ivory Palace with his mother, he'd always worn an open vest so it wasn't something she hadn't seen before. But a flame ignited in her chest anyway.

Taking a steady breath, she blew out that flame and lifted her viola from the mattress. She let a Chopin song fill the space around them as her bow slid across the strings.

Chess lowered himself to the floor on his stomach, his hands tucked beneath his head while he studied her. She waited for him to tell her to quit playing the damn instrument, but he didn't. Instead, he murmured, "You're quite lovely with that thing." Then he closed his eyes, his breathing growing even. It wasn't anywhere close to morning for them to be tired, but she knew he hadn't slept well in days.

Ever halted her playing. This was her chance. She thought she may have needed to knock him out again, and perhaps she should, but she chose to let him sleep.

With light steps, Ever crept up the ladder and opened the door. She turned the lock with a soft click after shutting it. Thunder rumbled in the distance, but no raindrops fell yet. Using her speed, she bolted through the trees to the park near one of the private schools. There were still hours before the sun rose, but this wouldn't take long.

On a picnic table across from a pair of swings lay a male, peering up at the darkened sky.

March.

Back at the club, Ever had given him the one finger hand signal, telling him to meet her at this park sometime tonight.

Another crack of thunder came as she stopped in front of him at the table.

"The prince?" He sighed, his gaze meeting hers. "Really?"

She sat on the table's bench, resting her elbows beside him. "I don't trust him, but he's going to make things easier. And he doesn't think I know he's wanted by Scarlet for his mother's death."

"I kind of figured that out." March chuckled.

His earlier clothing still appeared intact, no sign of a fight with any other vampires. "Did you see Rav at the club since we knew Chess was lying about intercepting anyone? One of the females followed Chess, but he killed her."

"Actually, good things may have come from this night."

March rolled to his side and propped his head in his hand.

"Oh?" Her interest was piqued. "Details."

"Your bastard brother did stumble upon me, and we feasted on the human together." His grin grew wolfish. "He offered me a position to be one of the guards at the Ivory Palace. Seems he's scouting the mortal world for rogue vampires who may want to side with him since he took out most of Ivory's guards who he didn't trust."

Her eyes widened. "Rav trusted you that easily?"

"I do turn on the charm when necessary." He paused. "But I don't believe he trusts me, just that he needs a few more hands there until he joins the territories. Apparently, he's still picky about who stays with him in Scarlet, though." Her blood boiled at the thought of the guards who betrayed her and wondered which ones remained in Ivory. They would all have to die regardless.

"Are you going to take the position?" This was like a dream come true. She would have him spy inside her palace in Ivory. He could then feed her necessary info about guard rotations and number of enemies so they could break into the palace, then take control of it.

"Of course. I'm headed there tomorrow." He peered up at her, his expression turning serious. "Be careful."

"I've been careful for nearly four years." It was time Ever used her carefulness for other things, like trying to take back her kingdom.

"I mean, with the prince."

Ever's heart pounded at his words and she took a deep swallow. "Don't worry. He's just a tool and once he betrays me, I'll rip out his heart as he'd planned to do with mine." And she would then feed it to the werewolves afterward. It wasn't a question of *if* he would turn on her but *when*.

March trailed a finger down her arm. "If you need me to do it, just give me the signal."

As she mulled over the wonderful news, the plan finally

fell into place. "In a few days, I'll head to the Ivory Palace. Meet me at the lake on the eastern side of the castle and we can go over anything you've learned." There was plenty of foliage in that location to keep her hidden as they discussed matters.

"I'll gather everything I can."

"Thank you." She placed a hand on his cheek. "If you decide to stay in Ivory after this is over, you always have a place inside the palace."

"Not now. But if you change your mind about me, I will in a heartbeat." He scooted closer and pressed his mouth to hers, dipping his tongue in between her lips. But all she could think about was when Chess's mouth had been on hers, the way his soft lips felt, the way he'd gripped her hips, the way his heart had pounded.

"I wish I could, but I can't." Not looking at what expression his face held, she pulled back. "See you soon."

"Until we meet again."

Ever hurried back to the safe house, being extra careful to make sure no one followed her. The next night, they would need to gather a few more weapons and get Chess some new clothing.

Once she was home, she locked the door behind her and found Chess still on his stomach, his lips parted, his chestnut hair covering his face. A tiny piece of her wanted to brush the strands from his eye. However, she did no such foolish thing and lifted her viola instead.

As she played a soft melody, her gaze lingered on his form, his naked upper body, her attention unable to fix on anything else. But he wouldn't have to know that.

CHAPTER ELEVEN

CHESS

Over the next several days, Chess had gone with Ever for supplies three times but never for more than an hour. It was too risky with him having killed Ari. Chess couldn't say he was sorry for murdering her—she'd been friends with his mother and was a decent fuck, but she'd also clung to him like bad cologne, always wanting more. More attention, more pleasure, more *him*, though he wasn't sure if she ever actually liked him or if she liked his position of power—as small as it was. Either way, he didn't have to worry about her anymore. He *did* have to worry about Rav trying to hunt her down now though. With Ari gone, he would be searching for her and whoever made her disappear. And he wouldn't be alone. Apparently, he'd recruited his mother's friends, including Anna. Anna who could've passed for Imogen's sister. Chess knew if he saw her it would stir up memories of his mother that he'd rather leave buried.

"Don't think too hard. I wouldn't want you to hurt

yourself," Ever quipped from where she sat on the floor, recounting their supplies. Guns had been impossible to find on short notice, but they had retrieved one more dagger for her collection and raided the blood bank.

Chess snorted, twisting the strings of the hoodie he'd stolen, and watched Ever carefully as she loaded her backpack, not sparing him a glance. He couldn't help thinking about the way Ari's appearance made him feel. Nervous, yes, because maybe Rav was right behind him, and then pissed because she could have blown his lie out of the water. But it was the rush of adrenaline urging him to protect Ever that irritated him. He'd hunted her for years to kill her. *Protect her?* Never. He huffed and turned his attention to the supplies still spread out neatly on the ground.

Seventeen blood bags, the three guns Ever already owned with a box of silver bullets, and four daggers. She'd packed two wigs into her backpack already—one with brown curls, another a dark bob—plus a change of clothes for them both.

"Are the costumes really necessary?" he asked.

"They're *disguises*, and do you really need to ask? Ari spotted you easily enough."

"Point taken," he grumbled. Ari had followed him with no trouble because he was so focused on Ever. *Damn.* He really needed to step up his game.

"Here." Ever tossed a blond wig at him. "I cut this into a style just for you."

Chess snatched the wig in the air and scowled. "I don't think this is my color."

"It's fit for a vampire prince." Ever grinned, seeming to know that the wig looked like shit. "Try it on and stop complaining."

"Demanding thing, aren't you?" Chess purred, slipping the wig over his chestnut hair, not bothering to tuck any strands beneath. "What do you think?"

"It will do." She pursed her lips in what appeared to be an

attempt not to laugh.

Chess reached for a hand mirror beside the mattress. Looking at his reflection, his eyes widened in horror. Stringy strands hung down his neck and back while choppier spikes rested on top. "What the fuck is this atrocity?"

"I believe the mortals call it a mullet."

"No." Chess ripped the wig from his head and glowered at it. "I've seen stylish mullets and *this* … this is an insult."

Ever batted her long lashes innocently at him. "No one could ever accuse you of being unstylish, Princeling, which makes it the perfect disguise."

"Yeah, fuck that," he grumbled and lunged for the scissors on the other side of the room.

"Don't you dare," Ever shouted, and leapt onto his back. "The whole point is to make you look different. Remember *you* were the one who was spotted the other night."

He grunted as her weight shoved him to the floor on his stomach. "Trust me, I'll look plenty different with this baggy-arse hoodie. The bad mullet is vetoed, Queenie." Everyone had their limits and he wouldn't be caught dead wearing that wig.

"We don't have time for you to fix it," she huffed, her warm breath brushing his ear. He shivered inwardly at the soft caress of it.

Chess rolled beneath her so she was straddling his abdomen, his fingers at her hips. It closely reminded him of the position they were in the other night. He imagined himself slowly slipping into her heat as she rolled her supple body forward. "We have time," he rasped. "Plenty of time, in fact, if you're interested in finishing what we started on the second floor of the club." He lifted a hand from her hips and traced her lips with his fingers, surprised when she didn't shove him away.

Ever drew in a sharp breath, her eyes flicking to his mouth. Then she snatched the wig from the floor and pushed herself up. "Time to go, Princeling."

Chess missed the weight of her on top of him. Damn, he needed a release—preferably by her hands. Or better yet, her mouth. Those perfect lips would undoubtedly feel like bliss running down his hard shaft. He eased his upper body up to lean on his elbows and watched her shove everything into her bag with a smirk on his face. She had considered his offer to continue, if only for half a moment. Which meant she had to want him too … wanted him to taste every inch of her, touch, tease, fill her up and wring out every drop of pleasure. The question was how much? Enough to have a tumble despite the loathing she harbored for him? The possibility felt a little closer every day they spent together. For once, he was glad he failed at assassinating her in the past.

Ever swung her bag over her shoulder and fished the key from her pocket. "Up, up," she urged, motioning for him to stand. "We're losing the night."

Chess's grin widened. "It's barely midnight."

"Yes, well…" She blew out a breath. "We're leaving. That's an order."

"Oh?" Chess was on his feet the next moment, moving fluidly until he was standing an inch from her. Taking her chin between his fingers, he laughed. "You may be a queen, but you are not *my* queen. Unless, of course, you'd like to be. Once I reclaim Scarlet, of course."

She stilled, her lips parting, her eyes widening at his words. They stared at each other for a moment too long before she batted his hand away and scurried up the ladder.

Chess stayed rooted to the spot. Had he really just suggested she become his wife? He'd meant to make her uncomfortable, to put her in her place and show how she couldn't control him. But he would *never* take her as a queen—in fact, he would never take a queen at all. There were too many souls out there left to ravage in his bed to let just one vampire lay claim to it. He shook his head. She took it as intended—as a bad joke.

"Chess!" Ever called from outside of the safe house.

He scrambled up the ladder and pulled himself out into the cool evening air. "Don't get your panties in a twist, Queenie."

She sighed heavily before closing and locking the hidden door again. "This is a mistake, isn't it?" she asked when she stood beside him.

"Care to be more specific? There are a lot of things that could be considered a mistake lately." Kissing each other, cohabitating with the enemy, murdering old acquaintances…

Ever began walking, her steps sure and brisk. Chess followed beside her while scanning the area in case any of Rav's spies were lurking about, but they seemed alone. Once they were back in Wonderland, vampires would be nearly everywhere, so he'd enjoy it while he could.

"So," Chess drawled to distract himself from the idea of his highly-probable impending capture. He wasn't quite ready to face Wonderland again, knowing his mother was no longer part of it. Knowing that everyone likely thought he was the murderer. "This mistake you spoke of. It's leaving your violin behind, isn't it?"

"Viola," she corrected. "Quit being a fool, you know what it is. But alas, it's too large to carry around with us so I'll come back for it later. The mistake is bringing *another* large, unnecessary thing instead."

Chess scanned her over, finding nothing that matched her description. Everything they had fit inside her one bag.

"You," she said slowly when it became obvious that he didn't understand. "I meant bringing you, of all people, with me to reclaim my throne is undoubtedly going to fuck me over in the end."

"I can fuck you any time you'd like." He flashed a playful grin, but her words rang true.

"You never stop, do you?" She leapt across a small stream and kicked aside a prickly bush, revealing a hole. *A portal.* "Try and take my heart again, and I'll take yours first, understand?”

“I’m content with your heart right where it is,” he said with a laugh. One day, that might change, but for now, her company was growing on him.

Ever then motioned toward the portal but Chess hesitated. “Are you waiting for a written invitation to my kingdom?” She cocked her head.

No—he was actively trying to justify returning to Wonderland when everyone would be hunting him down like a rabid werewolf. How would he hide the truth for long when he couldn’t be seen? “If you have one,” he answered. “Perhaps on embossed cardstock? With a little gold leaf on the invitation to make it *pop*.”

“Bloody hell,” she mumbled, grabbing hold of his hand.

“Well, if you wanted to touch me again all you had to do was ask.” Chess looked to the night sky, taking in the stars, and released a resigned breath.

Ever then yanked him forward, making him lose his footing. He stumbled into the hole and took one step forward through the mirror-like portal. White, glowing bugs crawled around the edges like a living frame. Vibrations ran along his skin, sending a shiver down his spine, but it ended in seconds as he stepped into a monochrome forest.

Most of the landscapes in Ivory were a mixture of white and silver, but there was none of the latter here. The bare trees were so white that they seemed almost fake, and the short grass blended into one giant blanket covering the ground. Even the dead leaves on the grass were pure alabaster. Like always, the pristine land brought the urge to ruin something. Chess wanted to dig in his heels, crush up the dried foliage and scatter their dust about. Instead, he scuffed his shoes on the ground, hoping there was something really nasty lodged into the soles.

“I hadn’t realized we were so close to a portal into Ivory,” Chess said. His voice was quiet, the atmosphere demanding their silence. It was oppressive here—the forest almost requiring perfection of anyone who laid eyes upon it. He recognized the staleness to the air, though, the coldness. The smell had taken over Ivory shortly after Ever disappeared.

Ever shrugged. "Why *would* you know?"

Because he'd traveled all through Ivory and Scarlet over the centuries, portals were one of his favorite things to discover. "The world is my oyster. I make a point of knowing where all the pearls are."

Ever released a quick breath. "We'll go to one of my safe houses next to the rendezvous point until it's time to meet with March."

"How would March know to meet us here?" Chess asked as she sauntered away from him. He quickly caught up with her and drew her back by the wrist.

She smiled wide. "Oh, did I forget to tell you? While you were getting your beauty rest the other night, I met up with March and he's to be one of Rav's shining white knights at the Ivory Palace."

Chess arched a brow. "Hold the fuck up. I'm going to ignore the fact that you snuck off into the night without me, but Rav is just inviting anyone to be a guard in Ivory now?"

"Seems so."

Bastard. Chess wasn't sure if he meant the thought for Rav or March, but it fit them both. After Imogen spent years planting spies, bribing Ever's guards, and plotting the White Queen's assassination, Rav was tossing any random bloke in the castle to protect it? And March… He was sure the male would come through on Ever's behalf, but Chess didn't relish the idea of seeing him again. "You're sure he'll meet us there then?" he asked, hoping to avoid it.

"I'm sure of my friends," she said without hesitation.

Chess glanced at her from the corner of his eyes. If she kissed all of her *friends* like she'd kissed March at the club, the rumors of her lack of experience wouldn't have spread. But if she claimed they weren't lovers, he would believe her.

Because, honestly, it didn't matter to him. He'd personally fucked a good portion of Wonderland himself.

Following Ever through Ivory, Chess continuously scanned their surroundings, but not a single vampire appeared to be in the forest where they entered. It was no wonder Chess had never stumbled upon the portal—there were only trees, trees, and more trees, none with leaves, as if this were a wasteland. The animals lurking about made it clear that there was plenty of life here though. Silver foxes with red eyes slunk into their den as they walked by, and albino birds watched them curiously from the bare branches. Angry squirrels with bared fangs chased each other through the dried leaves covering the ground, chittering back and forth.

When silver began to creep back in, breaking up the blinding white land—first as a handful of leaves still clinging to the branches, then as entire, glimmering trees—his heart beat a little faster. This was the Ivory he knew.

The ivory teeming with vampires.

Ever stopped at a small creek. Silver water flowed over opaque rocks with white tadpoles racing between them. The trees ended on one side and, on the other, were rolling hills. White grass and silver rocks as far as the eye could see. An ear-piercing screech filled the air, high-pitched yet brimming with power. Chess jumped—though he would've fully denied it if Ever pointed out that fact.

"The Jabberwocky," Ever said solemnly. "What's it doing here?"

Chess released a small chuckle. "At least something scares you more than my mother. Once Rav is dead, looks like you'll still have a nemesis to conquer."

"Your mother didn't scare me." Ever took a leaping step over the creek and walked softly down the path leading between swells of land. Chess hurried after her before she could disappear between the hills. Once he was at her side, she continued, "I didn't run because I was afraid. I ran because it was the smart thing to do. There would be no reclaiming the throne from the grave."

"If you say so, Queenie." He cringed as another screech rang out. At least it sounded farther away. The Jabberwocky was a problem neither of them could've planned for, but, even if they could've known the beast was traveling out of Red, he wouldn't have agreed to crossing its path. "For the record, I was scared of her on occasion myself."

Ever tilted her head to study him and opened her mouth when a shout rang out.

"Fuck!" an unseen male bellowed from farther down the path. "Fuck, fuck!"

"Calm down, Garrett!" a female hissed almost as loudly. Movement fluttered at the bend in the pathway ahead. "You'll attract its attention."

"Don't tell me to calm down, Dinah. We need to get out of here. If anyone was hiding around here, the Jabberwocky will have beat us to them."

Chess recognized those fucking voices. Vampires from Scarlet. He'd even enjoyed them both, separately, once or twice. *Dinah and Garrett.* They weren't part of Scarlet's guards—they would've been dead if they were, apparently— but they had been good friends with his mother. *Fuck this.*

Chess bolted up the side of a hill and pressed himself tightly against the wide trunk of a white tree, leaving Ever alone on the path. At least she had her disguise.

He grimaced. Maybe he should've worn her damn wig after all. If they attacked Ever, he'd be forced to step in to end things, but leaving a trail of bodies wasn't what he'd consider stealthy.

A stocky female wearing red leather trousers and an even stockier male with a metal bar pierced through the middle of his nose rounded the path and came to a dead stop. "Hello," Garrett called. "Are you lost?"

"No." Ever shifted her weight between her feet, keeping

her head down. "Just taking a short cut."

They prowled closer, circling her like she was prey, taking slow, purposeful steps as they eyed the White Queen over from head to toe. Ever stood perfectly still, looking far too relaxed for Chess's liking, but her calmness would likely save her. The pair had been fleeing the Jabberwocky a moment ago and her lack of obvious fear would send them on their way without much fuss.

Dinah smiled, baring her fangs. Chess tensed. That was *not* a good sort of smile. "All alone? A sweet thing like you."

Ever shrugged. "The Jabberwocky seems too busy tracking you at the moment to worry about me."

As if on cue, the beast let out a different sort of cry. One that shook the trees and the ground beneath Chess's feet. Judging by the excited—*terrifying*—note in the call, the Jabberwocky had picked up on the scent of its dinner. Dinah shared a petrified look with Garrett before speaking again. "Off you go then. Be sure to report any sightings of—" Another roar, closer this time. "Fuck it. Let's go." But Garrett was already fleeing from them. "Ya bleeding coward," Dinah shouted, and took off after him.

Chess loosened a breath and counted to ten before peeling himself away from the tree and scrambling back down the hill to Ever's side. "We should probably go too," he suggested.

Ever crossed her arms, smirking. "What's wrong, Princeling?"

Was she serious? The Jabberwocky was tracking Dinah and Garrett … who just happened to run straight past them. Something large, angry, and loud as shit. "Is there a problem with your hearing?"

"No, but I thought there was something wrong with my eyesight for a moment. Why did you hide?" she asked, almost smug.

"I may have fucked them. Both, if that was unclear," he said truthfully. It was clearly not the reason he didn't want to be seen, but he couldn't tell Ever that they were likely hunting *him*. They wouldn't be like Ari—they would certainly try and hand him over to Rav. He turned his gaze to the sky, expecting to see a beastly shape soar overhead. "It would've been a tad awkward."

Ever scowled. He could see it in her eyes—the knowledge that Chess would never find running into an old lover to be awkward. But then the Jabberwocky cried out again, saving him from her questions.

A loud *whoosh* of wind whipped around them, and Chess latched onto Ever's hand just as a shadow passed over them. He knew without looking what it was. He knew and he stared up anyway.

The Jabberwocky.

"Move," Ever snapped, and tore down the path, dragging Chess along with her.

CHAPTER TWELVE

EVER

Ever's heart was two seconds from exploding out of her chest. And no, she wasn't being melodramatic.

The Jabberwocky had never ventured into Ivory in the past. But perhaps with the Red Queen dead and the White Queen being gone for so long, the curious beastie was a bit more adventurous. Generally, it was only the rogue werewolves who attempted to slip into her territory and stir up problems. However, her guards had always shot them down before they could wreak havoc on her city.

Above them, bats flew from the trees, their wings pumping violently as they banded together in the air. The Jabberwocky tore toward them, the beat of its leathery wings shaking the trees, the entire forest. Ever's wig whipped around her head from the wind.

The Jabberwocky appeared the same as when she'd seen it last in Red, just before it had gobbled the hellion Red Queen up. Its massive bat-like leather wings cracked, its gnarled and curved talons ready to swipe a meal. Dark green, almost black, fur covered its entire body, thorns ran the length of its elongated tail, and thin spikes sprouted down its head. Barbed quills poked out from its fur—the creature's size could best compare with a dragon. Opening its large mouth, with rows of sharpened teeth, even wider, the creature shot forward, not leaving a single bat in the sky. The Jabberwocky then circled the air, swooping downward.

Ever yanked Chess toward the nearest tree, slipping behind several silver hanging vines that barely concealed them. Turning, he pushed her back against the bark, caging her in. She couldn't tell if the prince was trapping her in or *protecting* her.

Above them, the Jabberwocky continued to loop, cracking its tail like a whip as it searched for more prey. Ever clutched the front of Chess's shirt and didn't take a breath while his warm body held her still. With a shrill shriek that pierced her eardrums, would have shattered them if they'd belonged to a mortal, the creature darted away, the beat of its wings fading.

Once they were out of danger's way, Chess's chest heaved against hers as she finally took a breath. Then their eyes met, mischief shining in his yellow irises. A smirk crossed Chess's face as he peered down at her hand still grasping his shirt. "You're not pushing me away," he drawled.

Ever didn't want to shove him back like he expected her to do. So with a smirk of her own, she released his shirt and slowly trailed her finger down his chest, his taut abs, halting at his waistband. She partially dipped her digits inside, brushing warm skin, while toying with the ties of his trousers by using her thumb. "Do you want me to touch you?"

The prince's throat bobbed and his eyes became hooded. "Fuck yes."

"Nah, we don't have time for that, Princeling." She laughed, then playfully shoved him away. But a part of her yearned to see and feel what so many in Wonderland had, even though the thought should've revolted her.

Chess hauled her back to him, a wicked grin spreading across his face. He lowered his head beside her ear, a fluttering forming in her stomach, warming. "Perhaps if it's me touching you?" He paused, his voice deep with his next word. "Fingers, tongue, or cock. Your choice. Either way, I'll make you come like you never have before, Queenie."

The place that yearned for him to use all three of those tightened at his alluring words. Betraying her. She wanted him to touch, to circle, to lick, then to press inside her. Damn it.

"Who do we have here?" a female voice cooed from a gnarled tree across from them. Ever and Chess broke apart, her fangs lowering, as the two Scarlet vampires stepped out from behind the trunk. Dinah and Garrett. They must've hidden as well, knowing they couldn't outrun the beast.

"The traitorous prince and the cowardly queen." Garrett chuckled, pressing his fist to his mouth. "Together? Our king's been looking for you, Chess. And for what you did to your mother, you're going to pay dearly."

"You really will fuck anyone, won't you?" Dinah shook her head, wrinkling her nose in disgust. "It's now obvious why you killed your mother. Because you're the White Queen's lapdog. You'll turn on anyone."

Before the queen or Chess could speak, Dinah released her fangs and lunged for Ever. The queen whirled around her, then thrust the vampire against the trunk. She slammed her boot into Dinah's upper back. The female released a growl, but she was much weaker than Ever. The queen gripped the female's head and yanked it to the side, giving Dinah an extra rush of pain before tearing it from her shoulders. Hot blood sprayed the queen's face and shirt. Ever then tossed the head beside the body as thick crimson oozed down her hand.

She turned to Chess, who stood gripping Garrett's bloody heart in his hand, the vampire's body dead on the ground. The blood *drip, drip,* dripped while the prince stood frozen like a fool, not peering up at her, but studying the heart. An unreadable expression rested on his face.

"Tastes like victory." Ever swiped the tip of her tongue across the blood on her palm, wishing she could see into vampires' memories the way she could with a mortal's. Then maybe she would've been able to get some insight into Rav.

"The last time I held a heart," Chess whispered, "it was my mother's."

Ever's thoughts turned to Maddie, her friend telling her how she'd killed the queen. How Chess had come into the room and lifted his mother's dead heart, how tears had streamed down his cheeks. How Ever had believed the bastard prince didn't know how to cry.

A boisterous roar sounded, interrupting Ever's thoughts. The Jabberwocky was coming back. It must've smelled the blood that Ever and Chess had spilled, and if it didn't, then the beast surely would soon.

Thankfully the safe house wasn't too far away from their location. So the Jabberwocky wouldn't track them, Ever tore off her bloody T-shirt, leaving her wearing only her bra. She then ripped the heart that Chess was still holding out of his hand and tossed it beside the corpses.

"Come on, you idiot," Ever shouted, grabbing his hand.

The words must've drawn him from his thoughts because his legs started to move faster while she dragged him along with her. They skirted around trees, avoiding as many leaves and twigs as they could. She yanked Chess to the right, letting her enhanced speed take them across the rolling hills and through the luscious landscape.

The shimmering stream slid into view and she ran even faster. They came to a stop in front of the flowing water, sucking in gulps of air. She quickly washed the remaining blood from her arms, face, and neck as Chess did the same.

The Jabberwocky's sounds had vanished, but Ever still hurried to take out her key and unlock the secret door in the ground beside the stream. She didn't know what enemy might make an appearance next—there had been a few too many already in their brief time back in Wonderland. For all she knew, Rav would slink up soon since two of his Scarlet lackeys were here … and now dead.

As Ever opened the door, she motioned Chess inside. "Go."

Ever slipped into the safe house and closed the door behind them, locking them in. Her heart continued to beat wildly as she walked down the stone steps into an almost bare ivory room that held an earthy scent. A few blankets rested atop a mattress against the wall, and a wooden chair tucked into a small table, with a crate containing packets of dried blood atop it, sat in the corner. She fished out a clean shirt from her backpack and tossed her wig to the floor before sliding the fabric on.

"Told you we would need spare clothing," she said as she ran a hand over her pinned-up hair.

Chess peeled off his blood-speckled hoodie and lowered himself on the mattress, not glancing up at her.

"What is it?" Ever asked. "Cat got your tongue?"

"It's got a lot of things actually." For once, his voice wasn't assured while he stayed peering at his clasped hands. "About what happened back there, about what they said, it's not—"

Ever had wondered if he was going to say anything about his mother's death first. She folded her arms over her chest and took a step toward him. "Don't try and lie. We're past that and this part of your game needs to come to an end. You think I'm a *fool*? You believed that March really wouldn't know about what was happening in Wonderland? That he wouldn't tell me Rav killed his guards and how he's now recruiting your mother's friends to replace them? That he isn't turning mortals into vampires anymore but leaving them in a trance? And that every vampire knows you're wanted by my brother for the murder of his queen?"

"I didn't know any of that and I *didn't* murder my mother." His gaze met hers then, his voice steady. "At first I thought Rav blamed me on purpose, but it seems he really believes it was me. It wasn't."

"I know it wasn't," Ever bit back. And she knew the mistake as soon as she said it, but she hadn't been thinking about Maddie.

"You know?" He eyed her suspiciously.

"I know because, back there? When you were holding Garrett's heart, I know why you stood so still. You were thinking about your mother. You loved her."

"And you hated her," he accused, his voice bitter.

"I did." Anger coursed through her veins as she started to think about that bitch, truly think about all she'd done. "For her sending you to kill me. For hurting my friends. For turning mortals without a fucking care. For murdering anyone who wouldn't do what she wanted. I understand that you loved her, because I still love my brother, but I can see when my own flesh and blood is a monster." She slapped her hand to her chest, right over her heart. "We may be monsters, too, but your mother was the greatest one of all. She abandoned you as a child, then showed up in your life years later, turned you, and hauled you back to Wonderland without your consent. Did you even *want* to be a vampire? Don't you care that she murdered your own damn father? He was a good male who wanted to give you a choice of what life you wanted. Instead of giving you that opportunity, she murdered him with my fucking brother's help, then dragged you to her hell."

"Shut up," he whispered, his nostrils flaring as his fists shook.

"No." She gritted her teeth and knelt in front of him. "I will not. My brother is a bastard and I know it, so how can you not see it? How can you not have feelings about what she's done?"

"I see it, damn it." His jaw tightened, his hand slamming

against the mattress. "I know what my mother was. But she loved me. Who the fuck else ever would?"

Even though her stomach sank at what he'd spoken, she had to continue. These were words she'd held inside her chest for years. Words she should've spewed at him in that garden instead of fleeing. "She did in her own way, but to her, you were *her* tool. Would she have still loved you if you had told her no? What would she have done to you if you'd refused to take my heart?"

"And isn't that what I am to you right now?" he seethed. "A tool?"

"Don't." Ever held up a finger. "Don't pretend for a second that you weren't trying to use me." She needed to get up and walk away before she said something worse, before she admitted that Maddie had been the one to kill his mother and she was glad for it.

Ever stood and padded halfway across the room, when Chess's hand clasped her wrist. He tightened his grip, then backed her into a wall so his firm body was once again pressed to hers. "You're a fool." He narrowed his eyes at her, then lowered his face, his nose brushing hers. "After everything, after our past, you turned your back on me. If I'd wanted, I could've easily ripped your fucking heart out."

"Is that your end game?" she spat. "Tearing it out because you didn't get the chance to before? Even after all you've done, when I could've easily killed your foolish arse a hundred times in the mortal world, I didn't." *Not to say I won't.*

The prince's chest heaved—the vein at his jaw feathered, the one at his neck thrumming harder. She was prepared to spew more spiteful words with whatever asinine reply that came out of his mouth next, but instead, he brought her to him and folded his arms around her, his body trembling while he cried.

Ever's eyes widened, and she didn't know what the bloody hell was happening as her head rested on his chest. She knew she could've been anyone in that moment, but he apparently just needed this. Over the past several days, she hadn't hated him as she should've, yet she didn't think she liked him either. Perhaps she did a little, though, because she lifted her arms around him, holding him as he cried. The prince of Scarlet, who always had a smirk on his face, was vulnerable for once.

After a long while, when he stopped shaking, she took a step back from him. Her gaze locked onto Chess's, his eyes red-rimmed from crying. "Now that your lies are out in the open, you can continue with me or go back into hiding. If you decide to leave, I promise I won't tell my brother I saw you. Unless you turn on me, that is." There was one thing he still wasn't telling her—he knew Maddie had killed his mother. But Ever would never put her friend at risk by admitting that.

"Rav has to die, and the only way it will happen is if you and I continue to stay aligned." He paused, eyeing her warily. "However, I'm not much of a prince at the moment."

In response, Ever could have said so many awful things, yet she chose to speak the truth. "No, Chess. You're the king of Scarlet. Its rightful heir. And if my viola were here, I'd play us a song to prepare for our destinies."

CHAPTER THIRTEEN

CHESS

Chess followed Ever along the crest of a ridge toward a sparkling silver lake where they were meant to meet March. Four white gazebos with scrolling silver iron railings were spaced around it and a dock reached a few feet into the water where a canoe was tethered. He imagined parties took place here in the past.

But now, despite the beauty, it felt lifeless. As if no one had visited in ages. He couldn't put his finger on why it felt that way—perhaps it was that the air was too still or the temperature was cooler than it had been when he and Ever had exited the safe house moments ago. Or maybe it was all in his head.

Since he'd broken down and cried the night before, the whole world seemed off. Just slightly—like someone had tilted the earth a degree or two—but there wasn't time to get his footing. He'd fucking *cried*. In front of Ever, no less. *Bloody idiot.* He'd learned on the streets at a young age not to show his feelings or weaknesses. Then no one could use them against him. Now his enemy held that power.

Well… He glanced down at Ever as she walked beside him. The curls of her brunette wig bounced gently around her cheeks, and the urge to brush them away filled him. *Maybe she wasn't exactly his enemy.* There had been a subtle shift between them. An unspoken understanding after seeing another side of each other. Chess vulnerable and Ever comforting. It was strange and yet he didn't loathe it. He sure as hell didn't understand it, but it wasn't unwelcome. Why had he hated her for so long?

Because of his mother…

"I'm surprised they haven't torn any of this down," Ever whispered as they reached the nearest gazebo. Marble benches ran along the interior walls with a small, empty brazier at the center. "This used to be one of my favorite places. The music from my viola traveled so well here and everyone would sing and dance the night away."

"Even the humans?" Chess asked, genuinely curious. In Scarlet, no one danced unless it was in someone's blood.

"Sometimes." Ever sank onto the bench and looked out over the lake. "Most of the time they were … *busy* after feeding a vampire."

Chess smirked, knowing exactly what sort of activity usually followed. "At least Scarlet has something in common with this place. A good fucking after a good feeding."

Ever snorted. "No, Princeling, both the feeding and the fucking in Ivory are never simply *good.* They're always amazing. What sort of court were you running?"

"To be fair, I wasn't running anything. If I had been home more often, maybe I could've saved those poor souls from mediocre pleasure." He winked as he sat down beside her and scanned the area, looking for any sign of vampires, finding none. As much as he would love to tell Ever tales of his prowess and watch her reaction, they were there with a purpose. "Your friend is late."

Ever drew in a steadying breath. "March will be here."

If he wasn't discovered. Or killed. Or a traitor.

Ever said she trusted the male but she seemed to trust Chess too. Obviously, she was mistaken with Chess since he planned to betray her by killing Maddie, so she could be wrong twice. He looked at her again and sucked on his bottom lip. The thought of seeing her dead—or worse, alive and aware of his duplicity—made him shift uncomfortably on the bench. His blood warmed in shame. Was he really going to go through with it? Ever wouldn't forgive him once he killed Maddie, but that was the only reason he could think of for continuing down this path. They both wanted Rav dead and, once he was, his gut told him that they would be able to rule their respective kingdoms without too many issues. Maybe if he gave up his revenge…

Don't go getting soft, he warned himself. Imogen had been a shit mother, sure, but she still needed to be avenged. Even if she had forced immortality on him—he liked it now, after all—and lied to him. Ever said his father had been a good male, wanted Chess to have a choice about immortality, while his mother only ever disparaged the male. It was too late to know for sure now that he was dead. His mother had been his only blood relation for centuries and that counted for something.

Right?

Regardless of what he decided to do about Ever, the truth was he might not get the chance to double-cross her now that she knew the truth about him. Apparently Ever knew the *entire* time. She'd been playing with him, letting him spin his lies. She must've just *loved* that. Allowing him to look like a fool. Embarrassment burned beneath his skin, but the fact that she hadn't actually cared about his predicament cooled him slightly. She hadn't treated him any differently now that the truth was out. In fact, the wall he had created seemed to have crumbled, allowing them to see each other over the ruins. Somehow. He scowled. Was that normal? During his long life, he hadn't bothered to connect with anyone on an emotional level…

"He's here," Ever whispered.

Chess sat up straight and shifted a bit closer to her. A blur of motion came from the other side of the lake, a quick flash of red. Then March stood before them in his guard uniform, crimson with black piping along the front. They were very different than the stark white ones Chess had seen at the ball four years ago.

"Your Majesty," March said, bowing slightly, his braids slipping over his shoulders. "It's so good to see you."

Ever leapt up from her seat and hugged him tightly. When he returned the hug, Chess gripped the edge of the bench to keep himself seated. "It's good to see you too," she said with so much sincerity that Chess rolled his eyes.

"All right, all right," he snapped from his seat. "Enough with the touchy-feely. What information do you have?"

The two broke apart and March glowered down at him. Chess gripped the marble harder—he would *not* give the male the satisfaction of knowing how agitating his presence was. Though agitated might be too mild a term for the growing emotion inside of him. The sight of March's hand still on Ever's waist woke a territorial part of Chess that he hadn't known existed.

"I don't take orders from you," March said calmly.

"Who *do* you take them from, then?" Chess arched a brow. "Your queen? Or have Rav's cohorts put you under their spell yet? I know from experience just how alluring it can be to strive for Scarlet's ideals. All that gorging on blood, the death, the carefree—"

"Chess," Ever said in a flat tone. "Not now."

He narrowed his eyes at her and, reluctantly, snapped his mouth shut. It wasn't like him to take orders from anyone—

especially her—but the faster they got March's intel, the faster they could get away from him. Leaning back into the gazebo's railing, he motioned to March for them to continue.

"I have to be quick in case I was followed. They're keeping a close eye on me since I'm new," March said in a low voice. No one outside of the lake area would be able to pick up on his words. "As we already knew, Rav took out a lot of the guards here."

"How many are left of the ones who betrayed me?" Ever asked.

March cast a wary glance at Chess and hesitated before speaking. "Three, that I know of. They're the ones in charge of the new vampires Rav's been sending as replacements. One of them is on duty at all times. The good news is that the rest of us aren't trained as guards—we're given uniforms and told where to stand watch. The bad news is that the palace is now run by cutthroats with no morals and have no problem murdering citizens if they look at them sideways."

Ever's expression turned stony. "How many guards in all?"

"Twelve." March took Ever's hand and tugged her a few steps away from Chess, toward the opening to the gazebo. "Are you *sure* he should be hearing this?"

"He's fine," Ever assured him with a distracted wave of her hand. "What's the best way to get inside?"

"The—"

Chess leaned forward, resting his elbows on his knees and tilting his head as if this answer were particularly intriguing. It wasn't—he was simply along for the ride on this part of their journey—but he knew it would make March squirm. And squirm he did. The vampire leaned closer to Ever, wrapping a protective arm around her shoulders, and positioned her so they could flee together. As if Chess would suddenly decide to murder the White Queen after all this time when she had back up.

"Go on," Chess urged with a vicious smirk. "Tell us how to get into the castle, pretty boy."

March sneered and his fangs dropped. "I can't do this, Ever. How can you trust him? I'm about to tell you the greatest weakness to the castle's defenses *in front of the enemy*."

Ever released an exasperated sigh. "What do you think he'll do, March? Run and tattle to Rav? Do you think my brother will let him live long enough to tell him our secrets?"

"Technically, he's only ordered my arrest," Chess said with a shrug. Unless Rav had upgraded the order from throwing him in the dungeon to lopping off his head. "I'd have *plenty* of time to wag my tongue. And I'm good with my tongue, aren't I?" He licked his lips suggestively, eyeing Ever, knowing full well that March would misunderstand. Then, from their earlier conversation, he added, "Some would even say *more* than good, despite my being from Scarlet."

Ever turned toward him, meeting his gaze straight on with an icy stare that seemed to say *don't lie just to rile him up*. But he couldn't help himself. March made it too easy. If the male had only hugged Ever, clung to her hand and whispered in her ear, he would've behaved. Mostly. But Chess wasn't one to lie down and take personal insults from anyone, let alone someone as inferior as—

Ever opened her mouth, but before a word could pass through her lips, March lunged forward. Chess leapt from the bench and met him midair, fangs dropping. Together, they landed, slamming into the brazier, the metal clanging as it flew out from beneath their bodies. Everything that happened next was a blur of fists and fangs.

Chess took a particularly solid punch to the jaw that knocked his head into the edge of the bench. Stars burst behind his eyes. He shook his head to clear his vision, but before he could, March's fangs were lodged in the side of his neck. *Fuck.* He leaned into the bite so March couldn't rip the flesh from him and rolled, dragging March closer to the fallen brazier.

Grabbing a metal leg of the brazier, Chess swung the entire firepit at the back of March's head. It slammed against his skull, jostling him enough for Chess to free his throat. Hot blood flowed down from the wound. With a hiss, he lunged for March, mouth open, ready to tear out his throat.

A forearm suddenly appeared between them. It was too close for Chess to stop himself before chomping down on the flesh. Blood burst in his mouth, rich and … familiar. He unclenched his jaw, removing his fangs from Ever, and fell backward onto his arse, chest heaving.

"Enough," she growled, her gaze darting all around. "Not only are you two completely out of line, you're putting us in danger. Do you *want* us to get caught?"

"Sorry," both Chess and March mumbled, and shot scathing looks at each other.

Chess stood gracefully and wiped Ever's blood from his lips. "I—"

"I don't want to hear it. Play nice—end of story," she snapped at him before rounding on March. "Now, I'll ask again. How do we get into the castle?"

March got to his feet and straightened his uniform as best he could. "There's a loose grate hidden behind some bushes that leads into the cellar baths."

"Perfect. And when is the next shift change?"

March balled his hands into fists and flexed them again. "Two hours from now."

"We'll meet you in the baths in two hours then," she said with a note of finality. "Go before someone notices you're missing."

March gave a stiff bow. "Be careful around him," he warned before stomping out of the gazebo and racing away from the lake.

"That was eventful," Chess said once they were alone. Ever folded her arms over her chest, drawing his attention to her breasts instead of her pursed lips. The fabric of her T-shirt was taut, showing the swells perfectly behind the graphic of a skull that read *dead inside*. He couldn't help wondering what the tempting globes would feel like in his hands, against his tongue, the sound she would make when he sucked her nipple into his mouth. A rush of heat soared through him, straight to his cock. "You know, the only thing better than feeding and fucking is fighting and—"

Ever placed a finger to his lips, her skin soft, her lily scent caressing his nostrils. "Don't finish that sentence. If you screw this up for me when I'm finally close to regaining my castle, I won't forgive you. I already shouldn't after that ridiculous scene."

A grin grew on Chess's face. "I can think of a few ways to make it up to you."

"I'm in no mood to talk about your cock right now, you arse," she snarled and stepped out of the gazebo.

Chess licked the last traces of her blood from his lips and watched her hips sway as she stormed away from him. *Damn.* She had no business looking so fuckable when she was pissed. "Wait for me, Queenie," he called, chuckling to himself.

CHAPTER FOURTEEN

EVER

"Are you going to talk to me yet, my prickly white rose?" Chess purred from a tree limb directly above Ever.

She peered up at him in his crouched position and cocked her head. "Why are you hovering in the branch like a cat?"

"I can see all from this angle." He dropped to a hanging position from the branch, swinging with a smirk on his face before dropping and landing on his feet in front of her.

After the "brawl" between Chess and March, Ever had been frustrated, not only because their plan was put at risk from their foolishness, but because she'd been aroused by the way Chess's lithe body had moved, even when ridiculous words had poured out of his mouth.

Ever's fingers, restless, wished to play the viola to release her emotions instead of squeezing the chess piece in her pocket. Once they took out the guards in the palace, she would retrieve her favorite viola from under her bed. Unless Rav had cleared out her room and given her things away, which was most likely the case. Still, she hoped her prized instrument was there.

"So how long have you and March been lovers?" Chess asked, plopping down beside her and ignoring personal space. They had seemed to have passed that point a while ago, though.

She sighed. "Enough of that. March isn't my lover."

Chess perked up like a flower under sunshine, his grin growing wide. "Do tell. He clearly adores you."

Ever didn't know why she was telling him any of this, but perhaps she owed him more truths after his revelations the night before. "March wants more than I can give, so we aren't together in a pleasureful way anymore."

"You were literally kissing each other at the club," Chess pointed out.

And at the park when she'd went to secretly meet him. "There won't be any more of that."

"A pity for him." His grin grew even wider as he took a lock of her wig and twirled it around his finger. "So, who's the better kisser? Me or March?"

"Seriously?" She smacked his hand away from her hair.

"It's me." He chuckled. "If it were March, you would've easily said it."

"Bloody hell, you're a pest." A smile tugged at her lips as she found herself laughing too.

"Trust me, I'm no pest." He leaned close, his warm breath mingling with hers.

Ever fought against the desire to press her lips to his and pulled her thoughts together into a coherent sentence. "We need to go—we don't want to be late for our *very* important date with the guards."

"Ah, yes, a blood bath it will be." Chess stood and drew her up from the ground. Her eyes widened, but she didn't say anything.

They then skirted around trees and slinked out of the forest. The ivory garden came into view, its flowers overgrown—it clearly hadn't been wandered through, even by guards. Their steps remained light and their eyes stayed peeled for guards passing by in the grime-covered windows. The untrimmed bushes near the back of the castle were only a short distance away so they used their enhanced speed to get across. Ever pushed the daisy bushes aside and located the silver grate March had mentioned. When she'd ruled here last, it had been sealed, or at least she believed it had been. Her previous guards' words were no longer trustworthy.

She lifted the loose metal, revealing a hole big enough for them to fit through. Chess didn't hesitate and slipped in first. Keeping as quiet as she could, she climbed in next, then shut the grate behind her before her feet lost purchase against the stone and she fell.

Her heart pounded and she prepared to hit the hard floor, but two waiting hands caught her.

"And you consider me a villain." The prince smirked, his yellow gaze dancing.

"That's exactly what you are," March interrupted as he walked toward them.

Ever leapt from Chess's arms and peered around the cellar baths. It looked much more unkempt than usual—the sparkling white stone floor was covered in muddy boot prints and dirty guard uniforms were piled around the room. The silver walls, ivory clawfoot baths, and several ornate wardrobes that were once filled with towels and scented soaps still appeared the same, though the fur rugs resting in front of each bathtub were covered in brown stains.

"So where are we starting?" Chess asked, rubbing his hands together in anticipation.

"The only door leading out of here," March said with sarcasm, pointing to the wooden door at the opposite side of the room. He then turned to Ever. "Two of your original traitors are just outside this door, Sonny is in the back, and the other nine newer guards are scattered throughout the palace."

"That's good. We should be able to easily pick them off one by one." Ever shrugged. She couldn't risk what occurred last time to happen again. Soon, she would have to rebuild a new guard on her own, one that wouldn't deceive her again.

"I like when you're bloodthirsty," Chess purred in her ear.

March's eyes lingered on Chess a beat too long before motioning them forward. Ever opened the door and Chess bolted through it first. She was going to hiss at him to hold the fuck on, but he already had her old guard Kopa's bloodied head in his hands. When the other bastard guard, Leslie, shot across the room, Ever stepped between her and Chess.

"I bet you weren't expecting us to meet again," Ever seethed at the surprised guard's face, thrusting her hand into the vampire's chest with a sickening squelch and tearing out her beating heart.

The door flew open and two male guards wearing Scarlet uniforms came barreling in. Their gazes widened when they landed on the bodies and blood on the floor, leaving enough time for March to shoot forward, muscles flexing as he swung his sword, cutting cleanly through their necks. Blood sprayed the walls and Chess gave quiet applause.

"Not yet, Princeling," she said, tossing down the heart and rushing up the stairs to the sitting room. Chess and March's feet echoed behind her.

The door at the top of the stairs was locked, but March used his key and shoved it open with a bang. A female guard growled and leapt at March, but her head was already gone before she could touch him, blood oozing like a necklace down her chest.

Ever's pulse raced as they hurried down the narrow hall filled with dead flowers in vases on the walls. They cut through two more empty areas, the silver and white furniture covered in dust. Three guards darted into the sitting room as soon as they entered, hissing and pausing when they spotted Ever and Chess. She didn't think it would be an advantage for her and Chess to be seen together, but apparently it was quite the game-changer.

Ever tore the head from a stocky female, most of the spine coming away with her prize, blood dripping from the bones. A hand gripped her shoulder, but when Ever turned around, the head was gone, the body buckling and falling to the floor beside March and his bloody sword. The third, Chess had already taken care of. A guard flew down the steps and Chess moved like a tiger as he leapt over the handrail and snatched the heart from the male's chest, the rest of the vampire rolling down the stairs to the floor, the sounds building like a crescendo.

Three more left.

As if in answer, two more barreled down the stairs, a female and male, looked at Chess drenched in blood, then started running back up them like cowards. March and Chess went after them as Ever caught her eye on the last living betrayer, Sonny.

Her old guard walked through the door and paused, a smile on his tan face. "Look who's back," he grunted, "but not for long."

Too bad Ever knew all her guards' moves since she'd watched them train over the years, so with him alone, she could do this. She ducked as he reached for her head and she kicked her leg out, tripping him. He fell flat on his stomach with a low grunt and before he could push up, she was on his back, pulling his head toward her. A loud snap reverberated through the room.

Ever landed on her back from the hard yank, the guard's head in her hands, blood drenching her clothing as her chest heaved.

Victory. Or so she hoped.

She hurled the head, then hurried to see if Chess and March

needed help, but they stood at the bottom of the stairs. March wiped his sword on his uniform and Chess was polishing his nails against his bloody hoodie as in a job well done.

"So, that was entertaining," Ever said with a small laugh. "And a bit satisfying. Now you may clap, Chess."

"We need you to play your viola as well." Chess winked at her and March frowned at him.

"Perhaps later if it's still here." She smiled and focused on March. "Do you mind staying here as a guard, at least until Rav's dead?"

"Of course. I wouldn't leave you in a predicament without any guards here."

Ever caught Chess rolling his eyes and she ignored him.

"For now, we'll dispose of the bodies in the cellar," she instructed.

Chess nodded, stacking several and carrying them out of the room. Ever drew March back by his arm. "Tonight, I'm going to tell Maddie we reclaimed the palace and have them come here to help you once Chess and I leave."

"Are you telling him what you're doing?" March whispered.

She shook her head. No, she couldn't put Maddie's life at risk.

"Good," he said and scooped up a dead guard.

They then dumped all the bodies and bloodied pieces down in the cellar before March offered to clean the scarlet from the areas. She wasn't going to let him do it by himself, so she grabbed some cloths to help.

Chess looked at them both while they cleaned as if he'd never done a chore in his entire life. He probably hadn't, at least not since becoming immortal.

"You're not too good, Princeling. Come on." She threw a wet rag at his face and he caught it.

He puckered his lips but sank down beside a pool of blood then started on the task, although he moved much slower with it.

Once everything was spotless, Ever bid March a goodnight and led Chess up the spiral staircase to her room.

"I never had the royal tour of your palace before." He trailed a finger across the rail as if he just needed to always be touching something. "So where are we staying?"

We... "The royal quarters." She held up a finger. "But it's split into two rooms, so you get one and I get one."

She'd been gone for nearly four years and it looked it, without having any servants around to clean and dust. Same as before, pearl chandeliers hung from the ceilings, white chess piece statues rested in the corners, but her famous paintings of musicians hanging across the walls were gone. At the top of the stairs, the portraits of the old king and queen still remained. Her heart sank at the sight of their warm smiles—she still missed them, but it was good to see their faces again.

Ever opened the door, a flowery scent hitting her nose, and locked it behind them. The room was now bare of any of her musical decorations, only white and black walls, like a checkerboard, the floor a sparkling white and the ceiling a glistening obsidian. Her looming wardrobe rested across from the canopy bed covered in silky black sheets, the desk clear of all her notebooks.

She opened one of the two other doors in her room and glanced at Chess, who was studying her bed. "This is an adjoining door to Rav's old rooms. It hasn't been used in a while, unless the Scarlet guards slept there, but you can get some rest in here. A bathroom is attached inside for you to get cleaned up." He was covered in as much blood as she was, yet maybe even a little more.

"You know we can share a bath," he cooed, leaning against a doorframe and gazing at her beneath hooded eyes.

"And what filthy water that would be. We would hardly get cleaned." She chewed on her lip and took a step toward him. "Thank you for your help today. It might have taken me a teeny bit longer to do without you."

Chess chuckled and shrugged. "It was necessary." He turned on his heel and glanced over his shoulder at her with a big smile. "The door to my bathroom will be open, though."

She rolled her eyes and shut the door between them before heading into her own bathing chamber. Not surprisingly, all her things were gone, the counters bare, yet towels hung from the hooks on the wall.

Tossing her backpack in a corner, she peeled her bloody clothing from her body as she let the warm water fill the bath. With a sigh, she sank into the liquid and washed every part of her skin clean with a lavender soap bar until the water was no longer clear. She wondered what Chess would be doing after his bath, most likely lazily sprawled across Rav's old bed. Naked? She shook away the thought of his lithe body, his toned abs, his beautifully sculpted face...

Stop. That.

Ever left her wet hair hanging down her back as she wrapped a fluffy towel around her body. A giddiness filled her that she hadn't felt in a long while. Maybe, just maybe, one of her lacy dresses would be left behind. She opened her wardrobe and blinked. Her clothing wasn't gone—it was all still there. But every piece of fabric was ripped and ruined. A sinking feeling washed over her as she slammed the wardrobe shut and dove for her bed. She lifted the bed skirt and reached beneath it, expecting to touch emptiness. Except she didn't. She sighed as her hand brushed wood, but when she drew her beloved instrument out from the bed, horror filled her.

It was smashed and broken, covered in dust. This was her first instrument, a gift from her Italian uncle, the viola she'd traded with Rav, the one she loved so much. She reached under the bed again and took out the bow ... snapped in half. Tears pricked her eyes. Had Chess come in and done this after she fled? Had one of the guards? Or Imogen? She shoved open the door, finding Chess with a towel around his waist, digging through Rav's full wardrobe of unruined clothing.

"Do you know who did this?" Ever stuttered, hating the sound of her voice as she held up her broken instrument. "Did *you* do this?"

Chess whirled around to face her, his brow furrowed while studying the viola in her hand. He then shook his head. "I remember Rav said he was going to take care of some of your things, but I didn't know what that meant. I thought he was just clearing them out." That would have been better. If she'd found the instrument gone, like she'd thought it was going to be, that would have been better than this. But Rav had wanted to hurt her, in case she ever did try and come back. And he had.

Ever sank to her knees, the instrument clacking to the ground, as she held her face in her hands. She didn't want to cry, not in front of him, but she couldn't control it. "My brother knew how much this meant to me. I can get new clothes, I can build a new palace, but this viola will never play again. I can't get this back. It was what reminded me of home, my parents, a gift from my uncle." Sobs escaped her and she couldn't get them to stop.

Ever waited for Chess to make a joke but he didn't. Instead, he crouched in front of her and tucked a lock of wet hair behind her ear. "I'm sorry."

"It wasn't you who broke it," she whispered.

"No, but I should've tried to kill Rav a long time ago." For the first time, something like guilt crossed his expression.

Ever clasped his face in her hands, drawing him close, taking in the smell of pine. "You're going to do it now, and so am I." She then pressed her lips to his and she told herself she was a fool and to stop. But she didn't want to stop, not as he kissed her back, not as his tongue slipped between her lips and danced with hers, and not as he drew her into his lap.

Chess's lips left her mouth, trailing flames of desire down her throat while he kissed and nipped. She could feel the soft graze of his fangs drifting over her flesh. His fingers fell to her towel, dipping in to remove it, his gaze meeting hers, asking. She nodded and he took the layer of fabric from her skin, exposing her to the cool air of the room. His eyes hungrily roamed over her body—he then lifted her so she could wrap her legs around him, absorbing his warmth. She glided her lips across his again, drinking the sweet nectar that was all him.

Chess lay her gently on the bed, his hand lightly venturing over her breasts and down her stomach to between her thighs, where he cupped her mound. Her heart accelerated at his touch and she moaned when he drew a nipple into his mouth, softly sucking. His fangs then grazed her flesh, following to where his hand rested. They stopped at her inner thigh and he sank his teeth in, her body arching in pleasure. He flicked his tongue over the spot he bit before kissing his way to her core. She moaned as he licked his way up her center before pushing a finger inside her, then another. It had been so long since she'd been in this position with someone, but she couldn't remember it ever feeling like this. His movements were practiced yet tender and wickedly delightful as he caressed with his lips, swirled with his tongue.

A blissful feeling swam through her and she grasped his hair when her body quaked beneath his mouth, her fangs sliding out. He grinned that maddeningly wide grin of his while he crawled up her, caging her in and she *liked* that too. Especially the feel of his hard cock against her, but even the layer of his towel was too much.

She reached for the fabric and unraveled it, then grasped his velvety cock, pumping and stroking, her thumb circling his tip. The prince's head rested on her shoulder for a moment before he sank his fangs into her while she continued her movements. His bites were delectable and she wanted more when he drew back, his breath warm and tickling her neck.

Chess groaned, his body spasming as he spilled himself. "I don't … fall in love," he rasped, his breaths ragged.

"Good." She smiled, trailing her finger up his spine. "Because neither do I."

Chess chuckled, his lips softly kissing hers. He lifted her chin, peering into her eyes. "Just give me a minute and I'll make it so any past lover will be ruined for you."

Ever was tempted, so very tempted. She wanted to feel him slide his hard length into her heat, feel what it would be like to be fucked into oblivion. But she remembered what she'd always told herself because betrayal was always an option. "I don't go past this point. Ever," she breathed.

"Excuse me?" Chess's eyebrows flew up his forehead.

"I don't do more than this," she said, cocking her head. "With anyone. I never have."

He sucked in a sharp breath. "It isn't just a rumor? You're a virgin?"

"Yes. Is that an issue, Princeling?" She smiled at his dumbfounded expression.

"For *centuries*?"

"I've had plenty of pleasure in other ways, and I know how to take care of myself too."

"It's just, you're so … beautiful." His throat bobbed. A second later his expression turned back into a sly one. "Well then, I can show you other ways of pleasure the next time, if you wish. I just never imagined you and I…"

She laughed and tucked a lock of hair behind his ear. "We're quite a mess, aren't we?"

A knock came at the door leading to her room and she jerked up. Ever shoved Chess away and leapt from the bed, grabbing her towel and shutting the door between their rooms. She wiped Chess's pleasure from her hand against the fabric as she wrapped it around herself and hurried to the door.

March stood there, wearing a fresh Scarlet uniform, his eyes widening as he studied her. He took a whiff and she knew he could smell Chess all over her. "I heard noises and just wanted to see if everything was okay."

"It is. Thank you," she said, not meeting his gaze.

"I'll see you soon," he whispered, his shoulders sagging as he turned away.

Ever nodded and shut the door. Guilt washed over her and she didn't understand it. She wasn't with March, and he knew she only wanted to be his friend. But it wasn't only that. Guilt was there because of Maddie. What would she think of what Ever had just done? With someone who wanted her friend dead, who had tried to kill Ever…

A part of her wanted to open the door back to Chess's room and see what would happen next. But she might do something even more foolish. Yet she couldn't stop imagining what it would feel like for him to press inside her and thrust until she could barely remember her own name.

She didn't open the door between their rooms though. There were bigger things in the works than quenching her physical curiosities. Instead, she would wait for him to sleep and once he was, she would leave.

CHAPTER FIFTEEN

CHESS

Chess laid beneath the down-filled duvet, trying to fall asleep in a strange bed, for hours. Not that he hadn't slept in dubious places before, but this was the heart of Ivory. The soft mattress and lingering scent of lilies wouldn't allow him to forget that fact, so he'd noticed when Ever's soft footfalls paced her room. Felt her gaze when she'd cracked the door to peek in on him.

Part of Chess wondered if she was simply having trouble sleeping in case anyone snuck in to assassinate her, but his intuition told him there was more to it. The air was full of static, crackling with distrust. Things hadn't been that way between them since they'd first been forced together in the mortal world safe house. But maybe he was imagining things…

Should I check on her?

If all she needed was a little comfort, a *distraction,* he was more than willing to comply a second time. By spreading those creamy thighs, tasting her, bringing her over the edge over and over. She'd been so responsive when he'd licked her slit and had tasted so fucking good. Both her sex and her blood. Sweet. Like how he remembered candy tasting when he was a mortal. It would be no hardship to have her hands on him once more. Ever may have been a virgin, but that didn't mean she didn't know what she was doing. If she ever granted him the honor of taking her fully, he wasn't sure they would ever leave a bed again.

Unless it was to fuck in the bath or on a table or against a wall ... *oh* the things they would do together. They could explore each other all night until March came searching for her *again*—because he undoubtedly would. Clingy bastard. There were many other things to do now that Ever had reclaimed the castle and they couldn't afford to lose momentum by reveling in their victory. Rav could show up at any moment for all they knew. They'd killed his guards with a glorious swiftness, but the news was bound to get back to him soon. March could busy himself with that instead of worrying about Ever.

But perhaps March was right to worry about her. The gut feeling that she was up to something only increased along with the padding of her feet.

Chess purposely evened out his breathing and snuggled into the pillow to appear as if he were asleep. It only took ten minutes of pretending for him to get his answer. The soft *click* of her door shutting in the adjoining room told him everything he needed to know—Ever was sneaking out.

But to where? Why?

Chess eased from the bed, threw his clothes and boots on, and slipped into the hallway. Ever was already out of sight. He cursed silently and listened closely. Her rapid footsteps came from the right, descending stairs, if he was hearing correctly. Light on his feet, Chess followed.

He kept his distance, not allowing himself to get closer

than to see a blur of deep brown hair in the dark, as she traversed the castle. She'd put on a black skirt and a light blue T-shirt, though he much preferred the towel. When she snuck out a side door, he did the same.

Outside, the night swallowed them both. There was no moonlight tonight, but he could still see everything clearly. Bats flew overhead, swooping through the air, and the rustle of feathers floated down from the trees. Most importantly, he followed Ever's silhouette with ease. *Where the fuck are you going?* She wouldn't abandon him in her castle, would she? He could imagine March's reaction to *that* in the morning— so her destination couldn't be far.

They passed through the palace gardens and patches of forest. He couldn't stop to examine the surroundings as he needed to make sure he didn't lose sight of the White Queen, but if he didn't know any better, he'd say they were heading toward Scarlet. He narrowed his eyes at the figure weaving between trees. His stomach sank. No way would Ever have made a deal with her brother, even if it was to rid herself of Chess's presence. Only hours ago, she'd let him between her legs for fuck's sake. She had her castle back so what was left for Rav to barter anyway?

Then what—

Not more than a five minutes' run from the castle, Ever glanced over both shoulders before raising her hand to knock on an old, mossy tree. She rapped out a rhythm and stepped back. A few moments later, a door swung inward, expertly disguised to look like bark. Chess's eyes widened and his jaw clenched at *who* stood before Ever.

The mad, violet-haired twat who murdered his mother. *Maddie.*

Chess's vision went red. *Kill her* echoed through his head. *Kill her like she killed your mother.*

Fuck yes. She needed to die. *Now.* Before he could think better of charging rashly into the situation, Chess barreled from the trees at full speed. He knocked both Ever and Maddie down a staircase inside the hidden safe house before either of them could see him coming. They tumbled down in a heap, Ever's wig sailing past him in the process, and struck the edges of stairs. Chess's arm gave a sharp *crack*, but he ignored the blast of pain as he scrambled to get his hands around Maddie's neck. He still wasn't able to manage it before they landed in a pile at the bottom of the staircase. Ever was trapped face down beneath Maddie's body, Chess on top of them both.

The purple-clad vampire let out a shriek—part surprise, part fear—and snapped her fangs at his face. She clawed at his arms, raising her shoulders to protect her neck from his hands. The sound of a door slamming open and hitting a wall barely registered as he snatched her wrists. Chess hissed, spittle flying. He would rip her head off. Lick the blood from his lips. Send her heart back to Rav so he knew vengeance was had— just before Chess did the same to the bastard.

A muscled forearm pressed into Chess's neck from behind and ripped him off the female. He snarled and snapped while clawing at the arm hoisting him up until it bled freely.

"Don't kill him!" Ever yelled. Pins were slipping out of her white hair, the braids falling from where she had wound them against her head.

"Fucking prig!" Ferris shouted.

What the fuck is the Knave doing here? Not that it mattered. He drove his head back into the asshat's nose with a satisfying *crunch*.

"Fuck! Noah, grab his legs," Ferris growled.

Noah—Alice's damned brother—hurried forward, leaping over Maddie and Ever. Chess brought his legs back and kicked him square in the chest the moment he was close enough. Noah sailed into a glittering, white marble room with an ornate dining table. The force of the kick sent Ferris backward where he stumbled on the stairs, loosening his grip just enough for Chess to twist free.

His gaze went back to his prey. Maddie helped Ever off the ground, trusting the males to keep Chess away from her. *Foolish murderess.* Nothing would stop him from avenging his mother, no matter what she'd done to him as a child. *Nothing.* "You will *die* for what you've done!"

"No!" Ever shouted, and shoved Maddie behind her. Chess met her steely gaze, feeling irrationally betrayed that she would stop him. "You will not harm her."

"I will make it quick," Chess spat. It was all he could compromise on. Maddie deserved hours—no, days—of torture before she met her end, but for Ever, he would make it fast. There was no other option given the circumstances.

A figure moved in the open doorway behind the two females and Mouse stepped out, grabbing her sister's arm. The next moment Maddie was gone—inside the room, the door slammed shut. That was fine—there were no windows underground. He would simply need to finish off the vampires out here first, then rip off the fucking door and end the fucking she-devil. No problem. His eyes flickered to Ever. Perhaps a *slight* problem. But the males were completely dispensable.

He whirled around to face the Knave. Noah had joined him again and nervously bounced on the balls of his feet as if he was just *waiting* for the signal to attack. "You're an *infant*," Chess warned the new vampire. "Come at me and I will tear you apart."

"Maybe," Noah conceded. "But I like our odds."

Chess snarled. Noah was likely remembering the time he and Maddie managed to tie him to a tree on the edge of Ivory. But he failed to realize that Chess wasn't allowed to kill them at the time—or at least Maddie. His mother needed her to lead the way to Ever, and killing Maddie's boy-toy seemed detrimental to earning her cooperation. Now? He would see them both dead.

"There should be some reinforced handcuffs in the trunk at the foot of my bed," Ever said, her voice low. "Noah, if you wouldn't mind…"

He nodded and stepped out of the room, leaving only the Knave in front of him. "Your Highness," Chess said without turning around. "You never mentioned being so kinky. I would've happily obliged when we were together earlier … naked. My tongue—"

"Shut up," she growled in warning. The Knave's brows shot up as he looked from Chess to the queen. Ever kicked at the back of his knees and Chess buckled, catching himself. Ever huffed. "Incapacitate him and put him in one of the rooms. I don't want to see his face right now."

"With pleasure," Ferris said, his lips curling into a vengeful grin.

He leapt forward, but Chess sidestepped him. The Knave leapt again with the same result. Chess let out a small laugh as they seemed to dance with one another. Circling, ducking, sliding his feet against the marble floor to avoid the attacks. It was too easy. And he quickly grew bored of it. Maddie was right on the other side of that door. His revenge was so close and he wouldn't be denied.

"Enough," Chess snapped. "There is no quarrel with you, despite how you betrayed my mother. I just want the Hatter."

"She did all of Wonderland a favor by ripping out her heart," Ferris said spitefully.

Well, *now* there was a quarrel… His upper lip curled and he tensed for his first counter attack. The jangle of metal was his only warning before something heavy slammed into the back of his head. Chess's vision blurred and he stumbled.

Ferris took the opportunity to attack. He grabbed the sides of Chess's head and snapped his neck.

Chess jerked awake. Pain sliced up the back of his neck and his temples throbbed with a headache. He tried to raise a hand to his forehead but found them tightly bound behind his back. Cold metal dug into skin. And not only his wrists, but his ankles too. One side of each handcuff was attached to him, the others locked around the legs and back rungs of a steel chair. *Fucking bastards.*

He blinked the drowsiness away and scanned the room. A bed with messy, wrinkled sheets took up a majority of the space with two narrow tables on either side and a pile of clothes on the floor. The black wood of the furniture was carved with dainty lilies, and an empty vase sat on a long, thin table against one wall. Everything else was as white as the forest outside. Chess gave a sniff. It smelled stale, but a light scent of lilies lingered. How long ago had this space been used?

The door creaked open and Ever stepped inside, kicking the door shut. Strands of her hair stuck up at all angles. The pins were gone from around her face and her messy braids now hung over each shoulder. "You're awake," she drawled.

"This place seems a step up from the one in the mortal world," he said, purposefully glancing around. "You should've stayed here instead."

"You followed me," she accused matter-of-factly, ignoring his comments. But Chess didn't miss the hint of pain in her voice. "But this was where I stayed the night you tried to murder me in my own gardens. I gathered what I could and formulated my plan to stay in the human world right in this very room." She stalked around him, trailing her hand across the footboard as she passed the bed. "And now I get to come up with a new plan."

"You knew, didn't you? You knew she killed my mother all along and played me like a fool." His chest heaved.

"I knew, all right." Her nostrils flared. "What do you want me to say? She's my best friend. Of course, I would protect her."

"If you're trying to figure out how to let me kill your friend without shouldering the blame, I assure you, it will be *all* my fault. So, if you could just undo these cuffs…"

Ever whirled on him, eyes blazing. Her hand soared toward his face, cracking against his cheek. "How dare you do this? After everything? I don't know how, but something … something along the way changed between us."

"Between *us*, they have," he admitted. Though he wasn't sure what that meant exactly. He was fond of her, lusted for her, and for whatever forsaken reason, wanted to keep her safe. If it was anyone but himself, he would say *feelings* had developed. The type he'd never felt before and had no desire to experience now. Nevertheless, it was true. Murdering Maddie had nothing to do with how he felt about the White Queen though. "This has nothing to do with you. She killed *my* mother."

Ever leaned closer until her face was a breath from his. "Maddie took out the greatest threat to Wonderland and we should be *thanking* her for it."

Chess inhaled sharply. His mother was a vicious bitch with more problems than he could count but… "She. Was. My. Mother."

"That's all you have to say for yourself? You defend your actions even now that the moment of passion has passed?" She searched his face, perhaps hoping to find some sliver of remorse.

"If…" He swallowed hard. The fucking organ beating in his chest would be the ruin of him. "If my actions have hurt you, I *am* sorry for that. But I can't say I won't try again."

Ever stiffened and stepped back. "I'm sorry to hear that. Wait here while I talk to the others."

Chess tugged at his chains with a rueful smirk. As if he had a choice…

CHAPTER SIXTEEN

EVER

"**W**hat in all of Wonderland is going on here?" Maddie waved her hand in the air as she took a step toward Ever after the queen came out of Chess's room. "When you were here last, you said the time had come to reclaim Ivory and that Rav's heart would be intimately acquainted with a stake. I had assumed Chess would come next—I never thought you would *protect* the prince if you encountered him. He tried to *murder* you."

Ever hadn't expected any of this either—in her past, she'd thought of every single way she could kill Chess, viciously and slowly. She peered at the table where Noah pretended to observe his hands, Ferris watched her like a hawk, and Mouse played with her caterpillar.

"A lot has happened…" She pressed a palm to her forehead, not wanting to deal with this conversation. The way Maddie needed her hats when she was nervous was the way

Ever yearned for her viola, but there wasn't one around and there wasn't time to think about music or symphonies to distract.

"I would say so." Maddie arched a brow. "When you left, you hated Chess, and now? Now…" She covered her mouth with her hand as though coming to some sort of realization. "You *like* him? He's becoming your *friend*?"

Ever thought about earlier, how he'd run his tongue slowly, expertly, up her center, how he'd kissed her mouth with delicious hunger, how she'd wanted to do more than stroke his alluring cock. "It's a long story." She sighed, wanting to keep those moments that she should've regretted, but didn't, locked away for now. Forever.

"I'm pretty sure we have time for it," Ferris piped up, studying her as though he could read her thoughts, the way she had seen his history in his blood.

"Then afterward, I'm pretty sure he'll need to die," Noah added, running a hand through his thick blond hair, no longer able to hold his tongue. "When we were on our way to get the cure for my sister, we ran into Chess in Ivory. He tied Maddie and me together and was going to haul us back to Scarlet."

Ever blinked, her gaze locked on Noah's bright blue eyes. "To have you *killed*?"

"Well, no," Maddie sang. "Only because I wasn't 'allowed' in Ivory." She air-quoted, then adjusted her dark hat on the side of her head. "But we escaped and tied him to a tree after I knocked him out."

Ever would've done the same thing. She had also only learned that Maddie and Mouse hadn't been allowed in Ivory when she'd first arrived at the safe house after being gone for so long. Another reason why she wanted to hurt her brother, for keeping them away from their home and holding Mouse in a cage like an animal.

"Tell her," Mouse said, glancing up at Maddie, her voice barely audible. A mortal would not have been able to hear her soft words.

Maddie wrinkled her nose, staring at her sister in confusion. "Tell her what?"

Mouse stayed silent, letting Des crawl from one hand to the other before she spoke again. "Tell her how you were able to get me out from the Ruby Heart Palace."

"Oh, I already told her how I created this miraculous hat and—"

"No," Mouse drawled. "About the prince stopping by your cottage before you and Noah came to the palace."

"Oh yes, I did forget to tell you that part. The weeks have been a blur." Maddie shrugged. "So, Chess came to my cottage, somehow piecing together a part of my plan with Noah to get Mouse back. Instead of killing me or reporting it to his mother, he allowed me to hatch the plan..." The Hatter frowned as though she were uncomfortable admitting this.

"And?" Ever prodded when her friend stopped talking.

Maddie rolled her eyes. "He agreed to keep quiet in exchange for your hideout's location. I, of course, led him on a wild goose chase to Red." She cocked her head. "I suppose I can see why he's a teensy bit angry."

Chess was more than angry—he'd been livid when he'd stormed toward them, causing them to take a vexing tumble down the stairs. He could have been less brash and dramatic about it. Ferris had moved fast, and if she hadn't spoken up in time, Chess would've been like the damn Headless Horseman, except dead. Even though *he'd* attacked them, the thought sent a sinking feeling to the pit of her stomach.

As much as she loathed Imogen, Maddie had killed his mother. Although the bitch deserved it, she could see why Chess would be upset. By allowing Maddie to go through with her plan, he was part of the reason his mother was dead, and guilt had to be filling him.

Ever glanced to Ferris, who had been around him for two years, *lived* with him. "How was the prince at the palace?"

He groaned, glancing up at the ceiling. "A spoiled prince who fucked and fed constantly."

That wasn't surprising, but then her heart lodged in her throat at a thought. "Was he like Rav and Imogen? Dabbled in their disgusting hobby with mortals?" She'd discussed the turning of humans with Chess, yet this was a dire situation and there could be no more lies.

"No." Ferris shook his head. "He did the tasks Imogen assigned him, but the unwilling turning of mortals was a sick game between her and Rav only, as was your brother's experiments with them."

Rav had always enjoyed being some sort of deranged scientist. She didn't know what he had done with the unfortunate souls and preferred not to imagine the cruel things he concocted. Before Ever could ask another question, Mouse interrupted, "Chess would visit me at my cell."

Maddie whirled on her sister, her eyes wide. "For *what*?"

"To ask questions about Ever of course." Mouse set Des on the table, the caterpillar's head perking up as though it were listening too. "But, he would bring leaves for me to feed Des after he saw her with me one day."

Chess had brought Mouse leaves for her caterpillar to eat? Something was off about that. The only reason he would do that would be to get something in return. Information on Ever.

But that had been before. Before all this...

"A few leaves for your caterpillar doesn't erase everything he's done," Maddie said.

"He grew up differently than us." Mouse furrowed her brow. "People can change."

"I hate to say it," Ever started. "But Chess actually helped reclaim my castle, although his presence has been mostly accompanied by lies. He did come clean recently though. Of course, after being caught." She then went into more detail, discussing his lies, how he'd helped kill the vampires in the Ivory Palace, and how they both wanted Rav dead.

"You have the palace now?" Noah asked.

"Yes." Ever nodded. "My spy—March, who Maddie and Mouse are acquainted with—is there now. I had only come here to tell you the news, but since Chess now knows everything, I would like you all to come to the palace now. I trust you to help protect it, and I have to be more careful in the guards I pick this time. But if you choose not to, I understand."

"And Chess?" Maddie plopped down onto Noah's lap, one of his arms snaking protectively around her waist. "What are we going to do with him? I don't care what he wants to do to me, but, again, he tried to murder you."

He had. But from all their recent days together, he hadn't attempted to harm her. He'd been nothing but aggravating, yet he'd also been … caring? "I know he did. However, I have something to ask of you, Maddie. If you agree to come with me, I want to allow him an opportunity to join us. Will you allow it?"

By how red Noah's face was, she could tell he wanted to shout *fuck no*, but he waited for Maddie to give her answer.

"Only if I can personally escort him to your palace with his hands cuffed," she sang with a grin.

"Deal." Ever laughed. "Now, I need to have a word with the princeling." She gave a final look to Noah. "I also killed Osanna for you."

"One less vampire we have to kill." Maddie grinned.

Ever then left the group to themselves, Maddie patting Noah's cheek and telling him to calm down about the prince while Ferris watched Mouse scoop Des into her palm.

Pushing open the door, Ever found Chess still seated in the chair with his ankles cuffed to the legs and his wrists bound behind his back. Even then, he lazily rested his head against the back of the chair. He lifted his head, a smirk on his face as his yellow gaze met hers, as though he were tempting her to come closer.

Ever shut the door behind her and entered the room, taking

in the black and white walls, the obsidian wardrobe, the dark bed, the steel chair that made the prince look like a seductive devil luring her in. And bloody hell, she wanted to be lured in.

Focusing, she shook the blasted thought away. "I assume you were listening," she snapped. It may have been more at herself than him because she should've been wanting to rip his head off for trying to murder her best friend, and in turn, knocking them down a flight of stairs like a fool.

"To every word," he purred. "Osanna was always a cunt, so you taking her out doesn't bother me in the least. Now, what would you like to ask me first?"

"Why did you bring Mouse leaves for her caterpillar?"

Chess clucked his tongue and straightened. A line rested between the prince's brows, questioning. "Out of everything, that's what you're curious about? Ah, Queenie, I think you can do better than that."

"Just answer the question," she huffed.

"Poor little Mouse, all alone in her cell," he cooed. His gaze left hers and he studied the ceiling, as though, if he looked at her longer, she would discover the emotion he wanted to keep hidden. "I wanted her to think I was charming so she would tell me more about you. *Confess* where you were hiding."

"That's not the whole story though, is it?" Ever inched closer to him, then leaned forward, ignoring his lovely scent. He didn't speak as she pressed her hands to his warm cheeks, drawing his face to hers. She would keep his gaze focused on hers so he couldn't hide behind his lies.

The prince's yellow irises blazed, his breath hitching. "I had planned to toy with her like I did with Maddie. The Hatter was fun to get a rise out of, but Mouse… She was different. Always humming. Even when… Even when…" He paused, his nostrils flaring. "Even when Rav and my mother would bring her out for her *interrogations*."

The blood in Ever's veins boiled and she was about to slap

him, but then she remembered how he'd allowed Maddie to save her. A realization struck her—it wasn't only the leaves.

"You gave her the caterpillar, didn't you?" she whispered, her thumb stroking his cheek.

"And why the fuck would I do that?" he murmured.

"So you could bring her the leaves."

Chess stayed silent for a long moment before relenting. "Fine, I did. But don't believe for a second I was being a hero or that it was all out of the kindness of my heart."

"Yet the caterpillar was one of the things that helped her survive." And Ferris, but that wasn't a conversation to have now.

"The caterpillar helped me over the years, too, even though I was a bastard." Chess blew out a breath. "I told the furry little worm to crawl into a lonely vampire's cell and keep her company. Mouse doesn't know I gave the caterpillar to her."

Ever's brows shot up over the good deed, no matter if there was a bit of selfishness behind it. She'd bet anything that Mouse and the others had been listening and now knew what he'd done too.

"What would have happened if you'd found me in Red?" she said, changing the subject before she could think too much on the good deed he'd done. "Be honest."

"Don't slap me." His lips tilted at the edges. "I know I riled Maddie up on many occasions by testing her patience about you. But I never would've tortured you if I'd found you." His smile dropped, his throat bobbing. "If I'd discovered you, I would've taken your heart to my mother, just as I would've at your masquerade ball."

It wasn't a surprise, and for some reason, her stomach didn't drop at the words. That was the past, and what was more important was the present, the future. "Would you still now?" Her palms left his cheeks, his eyes questioning. "If Imogen were still alive, would you rip out my heart right now and give it to her."

"No," he whispered and shut his eyes for a brief moment. "I would hide you from her for an eternity if I had to."

Her heart pounded harder. She believed him, completely, wholly. This wasn't one of his lies. Everything was out in the open now, yet there was one thing he would have to agree to if they were to continue on their path. "We need to work together. *All* of us. But you must tell me now, Princeling, will you leave Maddie alone? Deep down, you know, that for Wonderland, it was for the best. As much as you loath what Maddie did, as much as it hurts inside here"—Ever placed her palm against his wildly beating heart—"it wasn't planned on her part, but somehow fate intervened and it happened. She did what needed to be done, for our world, just as it pains me to do the same thing to my brother. I know you loved your mother, yet you're free now because of it. You didn't deserve for her to make you jump through fire in order to remain in her good graces. You deserved to be treated like her son." She paused, taking a deep breath. "Let the hate and guilt go."

Chess bit his lip and remained quiet.

He wouldn't do it—he couldn't see what Ever wanted him to see, what she hoped he would believe. She took her hand from his chest and straightened. Letting out a sigh, she padded to the door before he called, "Wait."

Ever turned around as a loud squeaking echoed, finding Chess trying to move the chair toward her.

"I understand what you're saying, but you have them." He nodded toward the door where her friends all waited. "And I have no one. I only ever had my mother in Wonderland."

She moved back toward him until she was just as close as she'd been before. Peering at him, she understood that he was never a heartless prince—he'd just been lonely and hurting. And now, the heart could mend. "You have me, Chess. We're on each other's side."

The prince studied her for a long moment, as though battling something within himself before finally speaking,

"For you, I promise I won't hurt Maddie." Then he couldn't help himself and smirked. "Unless she tries to hurt me first."

"That's good enough, but know this—if you do, I'll have to kill you." Ever smiled. "I suppose we can uncuff you now but please play nice."

As she took the key from her pocket, he leaned forward and whispered in her ear, his breath warm on her neck, making her shiver. "Or we could leave them on a little longer. Let them hear how I made you feel at the Ivory Palace."

Heat flooded her cheeks as she unlocked his handcuffs at his wrists and ankles—wondering if her friends had heard his seductive words. "Let's not be hasty now." She then whirled around with Chess chuckling behind her.

CHAPTER SEVENTEEN

CHESS

Ever's gaze locked onto Chess when he sauntered out of the bedroom. Mouse watched on with her big eyes, while the caterpillar Chess had sent her way inched along her forearm. Maddie glowered from beneath her black hat, and fresh-faced Noah's scowl looked wrong on him. Then there was Ferris who appeared just as broody and suspicious as he had at the palace. How hadn't he noticed the Knave was a spy? The expressions of hate directed at his mother—the ones she mistook as lust, and how he skulked around places he had no business skulking. Not that it mattered now…

Chess gave them one of his cocky grins and held his hands up in mock surrender. "Consider me subdued."

Maddie tilted her head and studied him from where she was perched on Noah's lap. "Where are his cuffs?"

"About that…" Chess brushed past Ever and lazily sank into one of the empty chairs. Placing his elbow on the table, he wove his fingers together and cleared his throat. Ferris swiveled in the chair beside him and tensed. "I heard about your condition for me to return with Ever, Hatter, and there will be no more cuffs. At least, not for me. Well"—he gave Ever a seductive grin—"not under these circumstances."

Maddie rolled her eyes. "Ever already agreed. If you want to come—"

"The fuck if I care what was *agreed*," he growled, all traces of humor dissipating. "You killed my mother. You will not further insult me by parading me through Ivory like a prisoner when I've done nothing wrong." His gaze drifted to Ever. "At least, not lately."

Noah's grip tightened around Maddie's waist and Ferris's stare dug into him, but it was Mouse who spoke next. "You're selfish," she said softly. "But not incorrect, in this instance."

"Mouse," Maddie whispered, her lips set in a tight line.

"It's true. And we can all be selfish at times." She shrugged. Des perked her head up from the table, nodding in agreement. It was a name he wouldn't have chosen for the caterpillar, yet it somehow suited her.

"All right," Ever said in an even voice. "Now that this is settled, everyone will behave themselves. We all want the same thing—my brother dead. Gather what you will and we'll head to my palace. Home."

Slowly, Maddie slid from Noah's lap, taking his hand and leading him into one of the bedrooms. Ferris's chair scraped against the floor when he followed suit. Mouse, however, remained. "They're prickly for a reason, but you have a reason too." Her gaze softened for a moment before glaring, her voice coming out quiet. "Thank you for your kindness with Des at the palace. However, if you attack my sister, I will rip your throat out." She scooped Des off the table and patted his shoulder as though she hadn't threatened him. Maddie's sister was a strange little thing, but his heart lurched when he thought about what his mother and Rav had done to her over and *over*.

Ever grinned at Mouse, seeming proud of her. Once the

female shuffled away from the table, Ever grabbed Chess by the ear. "You can't hurt my friends."

He offered a small smile. "No, but you never said I had to be *nice.*"

"Taunting them into attacking you so you can defend yourself isn't allowed either."

"So many rules." He *tsked* and brushed her hand away. "You can only ask so much of me, Queenie. I won't attack them nor will I change who I am to appease them. Their anger management is their own problem."

Ever narrowed her eyes, studying his face. He wasn't sure what she found there, but he was determined not to budge a step further. Maddie murdered his mother *and* the queen of Scarlet. He wouldn't mind if the Hatter fell off a cliff and died, but he wasn't going to hurt her. The problem was that Rav would still want to end her life. Or, at least he would if he learned the truth before Ever killed him. There was still a chance someone else loyal to Imogen would solve the problem on Chess's behalf.

"We're ready," Maddie chirped.

Ever turned from Chess and nodded. "Come on, then."

Maddie adjusted her hat and fell behind Mouse, Ferris, and Noah as they climbed the stairs. Chess stood and followed behind the White Queen, keeping her between him and the others. There was no sense in tempting anyone's control by accidentally getting too close. Besides, he liked being behind her. Not only for the view of her arse in that black skirt, but he felt better knowing nothing would attack her from a blind spot. She'd protected him from her friends, had trusted him enough to let him be in the same room as his mother's killer. That thought warmed something inside him.

The Hatter halted in front of Ever and spun to look at him. "We have a truce then?" she asked hesitantly.

"For as long as Ever lives." Chess shot her a strained smile, forcing himself not to snarl instead. If anything happened to

Ever, all promises were null and void.

"Best keep me alive then," Ever said, her tone trying and failing to sound lighthearted. She nudged Maddie toward the stairs. "March will worry if I take too long."

Maddie bit her lip, casting a final wary look at Chess. He raised one brow in silent challenge before she said something he wasn't expecting. "I still loathe you, but thank you for giving my sister Des." She turned on her booted heel and rushed up the stairs.

Did … she just *thank* him? That was unexpected. Chess wasn't sure how to feel about that.

Pinning her hair back into place and forgoing the tangled wig, Ever followed wordlessly behind the Hatter, and Chess trudged after the group. Just what he needed … more people who loathed him. Was he *so* unlikable? He chuckled silently. *Certainly.* But perhaps he could change that one day and be slightly less antagonistic. On occasion. At least a few times a year, anyway.

As soon as he stepped out of the safe house, Ferris slammed the door shut and locked it back up with a key attached to a large ring. His nostrils flared at Chess's proximity which only made him want to step closer to the Knave. The male hadn't exactly been treated well by Imogen or Rav, but Chess had never touched him.

"I'm guilty by association, eh?" he said quietly to Ferris while the others started back toward the palace.

"Don't act innocent. Everyone knows who you are and that didn't change just because you helped Mouse," he snapped and brushed past Ever to walk at Mouse's side. The pink-haired vampire cast the prince an unreadable look over her shoulder.

"Are you joining us?" Ever asked when Chess didn't move. "You're welcome to go your own way if you choose."

He didn't want to go his own way—he wanted to stay with Ever. But the others…? Things were about to change. He could feel it in the air. Ever would withdraw as his presence drove a wedge between her and her friends, leaving him alone. Again.

"What do you prefer I do?" he asked softly.

"I want you to come." The corners of her mouth lifted. "And go back to being your cocky self."

He released a relieved breath, turning it into a chuckle to hide that he'd been worried about her answer. "I would have come regardless. Do you think it'll be that easy to get rid of me?" Leaning down to whisper in her ear, he added, "You taste too good for me to walk away now."

Ever drew in a sharp breath and he quickly nipped at her ear before straightening. Her widening eyes made his grin grow into a knowing smile. She remembered the pleasure he gave her just as well as he did and, if he wasn't mistaken, wanted another round. *Soon.* First, they had to get back to the castle and their conveniently adjoined rooms.

Chess nodded toward the group and started sauntering away. He knew the Knave and Maddie, had spent time with Mouse, but Noah was a stranger. While he seemed to listen to Maddie, Chess would need to watch him closely to make sure his newly-turned control was stable. The last time he'd seen Maddie and Noah together, they were walking through the forest in Ivory. He'd wondered where they were going when he'd found them, but their answer hadn't mattered much. Whatever their cause had been, his mother would've expected Chess to deliver the pair for questioning. Since he was Alice's brother, he probably knew where she was—possibly cured already from what he'd overheard while cuffed, not that he gave two shits anymore.

"Did you hear that?" Ever asked under her breath as she stilled, grabbing his arm.

Chess perked his ears up, listening hard. Everyone stopped moving. For a moment, all Chess could hear was his own breath. Then—

Snap.

They weren't alone in the forest, but there was nothing to be afraid of in Wonderland for six vampires. Except the Jabberwocky, of course, but it never came this far into Ivory. Chess scowled. He hadn't thought it would be in Ivory at all until they'd arrived on the outskirts, but the Jabberwocky wouldn't lurk about, snapping twigs. Perhaps it was one of Rav's spies. A low, rumbling growl filled the air.

Or a fucking werewolf.

"Not again," Noah said, tensing.

"Our bullets are low after our last werewolf situation and we don't want to attract more unless we have to," Maddie said.

He hadn't brought a gun from the palace and by the looks of it, Ever hadn't either. Perfect. Not that they would've trusted him with a weapon anyway. "Better get running then," he said, scanning the forest for any sign of the beast. Fighting a werewolf with his bare hands wasn't at the top of his bucket list.

A large black blur shot out from the shadows of the trees and tore straight for them. It was smaller than most, nearly as big as Chess. An adolescent that likely strayed too far from pack territory without realizing. *Fuck.* They were almost worse than the adults. *No, they* were *worse.* Hunting vampires down for sport, tearing them apart without bothering to eat them. Regardless, the adults would come looking for it, if they weren't already. Which meant they would get to deal with an arsehole child and an overprotective parent.

The werewolf released a deep roar and eyed its prey.

Eyed *them.*

Then its footsteps pounded against the ground, shaking the trees, its body snapping branches as it barreled past them.

The Knave lifted Mouse over his shoulder and dodged out of the werewolf's path. Noah and Maddie had already disappeared into the trees while Chess was focused on the charging beast. He bolted after them, following a flash of white that had to be Ever.

The thunderous rumble of galloping paws pounded behind him as he pushed himself faster, closing the distance between him and the queen. Only … it wasn't Ever. The white he'd seen was a shirt hanging out of Noah's backpack. Chess took a hard left behind a tree as the werewolf raced by. *Where the fuck is she?*

Doubling back, he frantically searched the woods for any clue to where Ever might be. Had she followed Ferris and Mouse instead? "Ever!" he shouted. Fuck the risk—he was faster than the werewolves. "Ever!"

"Shut up, Princeling," she snapped.

Whirling around, he nearly knocked her over. His heart caught in his chest and he pulled her to him. "I couldn't find you."

"I was running toward the castle, you big idiot." She pried herself out of his grip and took his hand. "Hurry."

Another growl came then, this one deeper, *angrier*. And from behind them. Ever took off toward the castle a second time, pulling Chess alongside her. A parent had come for their offspring and smelling vampires near their child would only make things more dangerous. They moved as fast as they could, weaving between trees, with the werewolf on their heels.

From nowhere, the young werewolf leapt in front of them, releasing a vicious roar that showcased its rows of sharp teeth. Ever stopped so fast that she fell forward. Chess's hand slipped from hers and she landed on her stomach. The younger werewolf chose that moment to surge forward. Chess bolted sideways in hopes the beast would follow.

And it did.

But the second werewolf had caught up—a female, judging by the narrower frame. Chess looked over Ever's shoulder just in time to see the adult beast yank her white hair and roll away. "Hey!" he shouted, turning on his heel. "Over here!"

The older werewolf's lips curled at the same time the younger pounced. Chess dug his feet into the ground and brought a fist back. "Get the fuck out of the way," the prince growled. He swung his fist upward, connecting with the underside of the younger werewolf's jaw. The teeth clacked together as the beast's head swung backward with a loud, pained yelp.

Ever thrashed, fangs exposed, clawing at the adult's snout when it snapped its head toward Chess. The werewolf released a deep growl, rattling the branches. At the sound of her offspring's agony, a malicious glint shone in her eyes. Dragging Ever by her hair as though she were a ragdoll, she sprinted toward Chess.

"Fuck," he hissed under his breath. How was he going to fight off two of them *and* save Ever? He jumped toward the nearest tree, scrambled up the trunk, and flung himself onto the first stable branch. Ever screamed, bucking her body wildly, when the adult stopped near the adolescent. The younger werewolf shook his head violently while Ever swiped at his mother to break free.

"Drop her, mutt," Chess warned the adult. *Fucking arse.* He was just toying with the werewolf now before he found a clean shot and went in for the kill.

The younger werewolf padded forward, head hung low, tilted to the side as if in pain. Even then, the adolescent's hungry gaze was focused on Ever. *Shit.* He was out of time. With a deep breath, he dropped from the branch and landed on the younger one's back as hard as he could. A bone snapped in its back under the impact—nothing that wouldn't heal—but the adult dropped Ever in response.

Ever scrambled to her feet with her hair a wild mess. Her gaze flicked between him and the beasts. *Run,* she mouthed.

"You first, Queenie," he said, climbing from the collapsed body, edging slowly away from the prowling werewolf. Ever hesitated as Chess sidestepped closer to her. "Any time now."

She bolted, but the werewolf must have anticipated it because she lunged, maw open wide. Chess didn't think—didn't question what he was about to do. He simply acted. Jumping in front of the werewolf, he shoved Ever out of danger's path.

A crushing pain burst in his shoulder and he cried out wordlessly. *Fuck!* The werewolf had his entire shoulder in her mouth. Her teeth carved through his shirt, the flesh, and crumbled the bone. Stars burst behind his eyes.

Boom!

The blast rattled his ears. And then … nothing. Silence rung through his head. The werewolf didn't shake him like she had Ever. Didn't gnaw on him or use her paws to rip at his body. He shook his head to clear his vision and found himself kneeling on the forest ground. Ever was in front of him, lightly slapping his cheeks.

"If … you wanted to hit me…" He tried to smirk but failed. "You could've saved it for the bedroom."

"Bloody hell, I think my ears are bleeding from that statement," Maddie scoffed from his side. The boom… She'd shot the werewolf. For him.

"Did you just *save me*?" Chess asked the Hatter as Ever helped him to his feet. Specks of fiery ash burned on the ground—all that remained of the werewolf.

"Someone needed to end our lovely feud. It was either that or shoot your arse," she sang, waving her hand in the air. "We waited for you at the edge of the forest and doubled back when it took too long for you to show up."

The queen wrapped his good arm around her shoulders. "Let's get you some blood."

"We need to move before more werewolves show up to investigate all this noise," Ferris called.

Chess glanced farther into the woods and found him waiting with Noah and Mouse. Noah approached the incapacitated werewolf. It whimpered where it lay.

"Leave him," Chess told Noah. It was only acting on instinct and was no danger to them in that condition. Coming into Ivory was foolish but he was young and had lost a mother as a result. That was enough punishment—he knew first hand. "If another werewolf comes, they will haul him home instead of chasing us down."

Noah lowered the gun and looked to Maddie who nodded. Chess released a breath. He cast the werewolf a knowing glance as Ever led him back toward the castle.

"That was really foolish of you," she whispered.

Chess chuckled. "I do a lot of foolish things." His chest warmed as he studied Ever's heart-shaped face and her deep brown eyes. The way they bantered, the way he felt when she touched him… Realization struck him like lightning, his heart pounding as if there were thunder beneath his rib cage.

He was falling in love with the fucking Queen of Ivory.

CHAPTER EIGHTEEN

EVER

Chess had saved Ever's life—the prince who'd once tried to murder her had risked himself. For *her*. Maddie had then killed the werewolf and saved Chess's life, even though she could've easily killed the prince instead. But she hadn't, and Ever knew it wasn't because she was a queen—it was because they were friends.

Yet if Chess had harmed a single hair on Mouse's head in the Ruby Heart Palace, a very different fate would've occurred by the Hatter's hand. Mouse had told Maddie she'd been treated fine in the palace, but after hearing Chess's confession, that wasn't the truth. Her stomach sank at what Rav and Imogen could've done to her during the "interrogations," but Mouse wasn't ready to talk about it and she wouldn't push her to.

"Thank you," Ever murmured to Chess as they came to a stop further away from the werewolf. Her scalp still ached from where her hair had been yanked, but it was quickly dissipating. "Truly."

The prince licked his lower lip. "It was nothing, Queenie."
It wasn't nothing. It was something.

Maddie handed Ever a scrap of blue silk from her
backpack to wrap around Chess's torn shoulder.

The prince eyed the fabric as though it were poison, and
shrugged it off. "It's just a bite and is already healing," he
muttered, his voice weak.

"Just take it, Princeling." Ever sighed as blood continued
to blossom across his shirt.

With a smirk, he took the silk and placed it over his wound.
"Only because you said it oh-so-nicely." The smile left his
face and he stumbled, beads of perspiration sliding down his
forehead.

"Quit wasting energy," she reprimanded, then peered
around the group. "Can someone get me some blood?"

Noah fished out a pouch and poured the contents into his
canteen, shoving it into Chess's face. "You owe me," he
grunted to the prince.

"Staying under the same roof shall be fun," Chess taunted,
taking the canteen and chugging it down as though he'd never
drank before in his life. He wiped a drizzle of crimson creeping
down his chin and drew his shoulders back, grinning.

Maddie rolled her eyes and Ever nudged him forward.
Even though they were tucked in the woods, she didn't want
to linger so close to the fresh blood, especially with everyone
in the group being wanted by Rav.

It wasn't long before they reached the palace and crossed
the bridge toward the door, the silver water of the moat
rippling from the wind. The smell here didn't seem as cold as
before, but that may have been in her head. Ivory remained
quiet as though the vampires in the city hadn't wanted to leave
their homes.

That would change soon.

"Finally, home sweet home," Maddie sang after Ever

unlocked the door and they entered the palace. "Hmm, it seems we will be redecorating." The Hatter studied the bare walls, the unkempt areas, and dirty furniture. A hint of blood from the dead guards still drifted through the air.

March rounded the corner, no longer wearing Scarlet's uniform but dark leather trousers and a tight white T-shirt. His eyes widened at the group, obviously not expecting Ever to have brought everyone home, then a bright smile formed on his face as his gaze settled on Ever, Maddie, and Mouse.

"It's been a while," he said to Maddie.

"Indeed, it has." The Hatter laughed and skipped to him. "But we can resume our tea parties now that you're back. Although, there will be a few new guests." She motioned to the side. "This is Noah and Ferris."

March's stare flicked to Chess, who'd been lingering behind them, and he scowled. "You're supposed to be in your room."

Chess smirked, slinking past the two males and stepping next to Ever. "I had a few things to take care of."

March shook his head. "You're a nuisance."

"I'm still royalty," Chess purred, picking at invisible lint on his tattered shirt.

"He did protect Ever from a werewolf," Mouse whispered, her caterpillar crawling up her arm.

March quirked a brow at her. "Did everyone forget he tried to *murder* her? He's one of the reasons you ended up in your cell, Mouse."

Ferris drew in a sharp breath and shifted protectively beside her. "That was Rav and Imogen's doing. Chess never touched her or he'd be dead," he said, his jaw clenched.

"If we're playing a game of forgiveness," Chess cooed. "I forgive Noah and Maddie for choking me until I passed out, then leaving me tied to a tree. Where I could've *starved*." He glanced at the duo with a wide grin.

"You tied us together first," Noah grumbled, balling his

fists at his sides as though he wanted to punch the prince in the face.

"Unimportant detail." Chess shrugged. "As delightful as this day has been, I'll retire to my quarters. The one attached to the *queen's* bedroom." He winked at Ever. "See you soon, Queenie."

Ever pursed her lips, knowing he was trying to rile everyone up as he turned around and sauntered up the stairs without glancing back. *Cocky bastard.* Yet she couldn't help but watch how his arse flexed in his tight trousers.

"You can't be serious." Maddie's voice rose an octave. "Sleeping in *your* room?"

"It's not *my* room. It's the adjacent room." Ever paused. "To keep an eye on him."

"Mm-hmm. We heard everything at the safe house during your conversation with him," she pointed out.

Before more questions ensued, Ever straightened, becoming the queen she needed to be. "March, will you discuss with Ferris and Noah everything that's been going on while I take Maddie and Mouse to their old rooms? Then you can assign shifts to guard the palace until we can locate trustworthy vampires who hate my brother."

March nodded, gesturing for Noah and Ferris to follow him while Ever led Maddie and Mouse up the stairs. Mouse remained quiet, her face expressionless, her eyes haunted, as though her mind were somewhere else, fighting something dark. Ever's heart sank at seeing her friend this hollow.

Mouse had always been quiet though, seeming as if she would never hurt a single thing, but that had never stopped her from taking lives when needed. If a problem arose, Ever knew, underneath it all, Mouse could easily become vicious. Helping guard the palace wouldn't be an issue for her, yet Mouse also didn't seem like she was in the right headspace, which was why Ever brought her and Maddie up together, as not to single the younger sister out.

At the top of the stairs, they turned down a hall opposite from Ever's. White and silver tile still covered the floor, only now, booted footprints marred the marble. The palace needed a thorough cleaning at some point.

No longer did Maddie's white and silver hats decorate the wall—instead, only nails poked out where they had once been.

They came to a halt in front of the sisters' old rooms that were across from one another, the obsidian handles covered in dust.

Ever broke the silence. "Are you two up for guarding tomorrow? I wouldn't ask this of either of you after all you've been through lately, but we're short on staff, as you can tell."

"What's tearing off a few more heads if I need to?" Maddie shrugged, studying the area from floor to ceiling.

"I'm fine," Mouse said softly, sounding anything but fine. "I'll do whatever you need me to."

"For now, rest." Ever placed a hand on her small shoulder. "I need to talk to Maddie about a few things."

Mouse nodded with a yawn and opened the door to her room, leaving it cracked.

Maddie smiled while sighing. Mouse had been sleeping with the door wide open, but maybe this was a step in the right direction, that she was feeling more at home, could start to heal.

Ever followed Maddie into her friend's mostly-empty room. The Hatter's bed was there, still covered in black and purple blankets, and the ornate obsidian wardrobe hugged a corner. Beside it rested her desk and chair where she'd created hats, but all her belongings were gone. Not even a needle lingered.

"Of course nothing I need is here," Maddie huffed. "Those fuckers probably sold my creations across Wonderland to make a few coins. When Mouse and I were taken to the cottage, Rav and Imogen barely let us gather anything before I had to slave away at making the queen a hat every damn month.”

Ever took a deep swallow at those words, guilt washing over her. She couldn’t change the past, but she could alter the future. “Eventually, you can return to the cottage and collect what you would like. All your hats.” Not until her brother was dead though.

“Although I do love a good discussion about hats, this is not the conversation we need to have.” Maddie cocked her head and dropped on her mattress, patting the spot beside her. “Now, what is going on with you and Chess exactly? Please deny there has been heavy petting of any kind.”

Ever ran a hand down the side of her face, avoiding eye contact as she sank down on the bed. “Something foolish.”

“Oh dear,” Maddie groaned. “Did you fuck him?”

“No,” Ever drawled, yet thinking how close they had been to that point.

“That sounded more like ‘not yet’.” She wrinkled her nose. “I may not like the arse, but he’s different than when I saw him in Scarlet last. Still cocky. I can’t put my finger on it though... Perhaps not selfish? No, no, he will always be that, but maybe less so.”

“We’ll see.” Ever smiled. However, she’d seen it. Thus far, she’d seen a change in the prince.

“Something else I noticed,” Maddie sang. “March seems to be a tad bit jealous. I don’t think he’ll ever stop carrying that blasted torch for you.”

“He knows I don’t want more than friendship with him.” Eventually, he would move on, find someone who felt the same way. One day.

“March never was the right one for you…” Maddie looked as though she wanted to say something else on that matter, but she changed the subject. “I should probably go chat with the others and start preparing in case some devious bastards show up.”

“I’m glad you’re here.” Ever grasped her friend’s hand and

gave it a gentle squeeze. "Unfortunately, I'll be leaving for the Ruby Heart Palace soon. And speaking of devious vampires, it won't be long before Rav discovers what has happened here. Whether he makes an appearance himself or sends new guards as he did with March, I'm unsure."

"We'll be ready"—Maddie tapped Ever's nose—"then have bloody fucking tea afterward."

"That's the spirit." Ever laughed. "I don't know much about Noah, but he seems a good match for you."

"He does, doesn't he?" Maddie grinned. "Who would've thought?"

Ever bid her friend goodnight and headed toward her bedroom. A strange feeling washed over her as she padded down the hall alone. In the past, there would always be a human or vampire servant around, cleaning. None were ever mistreated who served in the palace.

As Ever opened the door to her room, her gaze fell to Chess sprawled out on her bed, back against the headboard, his hair wet, shirt off, showing his chiseled abs. His shoulder was now almost fully healed with only raised pinkish marks. Once again, his trousers hung low, showing a patch of dark hair leading underneath the fabric.

She pushed down the heated feeling blooming inside her, pulsing harder, and placed her hands on her hips. "What are you doing?" Her voice came out more breathy than irritated.

"Being your knight for the day." He leaned forward, propping his elbow on his knee, his yellow eyes smoldering as he studied her with a seduction that must've lured half of Wonderland into his damn bed. For the first time, jealousy roared through her at the thought and she shoved the bothersome feeling away. "I did protect you earlier, didn't I?"

Ever took a step forward. "You could've gotten yourself killed."

Chess was off the bed in a split second, standing in front of her. "None of this would've happened if you'd told me the truth, Queenie." He pressed a warm finger to her lips and she hated that she was tempted to run her tongue up it instead of yearning to bite it off. "But I understand why you kept quiet about your rendezvous. Things are all out in the open now and we're one big happy family in your palace."

"That's a stretch." She laughed, a high-pitched sound that caused him to smile, only this smile was beautiful, captivating. That expression didn't make her want to push him away but pull him closer.

Chess must've sensed what she felt because he hoisted her up, then backed her against the wall. She squeaked in surprise, her legs betraying her and wrapping around his narrow waist. "Oh, Queenie," he murmured, "I wouldn't say that. I believe you like me plenty. Kiss me, then deny it."

She wouldn't deny him any damn thing right then.

His cock hardened in the precise place where she wanted it. Her eyes fluttered, and she inched closer, his breath mingling with hers.

"I'll play however you want tonight," he said, brushing the tip of her nose with his.

That shapely mouth of his wouldn't stop calling to her, and she was the first to give in, pressing her lips to his, gentle at first, then hungrier with each movement, each taste, until the hunger was all-consuming. His hips steadily rocked into her, making her moan in both pleasure and the need for more.

"How do you want me to touch you this time?" Chess purred in her ear. "With my fingers, my tongue, my lips, my cock? Tell me and I'll fucking do it. I won't stop until you come as many times as you damn well wish."

It was as though Ever could feel his invisible hands everywhere, touching her, devouring her, readying her. "All of them," she rasped, her fingers at the waist of his trousers, unfastening the button. He shoved them down and hiked up her skirt, drawing her panties to the side. His velvety cock slid against her warmth and she groaned in ecstasy, her fangs lowering. "I want to taste you this time," she breathed. At that moment, she could hear the symphony she would play for him, feel the way her fingers would press the viola strings, the way she would stroke them with her bow before she would let him glide slowly, deliciously, in between her lips, against her tongue.

He didn't hesitate as he carefully lowered her to her feet, their eyes meeting, something sparking. She was about to drop down to her knees, an act she thought she would never do with this male, when a sharp knock came at the door.

Ever froze and Chess growled in frustration but didn't tell her to ignore it. If it was important, then she had to take care of the matter. Yet disappointment stormed through her, her heart still pounding from what was happening between them.

She smoothed out her skirt and answered the door to March. His gaze narrowed as he glanced just past her to Chess, who was adjusting his trousers by the sound of the rustling.

"I'm sorry to break up whatever is going on here." March sighed. "But I have something important to show you, and it isn't good."

CHAPTER NINETEEN

CHESS

Fucking March.

If there was an award for impeccable timing, he would win, hands down. Chess scowled as he tucked his hard cock back into his trousers and adjusted himself as well as possible. There was no hiding the massive tent, but it wasn't as if March couldn't tell what he'd interrupted. The sweet scent of Ever's arousal filled the room from where she'd been rubbing herself up and down his cock. March had just apologized for interrupting a moment before, but he was a dirty liar.

Ever tensed. "What happened?"

"It will be easier to show you," the male said.

Ever nodded once and glanced over her shoulder at Chess. "Wait here."

Chess clenched his jaw. If there was a problem, he could help solve it, but she was the queen here. There would be things she had to deal with on her own that were none of his business and, as curious as he was, he had to accept that.

"Sure," he said with a sly grin. "We can finish what we started when you come back."

March clenched his jaw as he put an arm around Ever and ushered her out the door, murmuring that they needed to hurry. The door shut with a hard thud, leaving Chess alone. His lust was no longer an issue, but the image of Ever almost sinking to her knees lingered in his mind. He pushed the sensual budding image away—it was more important to deal with royal business, especially if Rav was on his way.

Oh shit.

What if it *was* Rav? Was Chess just supposed to sit around like a fool and wait for the bastard to storm the castle? He paced the room, his fingers flexing at his sides. Wait for Ever to be captured? Then find him lazing about in the bedroom as if there wasn't a care in the world?

"Maybe I should alert Mouse," he mused to himself. She loathed him the least and could pass the information along to the others. But what if it wasn't Rav? He didn't want to create a panic over nothing. Then Ever would be exasperated with him and her friends would trust him even less, if that were possible. There was only one solution…

Chess cracked the door open and slipped from the room. Fading footsteps came from the right so he sprinted in that direction, pausing at each corner to listen. His own steps were silent as he prowled closer and closer in the darker halls. They hadn't gotten as far as he expected which was odd. If March had something important to show Ever, they wouldn't have been taking their sweet time strolling through the palace.

Neither of them had spoken, but—finally—their steps increased with some unspoken urgency as they reached the first floor. Was there something he wasn't seeing?

"Out here," March said.

Chess pressed himself against the wall and peeked down the adjoining hallway. March opened the large glass door to a square courtyard. Ever stepped over the threshold, followed by

March, who conveniently left the door open. *Imbecile*.

Sneaking closer, Chess made out the details of the courtyard. An oval water fountain sat at the center—either not turned on or no longer working—and silver ivy climbed the walls to a terrace that ran around the second floor. Numerous flower pots were scattered across the brightly-colored mosaic floor, some broken, others turned over, spilling soil. Purple and ivory flowers still rested in larger pots, their leaves draping over the edges.

"What am I supposed to be seeing?" Ever asked, searching the courtyard.

March led her to the far side of the courtyard, drawing her closer. "Shh. I heard something."

Ever whirled around, scanning the terrace, but what March must've heard was Chess—though he hadn't moved then. Sighing, Chess stepped into the courtyard and shrugged, arms stretched outward. "Extra security," he purred with a smirk. Turning his gaze to the terrace, he did a quick sweep for danger, just in case.

Ever released a breath, shoulders relaxing. "I told you to wait in the room."

"And I decided not to listen," Chess cooed, sauntering up to the fountain and scooping out a handful of dead leaves, scattering them to the ground. "What's so wrong that couldn't wait until later?" He kept his voice light, curious, but a cloying sense of wrongness descended upon him. It wasn't the disrepair of the floral arrangements that had March's panties in a twist, so what was it? He rounded the fountain, trailing his fingers around the stone edge while scanning the space. Above them, the moon was bright, casting long shadows across the ground.

"Chess." Ever cocked her head.

"What?" he asked innocently. A shadow moved and his eyes snapped up. Was it the ivy moving? But there was no wind... "I think we should get back inside." Then, so as not to let March or any potential intruder know he was onto them, he added in a more serious tone, "And finish what we were doing before."

Ever's brow furrowed, ignoring Chess's innuendo per usual. "March, what's so important? Quit dallying around here."

The shadow slid along the wall, elongated limbs reaching out, creeping forward. It wasn't the ivy—ivy didn't bloody well have arms. Or *swords* for that matter. "Ever, now!" he snapped.

She blinked at Chess in surprise. March still held her elbow from when he'd guided her farther into the courtyard, tugging her closer. She scowled up at March, then her gaze flicked back to Chess and she opened her mouth to speak.

Before a single word could pass her lips, six figures dressed in all black leapt from behind the columns of the terrace. Swords rested in their hands and black fabric covered their heads so only the skin of their faces showed. Chess bolted toward Ever as they fell toward the courtyard in unison.

Horror painted her face when the intruders surrounded him, blocking him from reaching her. It was the only clue Chess had that he was completely fucked before a blade drove into his lower back. He stumbled forward and Ever struggled to pull herself free of March.

That bastard planned to have her killed.

Chess bared his fangs and punched the black-clad vampire in front of him. "Ever, run!" he urged as the others descended upon him.

The blade struck through his back once more, the agony spreading through his body. Again and again. Three, maybe four blades pierced him at once. An arm, a leg, his chest—all seemingly missing vital parts on purpose. He choked down the agonized scream. If they had wanted to cut off his head or slice through his heart, there was no doubt in Chess's mind they would've done it already.

Chess fell to his knees and another blade slammed into his calf, pinning him to the ground. "Fuck off," he snarled as they crowded him, blocking his view of the queen and March. "Ever!"

"Let *go!*" she shrieked. March released a harsh bellow the moment she finally tore herself free. The male directly in front of Chess was shoved aside and Ever ripped the sword out of his hand. She swung the blade, cutting off the male's head in one motion, crimson splashing the White Queen's face.

"Ever, stop!" March shouted.

Chess reached behind him for the sword pinning his leg to the ground, ignoring the other blades still shoved into his body. The taste of his own blood flooded his mouth and he spat it to the ground. This was going to hurt like a bitch.

The hilt of the sword was too high and too angled for him to reach, so he grabbed the blade. It sliced through his hand as he pried the steel upward. He ground his teeth against the pain radiating in his calf, yet it had barely moved at all before one of the attackers flicked a coiled whip toward him. The braided leather looped around his neck and the female yanked him forward. Chess gasped for a breath, but the whip was too tight for the oxygen to reach his lungs.

Ever screamed her fury wordlessly, backing toward Chess, holding her sword up in his defense. "March, what the fuck is this?"

"You were blinded by him," March said in a sympathetic voice. As if Chess had somehow manipulated her into giving a shit about him. "He's a danger to you. To all of Ivory. Your brother has accused him of murdering their queen and he needs to pay for that, at the very least."

"He didn't kill his mother!" she growled. "Now stop this."

"I knew he would follow you again." March stepped toward Ever and she pointed the sword at him so he held his hands up, placating her. "Don't you see how treacherous he is? If he'd listened to his queen's command, he wouldn't have walked into a trap."

"If *Chess* listened to me?" she screamed from where she stood in front of the prince. "*You're* not listening! Call them off."

The five assailants still remaining hadn't moved to further attack. Chess was pinned to the ground with a whip around his neck—trapped, his vision slowly growing fuzzy. They weren't sent to kill—they were sent to capture. He would be back in Scarlet tonight and at Rav's mercy. Ever wouldn't be able to stop this attack alone.

"What the actual fuck?" Ferris roared from the doorway.

"Bloody hell!" Maddie screeched, her violet curls bouncing as she pushed her way around him and raced to Ever's side. "We heard you screaming. What is this?"

The whip tightened and Chess swayed. *Fuck.* Far too many vampires had to be enjoying the sight of him so powerless. He clawed at the coil around his neck but it was too tight, biting into his skin.

"We didn't agree to fight the White Queen," one of the male assailants called to March. The others stood, stiff and ready to attack on cue from the one who spoke. Their leader, Chess assumed.

March scowled down at Ever and spoke to the leader. "Take him and go. No one will stop you."

"Like hell," Mouse chirped from the doorway. "No one deserves to be in the dungeons in Scarlet."

"Ever," Chess attempted to speak, but it was impossible. Darkness was creeping into his mind, his vision fading as Ferris stepped into the courtyard.

A moment later, a throbbing pain pulled Chess out of the darkness and he sat up with a gasp. Blood covered the mosaic floor of the courtyard. Ever was still before him with the sword, but March was now on his knees, head lowered. Ferris and Mouse were dragging a headless body toward the door and… Where the fuck were the rest of the attackers?

It hadn't only been a moment, Chess realized, though he had felt it was. He'd been unconscious long enough for five vampires to meet their demise—or flee—and March to surrender. He flicked his tongue against his parched lips and tasted his own blood.

A flash of purple approached from the side and Maddie bent down to speak in his ear. "I'm going to pull the sword from your leg now."

"Don't enjoy it too much," he said in a hoarse voice.

"Hmm." She grinned. "I can't promise that."

Ever glanced over her shoulder at him, healing scratch marks marred her cheek on one side, speckled blood on the other. Her breath came in heavy pants, but she offered him a weak smile anyway. Chess swallowed hard, bracing himself for the pain Maddie was about to inflict as she freed him. Guilt bubbled inside Chess. Ever's friend had betrayed her because of him, but March had never been a true friend if he was willing to do this. He hadn't wanted to be her *friend* at all. March wanted Ever as his lover, but Chess had taken that title as his own.

"Ready?" Maddie drawled.

He took a deep breath. "Not reall—"

The sword was yanked free and Chess cried out as a deep pain shot through him. Blindly, he fell to his side and rolled onto his back where, thankfully, the other weapons had already been pulled out. "Fucking hell," he grunted.

"You're welcome," Maddie sang. Then she tossed down the sword and approached Ever. "Are you okay?"

Ever's hands shook where she held the sword. "Is Noah still following the one who escaped?" she asked, ignoring the question.

"Yes, he'll catch him," Maddie assured her and motioned to March. "Do you want me to…"

"No." Ever drew in a shaky breath. "It's my duty to deal with traitors."

She was going to kill March. He deserved it, in Chess's opinion, but that would leave a mark on Ever. Killing friends always did. Not that Chess personally knew as he lived his life without getting close to anyone, but he'd seen it happen to those around him for centuries. Though she was killing him for betraying her, she could regret it later.

"Ever," he rasped. "Don't."

March's head snapped up to glare at him and Ever released a shocked laugh. "What?" she asked.

"Lock him up and think about this before you kill him," Chess urged. "He won't be any less dead if you wait a day or two. Besides, what if Noah doesn't catch up to the escapee? You should learn about everyone willing to betray you."

"I know my decision," Ever said. "Maddie, Ferris, can you please put March in the dungeon and I'll meet him there soon."

"Of course." Maddie took the sword from Ever and kept it pointed at March. Ferris walked around Chess and hoisted the male from his knees, leading him from the room.

Ever turned to loom over Chess, her hand gripping her hair. "Let me get you some blood before I have to deal with this. Wait here."

"This time, Queenie, I don't think I have any choice but to listen."

Ever shook her head and left him on the ground with only Mouse, who hovered near the entrance with the blue and yellow caterpillar in her hand.

"You all right over there?" Chess asked her. She had always been overly quiet when he visited, but it was no less worrisome outside of the dungeons.

Mouse met his gaze and something feral swirled in her eyes. "Hungry," was all she whispered.

CHAPTER TWENTY

EVER

The metal scent of the prince's blood permeated the air, but his wounds were slowly healing. He needed to drink to speed up the process, though. Ever handed Chess a basket holding a bundle of dried blood pouches and a couple of canteens. She then set the large jug of water beside him. He picked out a pouch and passed it to Mouse, who appeared hungrier than the prince did as she gnawed at her lip with her fangs. Ever studied the female for a long moment, but as her friend drank, a ravenous expression remained on her face. She wasn't certain how often Mouse fed when trapped in the Ruby Heart Palace, but it was clear that her friend would need a mortal to feed from soon.

In the distance, a blond head caught her attention. Noah. He picked up his pace and was beside Ever in only a few seconds.

"It's done," he said, chest heaving, his clothing covered in bright crimson. "I killed the last attacker and hid the body."

Ever didn't know Noah well, but she already liked him, as long as he treated Maddie like a queen. "Stay with them. I'm going to settle things with March."

Wiping her hands against her skirt, she headed inside the palace. She looped around the back, walking through hallway after hallway until she reached the ornate oval door leading to the dungeons. Her steps echoed down the stairs, the narrow walls seeming to close in on her before she came to the circular room filled with ivory cells. Above each one rested king and queen chess pieces that had represented the past royals before her. Ever had never removed them because she'd wanted parts of her caregivers to remain throughout the castle in their memory.

Maddie and Ferris stood near the back of the room, anger written across both their faces, her lips pursed and his set in a snarl. Ferris hadn't known March well, but Maddie had.

The cells here had never been filled like the ones in Scarlet—Ever's enemies were killed immediately and she didn't place humans in them either.

"Noah's back," Ever said, then glanced at Ferris. "I think you need to find Mouse a human to feed on. Sooner rather than later."

He bit his lip while nodding and slipped past her. Ever could see in Maddie's face that she agreed by the way her expression fell.

The Hatter handed Ever the bone key that usually hung on the wall. "I'll wait outside the door." She placed her palms on the queen's shoulders. "Be careful. I'm on your side, no matter your decision." Maddie was a good friend, ever since the day the Hatter had stumbled into Ivory, lost and broken, not knowing who Ever truly was.

"Thank you." Ever watched as Maddie shut the door, then turned to face March, who stood in the corner of the cell, his mouth set in a tight line. The only item in each cell was a dusty silver mattress on the floor.

Ever didn't say a word as she unlocked the door to his cell. She shut it behind her, this time prepared if he attempted anything deceitful.

March was the first to break the tense silence as his warm gaze latched onto her. "After everything that bastard did, we can't trust him."

"I know better than anyone what he's done, some of it right in my own garden, but I believe he can be trusted now or he wouldn't be alive." Ever took in a breath, flexing her fingers. "He didn't kill his mother." She wouldn't tell him it was Maddie who'd done the deed because that was irrelevant.

"It doesn't matter." March paused, his eyes pleading for something she couldn't return. "I love you."

Ever sighed, her heart lodging in her throat. "And I love you, you know this, but as a dear friend. Even when we pleasured each other, you knew this." She couldn't give him more now, just as she couldn't then.

"But this *bastard*?" March's fists clenched at his sides. "I've seen you with others, and I would be content if you were with anyone else. Forgive me if I can't get past him trying to murder you."

"It isn't something for you to get past or to forgive." She placed a hand on his chest, his heart beating rapidly against her palm. "It's for me. *My* decision. If he'd been the one to betray me before I got to know him, I wouldn't have been surprised, but it was you who did. The one male who was supposed to be on my side. You knew what I faced with my past guards, and yet—and yet—" she stuttered, fighting the emotion brewing in her chest. "You may not have physically tried to rip out my heart, but it was just the same."

"Rav doesn't know yet," he whispered. "I never would've risked him knowing you were here, alive. I only collected the few vampires who I could trust to bring Chess back to Scarlet."

"And what if Chess hadn't followed me outside?" She threw up her hands. "Then what? Would you have tried to play another game to see if he would listen?"

He hung his head. "No, they would've taken him from inside the palace."

"Damn it, March!" she snapped. "I wouldn't even give Chess a second chance if he'd done this tonight instead of you. How can I trust you won't do this again?"

"You can't. I trust you with my entire heart, but I won't ever accept him," March said softly, placing his hand against her cheek. "You made me a vampire because I wanted it. And I had asked because I loved you, even then. I left Wonderland to stop these feelings, yet in the mortal world, all those years away from you, I couldn't end the yearning. So kill me. Kill me before I make another mistake."

Her stomach sank, her eyes widening at his words, even though she'd been prepared to kill him if he'd forced her hand. "March, no…"

"Your mission is to let humans choose what they want. Do the same for me, and be the one to end my life. That's all I want."

"Is … is this what you really want?" Ever's heart pounded wildly, the blood rushing in her ears.

"It is." His voice was resigned, his shoulders falling. This was what he wanted, *needed*.

Taking a deep breath, she tried to steady her shaky hand on her friend's chest, his gaze fastened to hers. She didn't want him to suffer any longer, and perhaps it would've been better if she'd never met him, if she'd never turned him, yet she didn't want to take their friendship back. Because she did love him.

Tears slid down her cheeks, as he lowered his mouth to hers, a goodbye kiss that held everything they'd shared. Him dancing with her inside the palace, her walking with him outside in her garden, them laughing, sharing blood at the tea parties with Maddie and Mouse. So many blending together like a fading rainbow.

Then she thrust her hand into his chest, shattering his rib cage to get to his beating heart. A relieved gasp ripped from his throat as she tore the organ from his chest. She caught his body before it fell to the floor, then carefully lowered him to the mattress while she cradled his heart.

Ever didn't want to release it, and she held the organ until the warmth was gone, until *he* was gone. She wouldn't toss his heart down as though it meant nothing, so she tucked it back into his broken rib cage and kissed his forehead. Pressing her clean fingers into the pocket of her skirt, she fished out her lucky chess piece and placed it into his hand before leaving the cell.

Maddie stood outside the door, her expression solemn. "I'm sorry," the Hatter said.

"March wanted it this way." Ever wiped the tears from her cheeks. "Have Noah take his body to the mortal world. He would want the sun to turn it to ash instead of being buried here."

"We'll take care of everything. Go rest. You can't go to Scarlet like this."

Maddie was right. As much as Ever hated it, as much as she wanted more than anything to tear her brother apart, if she went like this, she wouldn't be able to save her kingdom or Chess's.

She nodded and headed toward her bedroom. When she opened the door, she found no sign of Chess, who was most likely still drinking blood.

Blood.

March's blood was still on her damn hands.

Stripping out from her clothing, she filled the bath and washed the blood from her body. Washed and washed until her skin was raw, until blood was no longer there. Tucking her knees into her chest, she sobbed, remaining in the water until it turned cold, just like March's heart had. She didn't even have an instrument to play her friend a goodbye song and that made her sob again, breaking her apart on the inside.

The door to her room opened and she didn't peer out into her space to see that it was Chess—she knew it was by his familiar scent, his movements.

"Are you all right?" he asked, stepping to the open door of the bathroom.

"No." Ever stared down at the swirling scarlet water.

Being Chess, he didn't leave her alone, yet stepped inside, their gazes locking. He was no longer covered in blood and ripped clothing but clean, his hair wet, his shirt off. The prince's wounds were still healing, pink lines decorating his skin.

"I killed him. He wanted me to," she whispered, trying to fight the uncontrollable sobs that still managed to escape her.

Chess didn't say anything, just scooped her out of the bath and held her to him. She cried into his chest as he took her to the bed and laid her down, covering her with the thick blankets.

"Sleep," he said softly. "I never promise anything, but I promise I won't ever betray you."

The prince lowered himself on top of the blankets, resting his back against the headboard. He ran his fingers through her wet hair, and Ever closed her eyes at the comforting touch. She then tried to sleep, even though the nightmares would take control, playing an angry melody inside her head.

Ever didn't know how long she'd stayed in bed. But it had been longer than she'd liked. *Days*. As she cracked open her eyes, Chess handed her a cool bag of blood. "Maddie got this for you, and Ferris was able to retrieve a human for Mouse to feed on." The prince wore one of Rav's old black vests, but it fit him better than it ever did her brother. It had been so long since she'd seen Chess in his usual style, but it suited him well.

"How is Mouse?"

He shrugged. "Not as hungry." *Good.*

"I'm surprised the others didn't give you a hard time for staying in here."

"What can I say? I do have an aura that makes everyone come around eventually, including a certain White Queen." He gave her a wide grin.

"You're so cocky." Ever rolled her eyes, then straightened, thinking about more important matters at hand. "Tomorrow morning, we leave for Scarlet. Only you and me. The others will guard here."

"Aw, you want to be alone with me some more, Queenie, is that it?"

"You're insufferable."

"Am I?" Chess arched a brow.

Holding the blankets to her chest, she leaned forward and grabbed him by the arm with her free hand. His lips parted in surprise as she pulled him beside her and pressed her mouth to the prince's. "Truly." Her forehead rested against his. Over the past few days, he'd stayed with her as she sulked, as she wept, and had brought her blood. It was different, and she couldn't thank him enough for sticking beside her.

He inched his body closer, capturing her lips with his, his tongue slipping inside, flirting with hers. Her heart accelerated, turning frenzied.

The kiss deepened, becoming more than the simple kiss she'd planned, and the way he was kissing her was different than before. He was gentle with her, his hands entwining in her hair. A heat spread through her, making her heart pound harder, thirsty for more, hungry for him. She pushed the blankets away, inviting him in. Her body was still bare from her bath, ever since he'd taken her from the bloody water and tucked her safely into bed as he guarded her, even though he'd been the one who had needed protection.

She unbuttoned his vest and drew it off. Her hand trailed down the length of his chiseled chest, taking in every sculpted curve. Her fingertips drifted to the laces of his trousers and loosened them, allowing him to shuck them the remainder of the way off.

Chess scooted closer, his lips slanting over hers, claiming them. Their bodies were now flesh to flesh, igniting a fierce warmth, not a single barrier between them. Ever rolled him to his back, trailing open-mouth kisses down his throat, his chest, his abdomen, then his thigh, wanting to explore every piece of him. Her fangs were eager to come out, and she sank them into his salty flesh, the way he had with her. She relished in the euphoric growl that escaped the prince as she tasted him, as her fingers skated to his cock and pumped him thoroughly.

While drinking in his metallic flavor, her body tightened, his growing taut. Ever released him, then slowly ran her tongue up the base of his length to the tip before taking him fully into her mouth. His hips slightly bucked in rhythm with her movements. She continued to lick, to taste, to stroke, to devour until he writhed beneath her, spilling himself onto her tongue.

With a smile after she swallowed, she glanced up at him, his yellow eyes pinned to hers, blazing with lust.

As they stared at one another for what seemed like an eternity, she knew this was what she'd saved herself for, *who* she'd saved herself for.

"I've never given myself to anyone," Ever breathed, "but I want to with you. It doesn't have to be today, it doesn't have to be tomorrow, just whenever you're ready."

In one swift motion, she was resting in his lap, a laugh escaping her as he purred, "Oh, I'm ready, Queenie." His lips crashed into hers, growing desperate, ferocious. She mirrored his movements, her hips rocking into his until he was hard once more.

Chess gently lay Ever on her back, kissing down her chest, her breast, flicking a peaked nipple with his tongue before sucking it between his teeth. Her back arched and her eyes fluttered at every single one of his licks, his touches.

The prince's fingers drifted between her thighs, circling her clit as he kissed his way to her ear. "Tell me if you need me to slow down," he rasped.

She cradled his face, bringing his mouth to hers again, never wanting it to leave. "Don't you dare. I want you inside me."

A wickedly delicious smile crossed his face and he did as she asked, sliding into her with one exquisite motion until she was full. It was harder than he would've moved with a mortal, but the perfect amount of force for what a vampire could handle. A slight ache burned, making her gasp, yet only for a moment before her body held a new sensation.

Chess's body shook as he slowly moved inside her, and she knew he was holding back, for her. "Faster," Ever said. She dug her fingers into his back and drove her fangs into his shoulder. In answer, his pace picked up, his thrusting growing harder, faster, exactly what she'd asked for and more. He was fucking her and she *liked* it, *loved* it. "More."

He flipped them both so she was in his lap, his fingers gripping her hips, then her arse, urging her to move faster this time, harder, while he sank his fangs into her neck.

The world was filled with music, as though all the musicians of the past and the present had come together, performing the loudest song she'd ever heard. One she wanted to be a part of, one she never wanted to end while it pulsed within her heart. And then the cymbals struck, a rush of ecstasy rolling through her, and she moaned Chess's name over and over again.

She rode him even harder, wanting him to feel the way she did. It only took a few pleasureful moments before he groaned, his sounds reverberating in the room.

Ever collapsed against him, their chests heaving. He wrapped his arms around her as he murmured in her ear, "Ah hell, Queenie. I suppose slow and gentle wasn't meant to be for your first time."

She smiled in the crook of his neck. "I wouldn't have wanted it any other way, Princeling."

CHAPTER TWENTY-ONE

CHESS

The scent of lilies greeted Chess as he stirred from sleep. A smile lifted the corners of his mouth before he opened his eyes. He shifted closer to Ever and inhaled deeply. Not only lily, but his pine scent mixed with the headiness of their late-night fucking. They'd stayed up nearly all day, exploring and enjoying each other's bodies. It wasn't until Chess was too exhausted to move that he'd drifted to sleep while Ever idly traced the lines of muscle on his stomach.

Chess cracked his eyes open and studied Ever's face. She looked at peace in a way she hadn't before, awake or asleep. She nuzzled closer and his heart thudded. The sensation of her skin brushing against his had his cock rising. She was so soft against him, so smooth. And she'd chosen him to give herself to. It was an honor he never thought much of before but, with her, it was different. After everything he'd done in the past for his mother, Ever had not only forgiven him, she'd *chosen* him. The sudden urge, that *need*, to be inside her again swept over him.

Chess rolled her onto her back and hovered over her, nipping at her ear to wake her. When she stirred, he ran his tongue along her neck and pressed a kiss at the hollow of her throat. Ever let out a small laugh, then spread her legs to allow him to settle between them.

"Good morning, Your Majesty," Chess whispered with a crooked smile.

"I could say the same to you," she replied, shifting her hips beneath him. "Is this how I should expect to be woken from now on?"

Chess's breath caught. Never once had a female expected him to linger before. Plenty of females had hopes of keeping him in their beds—for power or status or the multiple orgasms. Or all three. But he'd never wanted them for more than their bodies. This was different. Chess wanted Ever and that made him vulnerable. Honestly, he didn't hate that fact as much as he thought he would. Though how the fuck he managed to fall in love was beyond him.

"You should, yes," he said, lifting himself enough to look down at her. "Unless you object?"

"I certainly do not." She laced her fingers behind his head and drew him down to her.

Their lips met with tenderness, pressing softly, moving with reverence. Chess rubbed his hard length against her slick opening, eliciting a moan from his queen. He chuckled and trailed his kisses down her neck. Ever tilted her head back to allow him better access.

"Do you want me to bite you?" He nipped at her throat, but his fangs hadn't descended yet. "Or fuck you?"

"I think you know the answer, Princeling."

"Both then." His fangs dropped and he pierced her flesh at the same time he pressed inside.

A growl left him as his urges took over, sucking gently, fucking hard. She ground herself against him, met him thrust for thrust. Her moans were delicious, her fingernails biting against his back. *Fuck.* He wasn't going to last. Not when she was so fucking perfect.

"Chess!" she cried as her orgasm squeezed around him.

He pulled his fangs from her throat and kissed her fiercely as he came. Panting, he rolled off her a moment later and grinned. "It's unfortunate we don't have time to go again."

"It is unfortunate, but we would have to wait another day to murder my *beloved* brother…" She sighed and sat up. Chess's gaze focused on her flawless breasts and he fought the desire to lean forward, take a peaked nipple into his mouth while ravishing her with his fingers between her thighs. "We will have a concert to celebrate his death."

"Ah yes." Chess pressed his eyes closed for a moment before meeting her stare. "Shall we go kill the bastard then?"

Ever nodded silently. "Let's get washed up and say our goodbyes. I don't want to linger and risk him knowing I'm here. Surprise will be our greatest advantage."

Chances were high that *somehow* Rav already knew Ever had retaken the castle, but she was right not to want to wait. If Rav traveled to Ivory at the same time they journeyed to Scarlet, they might miss each other. The bastard wouldn't expect Ever to bring the fight to him after hiding away for nearly four years. While Chess knew she wasn't a coward, the rest of Wonderland wouldn't necessarily agree. They would remember a queen who'd fled her home, who'd abandoned them.

"I'll meet you here in thirty minutes," Chess said. That would be enough time to bathe and gather whatever weapons might be useful.

Ever slipped from the bed. He watched her arse as she walked away and gave a satisfied smirk. It quickly fell from his lips as he realized they were about to return to Scarlet. Where he was wanted for his mother's murder. Killing Rav wasn't going to make the accusation magically disappear, but it would be a start. If he made it that far…

Ever waltzed back into Chess's bedroom with a dark, curly wig on her head. She wore a clean pair of acid washed jeans and a plain black hooded jumper. Nothing she had on would draw attention, but she still looked delectable. The way her jeans hugged her thighs, the swell of her breasts beneath the jumper…

Ever cleared her throat. "Are you ready?"

Chess peered down at himself. Blue jeans and a white tunic weren't his style at all, but that was fine. He was trying not to be recognized and the black vest was too much of his signature outfit. "No wig for me?" he asked. As much as he'd teased with her about them before, he wouldn't deny wearing one now that they were going back to Scarlet.

"Sorry," she said, her lips growing into a wide grin. "We could give you a haircut before we leave. Maddie is quite talented with scissors."

"Something tells me different colored hair or a new style wouldn't make much difference," he admitted, slowly twirling a piece of his hair around his finger. Too many vampires knew him. Loved him, loathed him. No matter their feelings, turning him in now was likely to get them a huge bounty. Especially since Ever would be included in it. "I was thinking about how we should get to the Ruby Heart Palace."

Ever tilted her head thoughtfully. "Go on."

"Let's go back to the mortal realm and use the portal into the palace basement. No one will see us unless they're skulking around the park in London. And even if they are, the only ones allowed to use the portal into the palace are Rav, my—" He caught himself before he could include his mother.

"And myself."

The lower tunnels were always clear of guards because Rav didn't want anyone in his business, but past that point was where they lingered, prepared to throw anyone in the dungeon who ventured down. Any intruder would have their heart ripped out by his mother or become Rav's next experiment, which was enough deterrent to keep the castle safe.

"Great minds think alike." Ever trailed the tip of her finger across his bottom lip, and bloody hell, he wanted to suck on that too.

"Are you trying to take credit for my plan?" he asked with a chuckle.

"Technically it was my plan first—you just didn't know it yet." She laughed. "Now, come on before the mortal night fades."

Chess swiped his gun off the bed and strapped it to his boot, then followed her down the hallway. The others were waiting for them in the banquet room just off the main hall. Mouse was reading a Shakespeare play quietly to Des at the head of the table while Ferris and Noah played a game of cards. Maddie had acquired hat making material and the remainder of the table was strewn in ribbons and lace.

"Ever!" the Hatter chirped and held up a swath of sapphire satin. "What do you think of this shade of blue?"

"It's lovely."

Maddie nodded thoughtfully. "Mouse requested a hat that matched Des. I wasn't quite sure if this was better than the cobalt silk."

"The sapphire." Ever smiled at her friend, but it slowly faded from her face. Clearing her throat, she announced, "Chess and I are leaving."

"Only to kill her brother," he explained when the room remained silent.

Ever arched a brow at him, then looked to her friends once more. "I won't let Ivory be taken over again."

"We won't either. This is our home too," Maddie started. "But what about you, what if something happens to *you*?"

"We won't think about that now, will we?" Ever smoothed the front of her shirt and straightened.

"Do you need anything before you go?"

"Some blood, perhaps?" Mouse asked without looking up from the play.

"No, thank you." Ever cocked her head and smiled at Maddie. "Perhaps a hat for when I return."

"Ah, that I can do," Maddie sang.

Ever moved around the table to hug Maddie, then Ferris and Mouse. Noah, she simply ruffled his hair. "Stay safe."

Chess backed away from the room while they each offered Ever well on the journey and exchanged how much they cared. The emotions swirling in the air made his skin crawl. He never used to care if he had friends like that … or he hadn't *thought* he'd cared. Maybe he'd convinced himself he didn't need it, but seeing it now, he had to admit he wanted the same. Someone to miss him, to worry about him. Without all the verbalizing, of course—he didn't want to hear it, but *feel* it. Though, he supposed, he would need to start behaving slightly less like an arse for that to happen. He wrinkled his nose at the thought. *Not sure it's worth it.*

"I'm about to show you another secret portal, Princeling." Ever smiled, joining him in the hallway. "Tell anyone of it and you may lose a precious body part."

Chess perked up. "Go on."

Ever grabbed his hand and led him through the heavy front doors, into the dark, starless night. They paused on top of a large, silver stone medallion in the middle of the pathway. "Trace your finger over the crack in the wall."

Chess studied the castle entrance and found a fissure in the doorway. At first glance, it looked like a vein in the marble but now that he was paying attention, he could see it was more. He tilted his head and did as she instructed. The moment his finger reached the end, the floor shook. A rumbling filled the air just before the stone gave out beneath them. He sucked in a breath of musty air as they fell straight down into a portal, swallowed up by the silver, mirror-like surface, and were spat out in the middle of a cemetery.

The old, worn headstones were packed tightly together, some tilting, others cracked. Fog caressed the ground and an owl hooted overhead. Ever climbed to her feet and adjusted her wig. The corners of her lips curled in amusement as she cast a glance at Chess, who was still on the ground.

"You're not going to sit there all day, are you?"

Chess pried his boot from between two stones and stood, taking her chin between his thumb and finger. "You enjoyed that, didn't you?"

"I don't know what you mean." She grinned.

"You'll pay for that later." He chuckled and fuck it, he gave into quick temptation and drew her close, capturing her mouth with his. Just because he could. Just because he was the bloody prince of Scarlet. And just because he damn well loved her, even if she didn't know that. He'd bring her to the edge of pleasure again and again, and only let her fall off when she begged him for it. "Though, you'll probably enjoy the punishment far, *far* too much."

"You talk a lot." Amusement danced in her eyes, and he'd bet anything that between those pretty thighs of hers, she was aroused. "Lead the way to your portal into the Ruby Heart Palace."

Chess swallowed hard, knowing he needed to leave the distraction at this cemetery. There was no point in delaying the inevitable any longer. If his time was over, there was little he could do to change fate. He would die in Wonderland though—not in this forsaken mortal world. Wonderland was a brutal place, but at least they didn't hide that fact like the mortals did. As a child, he'd experienced more ill-intention hidden behind kind smiles than he'd care to admit. "Keep up," he said with a wink, and raced through the peaceful London streets.

Ever was right behind him the entire trip to the tree where the portal into the palace basement was. The entrance rested at the tree's base, hidden by leafy shrubs. She said nothing as he pulled aside the brush covering the opening and motioned her inside. Without hesitation, she hopped down into the hole. His pulse raced as he glanced over his shoulder to make sure they were alone, then he leapt down beside her.

Once they crossed into Scarlet, Chess would be hunted down like a bleeding human in a city of starving vampires. Ever, too, though she might be better at talking her way out of a death sentence than him. Rav might be willing to cut a deal with her with the right terms. But if they managed to kill Rav, Chess could live in relative peace … as soon as he cleared his mother's murder from his name, at least. He could easily blame his mother's servant, Rine, who had been dead in the same room, and claim he'd killed the female for the injustice.

"And the concert begins," Ever whispered to him.

He nodded.

They stepped through together and Chess drew in a deep breath. A mixture of scents—blood, hot summer air, and sulfur from the portal—filled him with a sense of home, but the Ruby Heart Palace didn't quite feel the same. The slate tunnels were so familiar yet less endearing.

"Are you all right?" Ever asked under her breath.

"Smashing." Chess swallowed hard as centuries of memories assaulted him. Some good, some bad. All tainted now. He led her down the black slate tunnel, then turned down another.

"Did ya hear that?" a bloke called from the far end.

"Hear what?" another male replied.

Chess froze. *Well, fuck me.* Rav had the guards in the lower tunnel levels now instead of at the top? What kind of shite was that? He glanced at Ever, whose fangs were already dropped, and he gave her a nod. They could easily take out two guards, then finish with their plan.

A loud sniff from the second guard, followed by an annoyed grunt as the strong sulfur smell must've reached them. "It's probably the king coming back," the first male said.

Chess's gaze snapped to Ever. Rav wasn't even here? *Bloody hell.*

"I thought he was staying in the mortal world for a few days." The male's voice jarred Chess's memory. If he wasn't mistaken, it was a vampire his mother turned about a century ago. *Michael? Micah?* Something like that. "Maybe he's coming back early with one of those groupies?"

"Nah, I overheard him mentioning Apex which is one of them fancy clubs."

"No shit?" The second sounded impressed, though given that Rav was king, it didn't seem that strange. "I've always wanted to go there."

Ever tugged at Chess's shirt and motioned for them to go back the way they came. He followed reluctantly. There was no getting in unannounced and Rav would simply find them when he came home if they didn't get out of the tunnel. If he had to fight Rav in the mortal world, so be it. At least he wouldn't have an entire palace worth of guards at his disposal.

CHAPTER TWENTY-TWO

EVER

Ever and Chess kept their feet light as they raced down the slate tunnels until they reached the portal. She hurled her body through, the barrier tickling her flesh, and stepped out into a small, dirt cavern. Six feet above her, moonlight shimmered down from a round opening. Chess stepped through behind her and lifted her by the hips without hesitation, thrusting her toward the mortal park. She dug her fingertips into the dirt around the edge of the hole and hoisted herself up. A grunt escaped her mouth—going up was more tedious than dropping down.

"I like my view right now, Queenie," the prince called up, and his smile translated in his tone. He said the most ridiculous things at the most inappropriate times.

Ever rolled her eyes as she threw herself from the hole, the fresh air hitting her nose. She stood and turned, smiling as she grabbed Chess's hand and drew him out. "Have you ever thought when we crawl out of these holes at night that we look like the zombies straight from the mortals' movies?"

"Ah, but aren't we the monsters of their movies?" Chess purred, brushing a lock of hair from her face. Her gaze focused on his gleaming yellow irises, and she remembered how he traced her entire body with delicate fingertips, how his lips moved slowly, *seductively*, up and down her flesh. How he thrust inside her from the front, from behind, then her riding him into bliss, him driving her into madness. She'd never felt something so … so … she couldn't grasp onto the words. Her damn fingers ached for a viola to draw the things from her mind.

Swallowing, she drew herself from those thoughts. "Some of us. But we need to get out of here before the guards investigate who used the portal."

"Those fools didn't sound the brightest."

She highly agreed with that statement.

The club awaited and more than a little blood would be spilled. Ever just prayed it wouldn't be her or Chess who ended up without their heads and hearts.

A bird cried out in the distance and the flap of another's wings tore through the air. The moon rested high in the sky, its color a pale silver as it cast its light upon the park. Ever and the prince jolted forward, barreling through the foggy area.

They wouldn't need to hail a taxi tonight since Rav's portal was an easy walking distance to the club scene. As they approached the road, a flood of cars passed, the night still being young.

Ever grasped Chess's hand and they continued at a casual pace once they reached the opposite side, as not to draw in any unwanted attention. Bright lights flickered from buildings just ahead, and chatting and music clashed together while they passed. She could pick out precisely who was going to the clubs by the flash of their clothing and the pep in their step.

As they turned down a sidewalk, a faded white building, covered in graffiti paintings, stood at the corner of the road.

This was it … the club the guards had mentioned where Rav was staying, though there were no guarantees he would be there. This wasn't a new club to Ever—this was where Rav had met Imogen.

Back then, they'd known of the Queen of Hearts, who she was, how she was married to a kind male. But this was where Rav had been lured in by her, or perhaps it was her to him.

The front glass door of the club opened and music boomed louder as two men, their arms draped around one another, walked out kissing while one reached for the button of the other's trousers.

If they couldn't find Rav tonight, then they would have to either wait here, go back to her brother's palace the following night, or go home. The last choice wasn't an option.

Chess held the door open for her and she walked inside, catching a whiff of blood, sweat, and something smoky. A tattooed woman at the front desk, wearing a black crop top, started to open her mouth when Ever met her gaze. She let her influence seep into the woman, grasping and tightening.

"Let us in," Ever demanded.

The young woman nodded, her red ponytail bobbing.

As they slipped through the hallway leading to the dance floor, the blood, as always, called to her, sending an intoxicating thrill deep into her bones, her marrow. Bodies gyrated around her, grinding, on the brink of pleasuring one another, but she didn't catch sight of white hair.

"I'm going to scout upstairs," Chess said. "Check around here for him, and keep your eye on the bar. He has the tendency to always show up near one."

"Be careful," Ever whispered. She didn't want to separate, but if Rav slipped past one of them, the other could catch him.

He winked and slinked away, his arse flexing against his tight jeans, just as Chess knew how to do best.

Pushing a lock of her wig forward, Ever covered her face a bit better while she searched the crowd. Blue and green lights flashed as a new hip-hop song poured out through the speakers. The club scene reminded her of the times she'd met March, but she placed the memories into a hidden box for now. He was gone because of her. *Because he'd wanted it*, she reminded herself.

Her gaze drifted through the crowd, searching, and found nothing. But then her heart picked up, her lungs pumping harder as she spotted someone who had once been dear to her. Farther ahead, near the edge of the crowd, long white hair wandered away, like a rabbit begging to be followed. Rav moved the same as he always did, silkily. She wanted to get Chess, but she also couldn't lose sight of her brother. Keeping her hand near the knife in her pocket, she broke through the crowd. She turned down a bare brick hallway, then another, finding two couples against the wall kissing, their hands roaming over each other's bodies.

Ever thought she had lost him, when her brother rounded the corner. Her shoulders fell—it wasn't Rav. The hair matched his, only it wasn't tipped with red. Something was off about him as he studied her with bright blue eyes and a knowing expression—he was a vampire, but that wasn't all...

Just as she drew out her knife, the couples—*vampires*—shoved off from the walls and locked onto her wrists, another with a blade at her throat. One of the vampires ripped the knife from her hand and Ever dropped her fangs as anger rolled off her in waves.

A mortal would've screamed. She knew what happened when one screamed while in the grips of a vampire—they wound up dead, and any mortals nearby would be influenced to forget.

"Rav's been looking for you," a female cooed, her dark braids pulled up into a bun atop her head. Ever recognized her as one of the females from the night she'd seen Rav at the club.

"Then take me to him," Ever demanded. She would try to find a way out of this, but if she didn't, at least she wasn't hiding away in a hole in the ground any longer.

The five vampires led her to the end of the hall and unlocked the door before bringing her down a flight of metal stairs. Blood and sex permeated the air of the room. The answer as to why came when her gaze drifted to three naked females wrapped around a male with white and red-tipped hair… Her brother.

"What is it?" Rav panted, his fingers digging into the waist of the female atop him, guiding her as she rode him, her breasts bouncing. The other two were taking care of each other, stroking between their legs, their opposite hand caressing Rav's arms. Ever wanted to spit in her brother's face.

"Seems we found a White Queen," the dark-haired vampire said.

"About fucking time," Rav groaned with ecstasy. "I'll see my lovely sister in a few moments."

Ever clenched her jaw, ignoring the sounds of her brother's growls, the females' moans. Once he shouted a long curse, he peeled his sweat-slicked body from the females to slip on a pair of leather trousers and approach her.

"I've been trying to find you for a very long time." Rav cocked his head, his brown irises pinned to hers. "Why would you stay hidden from your own brother for so long?"

"Stop with the games," Ever spat, the blade at her throat digging in further. "You turned my guards against me."

"It wasn't difficult." He shrugged. "You shouldn't have put your nose in Scarlet's business."

There was no use discussing how it was wrong to turn mortals without their consent. He knew her feelings on it, and he didn't give a damn. "If you're going to kill me, then just do it."

Rav removed her wig before patting her down, searching for her hidden weapons. He fished out the gun within her boot. As he lifted it, he glided a finger down the barrel. "Let me guess, you were going to try to shoot me from afar like a coward? Then rip out my heart? How cliché of you, sister." He swiped the tip of his tongue across his lower lip and chuckled.

She clenched her teeth. "Just repaying you for what you not only tried to do to me, but what you did to my viola."

"Ever, Ever, *Ever*." Rav trailed a finger down her cheek, drew close so his hot breath touched her ear. "I left you scraps of your instrument. I could've easily burned it. But I now know you reclaimed your palace, just the way I wanted."

She stilled, her breathing hitching. "What?"

"I knew once you heard word of Imogen's death, along with Mouse and Maddie now hidden somewhere, that you would come crawling out from your cowardly hole." He paused, his brown gaze boring into hers. "You're not the only one I want. I also want the one who has been obsessed with you. The bastard who killed my queen." Rav glanced past her, a vicious smile spreading across his face. "And right on time."

Two broad male vampires carried Chess through the door with three more females behind them. After murdering all his guards, it hadn't taken her brother long to find a whole new set.

Chess didn't show any of his cards as he smirked. "Pleasant seeing you again, *my king*." His eyes met hers and she looked away.

Rav ignored the prince, studying Ever with his lip curled in disgust. "I smell his arousal all over you. Chess has been obsessed with finding you for years. Honestly, his infatuation was ungodly. He killed Imogen after releasing Mouse to get you out of hiding. His obsession drove him to kill his own mother. *My* Imogen." Spittle flew from his mouth, red staining his face.

That was what her brother believed? He'd conjured up this reason for why he'd found Chess that day holding Imogen's bloody heart. She knew her brother's mind, when it got scientific, when it went elsewhere—he would build on a hypothesis and not shy away from it. In his mind, he was always right.

"I didn't kill her," Chess said through gritted teeth. Even now, after all they shared, she shouldn't have been surprised that he didn't confess the truth about Maddie, but she still was.

Rav continued to ignore the prince as he spoke to Ever, "I don't want you dead, sister. That's old news now."

What a pretentious bastard... "What do you want then? All you ever do is ramble on."

"Oh, Ever, you know I'll never stop that." He took a step back, fastening the button of his trousers. "You're my sister. You made mistakes. I made mistakes. We should make amends."

She wrinkled her nose. "Amends?"

"I'm uniting the territories and you will be my loyal subject, as it should've been to begin with. In the mortal world, I would've been the rightful heir. When we return to the palace, you'll have to earn your way back into my good graces. Be grateful—the little prince won't have the same chance as you."

She sucked in a sharp breath, but he continued, "I want my sister back. Do you agree to the terms?" His eyes, matching hers, stared at her, pleading.

Rav... He wanted her back as a sister? After everything he'd done? She remembered them as children, trading their instruments, laughing, playing, then as adults having tea with their parents, when they were mortal and everything was different.

Ever thought and thought, her mind spinning, her heart beating wildly, calming, focusing. "With pleasure," she finally said.

A shouted *no* poured out from Chess's lips, just before a female snapped his neck.

CHAPTER TWENTY-THREE

CHESS

A groan slipped from Chess's lips as he roused. *Fucking terrible nightmare.* Ever turning on him, Rav capturing him. His head throbbed with the aftereffects of having … died. *Fuck!*

Chess bolted upright, only to be jerked to a halt, his muscles aching. Metal cuffs bound his wrists over his head and heavy chains held his ankles in the lower corners of a table. If this were any other situation, he may have been excited to be bound, but then his predicament slowly sank in. "Oh, fuck no," he growled. Based on the stone ceiling and the blood splattering the walls, he was in the dungeon. Not to be unexpected, given the situation, but it was this particular table that had his pulse racing. He wasn't keen on the idea of having his limbs slowly torn off like the others who had been there before him.

"You're awake," Rav sang as he burst through the solid metal door and kicked it shut behind him. His white, red-tipped hair was pulled back in a ponytail and the sleeves of his black tunic were rolled to the elbow.

"You put me on the rack?" Chess seethed. "Is this the best you can do?"

Rav *tsked*. "We don't want to start with the big guns and ruin all the fun."

"I didn't kill my mother!" His roar echoed off the walls as he tugged at his bindings. Logically, he knew there was no getting out of them. Even if one broke, three more held him down. Rav would have the problem fixed before he could break free again. Same as it had been with other vampires Rav had toyed with in the past.

"There's no need to admit it." Rav strolled to the wheel positioned beneath the ledge of the table, out of Chess's sight, and gave it a turn.

The metal tugged at Chess's ankles. It wasn't painful—not yet. It was only a warning of what was to come when Rav inevitably stretched the prince's limbs to their breaking point. At least Rav wasn't using him in any of his science experiments at the moment. He'd seen vampires cut apart and allowed to heal around new appendages. Eyes plucked out, fucked with, and reinserted. Torture was definitely preferrable to any of that and the effects were only temporary.

"Don't you want to destroy who *actually* killed my mother?" Chess asked. He wouldn't give the Hatter up, not only because of how much it would hurt Ever, but because Maddie hadn't been the one to betray him. Ever had. He winced. *Fuck*. It didn't matter. For some reason, he still ... loved her. "It wasn't me," he said again, quieter this time.

"Chess." Rav chuckled humorlessly. "I walked in on you holding her heart."

"I picked it up, arsehole." He lifted his head and let it slam back to the table. "She was the only one who gave a shit about me—why would I rip out her heart?"

"Because I've always known you to be an ungrateful

bastard. And your mother? She said you reminded her too much of your father." He scoffed. "We should've ripped out your heart like we did him, but I'll remedy that soon enough."

Chess released an exaggerated sigh. "Yes, by all means. Use your toys. Break me apart. I still won't be guilty. Ask your sister—she knows the truth."

"My sister has agreed to align with me and believes you're guilty." Rav spun the wheel a few more clicks until Chess's joints were stretched, *burning*, then he circled the table in quick, predatory steps. When Rav stopped near the prince's head, he leaned down and whispered, "She's turned on you, it seems."

But she had claimed to believe him innocent. *No, she knew I was.* Maddie had done the deed… Which was why it made perfect sense for her to proclaim Chess guilty to Rav. Ever had betrayed Chess. Taken his heart and stomped on it. Perhaps it would've been better if he had remained alone and miserable. Whatever physical torture Rav planned to inflict was nothing compared to the invisible stake in his chest.

"Always the liar, you are," Chess quipped. "Given your exceptional skill, I would think you'd be able to tell when other people were being truthful or not."

A blade sliced Chess's cheek before he could even register one rested in Rav's hand. He hissed at the sudden sting, yet it didn't matter—he'd been through worse and it would heal in moments. The blade cut again, this time his neck.

"Before the fun begins, we need to bleed you a bit," Rav explained as if he were bored. "Can't have you healing too fast."

Starving while being wounded would be physiological torture. Each new cut or break would drive him closer to the brink of madness. Chess had seen a few torture sessions in the past and found them rather unnecessary. The repeated stabbings, acid baths, fang extractions… There was no reason not to kill them and be done with it. Though, he supposed, some did deserve it. The mortals who had mistreated him after his mother left for Wonderland would have earned themselves some time in this dungeon.

Rav began humming "Waltz Of The Flowers," starting the melody low then higher, a deadly edge to it as he cut and cut *and cut* again. Warm blood trickled from the slices, gliding over the skin on his face, neck, and arms. He fought against the bindings, struggling to break free, despite knowing there was no escape.

He would die there.

Perhaps not on the rack or even in the dungeon if Rav decided to make his execution public, but what did it matter? Ever betrayed him. His mother was gone. All of Scarlet thought he was a traitor and everyone in Ivory loathed him. He was alone for the third time in his life, and he wasn't sure if he had the same strength he'd summoned as a child. The same will to survive.

Fucking hell.

What was he thinking? Chess was *not* going to accept his own death. That was the heartbreak talking and that was not like him. A smirk tugged at his lips. All he had to do was wait until Rav thought he was weak enough to remove him from the rack. Once he was transferred to the next torture device, he would make his move. Kill Rav, find Ever… Deal with her somehow. He wasn't sure what he would do when he saw her again, if anything, but he would fight his way out of this damned place, fang and nail.

"You won't find this amusing for long," Rav warned. He stared down at Chess with a malicious glint in his eyes. Then he slit Chess's throat.

Chess tried to drag in a breath. Blood filled his mouth instead of air and it sprayed outward when he coughed, splattering across his face. The room spun, but not for long as he succumbed to his second death that day.

When he woke again, his throat was drier than chalk. Chess shifted on the table only to, once again, find himself strapped to the rack. How had he forgotten that bit? His shoulders ached from being stretched upward, while the metal dug into his ankles. The dried blood from Rav's cuts itched his skin. He let out a sharp breath and tried to focus on the stone ceiling, but the details were fuzzy.

Hunger consumed him, ravenous, as his head throbbed, his veins pulsing. "Fuck," he rasped.

The door opened as if someone had heard him speak. He rolled his head to the side expecting to see Rav returning for another bloody round. Instead, a female with vibrant red hair, spilling down her shoulders over a lacy black gown, approached. His heart leapt in his chest.

"Mother?" he croaked.

As she inched closer and leaned over him, her face took shape. It didn't have the familiar angles of his mother but was round, soft... Of course. Because his mother was dead. He squeezed his eyes shut and shook away the delusion.

When he opened them again, the female gave him a lopsided smile full of pity. "Sorry, Prince. It's just me."

"A—Anna?" he asked, barely remembering her name. She had been one of his mother's friends who lived outside of the inner city and only came to the palace for the parties. "What are you doing here?"

"Rav asked me to come," she said in a soft voice. "He wanted vampires he could trust around him after Imogen's death."

"Oh, right." Ari had mentioned that before he killed her. Chess tried to clear his throat, but the motion only made it worse. "I suppose you're here to exact a bit of revenge for yourself then? Should I be expecting all of my mother's friends to stop by?" Wouldn't that be just like Rav? To let everyone have a piece of the murderous prince.

"I hold no ill-will for what you did. We are what we are." She brandished a large ice pick. "However, I did come here to help Rav and I've been instructed to kill you again."

"Of course, though for the record, I didn't murder her." He grunted. "Before you carry out your orders, how long has it been?"

"Since they brought you here? Two days. Most of it, you've spent dead and bleeding." She patted the top of his head. "This should be the last false death for you. Next time you wake, I imagine you'll be weak enough for Rav to do what he wishes."

Torture him. Ruin him. Kill him.

"And Ever?" He swallowed deeply.

"The White Queen and her brother are getting along well. With any luck, they will unite the kingdoms in no time." She smiled as if Rav was actually doing something beneficial for Wonderland. Chess knew better—anything his mother's lover did was for his own benefit. But what was he getting out of reconciling with Ever? She wouldn't give him Ivory.

Shit. His mind was too muddled to think clearly. Who was telling the truth? He supposed it wouldn't matter once he freed himself and killed Rav. Then the only truth that mattered would be his own. All he had to do was hold onto enough strength. Not impossible… Not probable, but this was life or death.

"You better get on with it then," he said with a smirk.

Anna lifted the ice pick and adjusted her grip. "Apologies," she said and drove it into his chest.

It was the scent of blood that woke Chess next. Fresh, and from the source, based on the richness. His hunger roared to life. It clawed through him like an angry beast, demanding he partake in the feeding.

His limbs jerked against the chains as he lurched upward. A feral snarl ripped from his chest. Rav stood at the foot of the table, fangs deep in a mortal woman's neck. One of the slaves who stayed in a trance, Chess assumed. Their gazes locked and Rav smirked as he drank. A stream of crimson flowed down the column of her neck when she leaned into Rav's chest, her head thrown back in pleasure.

Chess pulled harder against his shackles, which, if he wasn't mistaken, had been drawn tighter. The pain radiating from his shoulder made him think it was dislocated already, but fuck if he cared. The metallic scent wafted through the air, caressing his nostrils, luring him in to the seductive odor. He zeroed in on the blood pulsing beneath the female's dark flesh. As his cravings increased, he would do anything for a simple taste, even if it meant gnawing off his arm.

"Now, brother. That's just selfish," Ever said from the doorway. Her white hair was carefully pinned like a crown around her head and she wore a stark white, formfitting dress that hugged every curve. His cock stirred in anticipation, not only for a meal but for a pleasureful fuck.

A hate-fuck.

Rav dropped his fangs, letting the woman slump to the floor with a dazed expression on her face. "Isn't it?" He laughed and turned to leer at Chess. "Come, sister." Ever stepped into the room, keeping her gaze averted, and up to her brother's side. He wrapped an arm around her shoulders and licked the blood from his lips. "Are you ready to dole out a bit of justice?"

Her gaze pierced Chess and his pulse spiked. A deep growl vibrated through the room as his hunger fed his fury.

"I am," Ever said, her lips curling into a vicious smile.

CHAPTER TWENTY-FOUR

EVER

"Stab him in the heart with this," Rav said, shoving a lock of hair over his shoulder. He then handed Ever an obsidian dagger encrusted in ruby jewels from his boot. "I think he deserves one more false death before we bring him to Imogen's gardens. I don't care how weak he is."

"Wouldn't want him to struggle even a little now, would we?" Ever grinned, taking the blade from her brother. She turned to Chess, looking straight into his yellow irises. He didn't say a bloody word as she drifted closer, rotating the dagger in her grasp while inhaling his pine scent. Lifting the blade in both hands, she plunged it directly into his heart with a sickening squelch, just as she'd always planned to do, right before ripping out his heart.

Only, Ever hadn't ripped his heart out as she'd dreamt about for almost four years. Not yet. Her pulse pounded feverishly, and the thought of what she'd just done brought her no pleasure, only a sickness swirling in her stomach. Yet she excelled at hiding her true emotions—that was what a royal was always taught to do. She continued to neutralize her expression as she wiped the prince's blood on the ivory skirt of her silk dress. "Now what, brother?"

Rav took the blade from her and shouted, his deep voice booming off the walls, "Guards!" The door opened to the familiar vampire with red hair, loose curls cascading down to her waist. Four other guards stood behind her. Lifting a long finger, Rav motioned at the female. "Anna, undo the traitorous prince's bindings." He stepped beside Ever, tucking the dagger back in his boot. "Now, sister, we need to discuss what will happen after the kingdoms are united."

Ever folded her arms, a line forming between her brows. "Are you going to continue the unwilling turning?" She knew if she agreed with him on everything, he would see through her. Rav was no fool though—that was why he'd kept her in the dungeon these past few days instead of allowing her to walk around the palace freely. While being held as a prisoner, she wasn't completely treated as such. She was fed properly, given new attire, and guarded by the red-headed vampire, Anna, who had remained silent, even when braiding Ever's hair into a crown. Even the blankets in her cell were made of silk while the other prisoners had none at all. Yet her brother had only visited her briefly each day since, she assumed, he was busy torturing Chess or fucking his female vampires.

"No," Rav finally answered. "I do believe if we are to start fresh, I'm going to have to make a change myself. Instead of turning mortals unwillingly, I will focus more on my sciences and toy with the humans, do more than leave them in a trance. Perhaps I'll come up with new theories and hypotheses about vampire creation and alteration. Maybe even *create* something new altogether." His eyes grew wild as they did when they'd been children, when he would experiment with dead animals.

Ever took a deep swallow. He was sounding positively

mad, like one of the doctors from a mortal's horror book. This was even worse than turning an unwilling mortal into a vampire.

Before she could speak, Rav snatched her by the wrist and drew her to him, squeezing her flesh roughly. "After Chess is murdered, you'll retrieve the Hatter and her sister, then bring them to me. The prince helped Mouse escape and that means you know where they are. They'll be executed next. We shall give them a swift death and then, finally, we'll hunt down Imogen's bastard Knave, for betraying her. Since we never found the newly-turned vampire he helped escape, we'll need to get her location out of him before he dies. Our slates will be wiped clean, and you and I will start anew." Rav's eyes beamed, a dysfunctional sort of gleam. He still didn't know that Ferris was connected to Maddie and Mouse, and he hadn't discovered that Alice was human again or Noah's sister either.

"The prince is untied, Your Majesty," Anna said, bowing her head before standing in line with the four other vampire guards.

Rav released Ever and grabbed Anna by the chin, inspecting her face. "I never noticed before, but you look a lot like Imogen, especially in that black dress. Tonight, you'll put on one of her gowns and stay in my bed."

"My pleasure." Anna bowed again, but Ever could've sworn she'd seen the vampire curl her lips in disgust. Ever continued to keep her expression blank as Rav hoisted Chess's limp and bloody body over his shoulder. Even though his only visible wound was the one she created, she would never forget hearing his growls of pain through the wall beside her cell as Rav tormented the prince. Ever loathed herself for not standing up to her brother sooner, for getting caught at the club before killing him.

The guards led them through the palace hall, two vampires in front of them and three behind. Several of the entranced human servants paced up and down the halls, causing Ever's chest to tighten. All the décor had been taken off the walls from when she'd been there last, and in its place were anatomical hearts, *hundreds*, painted across the entire surface. It looked more like an obsession than a decoration. By the fresh smell of paint, they were added not long ago. She was surprised Rav hadn't covered the walls in Imogen's portraits that the Queen of Hearts had commissioned to be painted every year. The palace's attic was full of the finished pieces, where Ever assumed they'd been collecting dust.

Over the past several days, Ever hadn't slept, not once. It had felt just as it had the last time she fled her castle, like she was powerless. As she mulled things over again and again while walking down hall after hall of anatomical hearts, she wasn't certain how to get out of this blasted situation, how to save Chess. Even if she were to confess the truth about Maddie murdering Imogen, Rav wouldn't believe it—he would think she was admitting that only to save Chess. At this point, she needed a damn miracle, and she didn't know if she would be blessed enough to gain one of those. What she did believe was that Chess would die hating her, thinking she'd betrayed him, and that she'd pleasured him just to get him in this position.

A stocky guard with blue dreadlocks opened the door outside. The warm breeze rumpled Ever's hair and dress as they trudged through the rose gardens. A whiff of the overwhelming flowery scent tickled her senses. Thick crimson vines, with obsidian thorns, wrapped around the gazebos, and near the one in the center, stood two vampire guards.

They stopped in front of the garden structure, dark red blood staining most of its gray color. By the rich smell mixed with decay, some of the blood was fresh.

"Tie him up," Rav demanded, handing Chess to two females. They grabbed the chains attached to the poles on the gazebo and cuffed his arms, then stretched out his legs to bind them to the chains at the bottom, his body appearing in the shape of a hollow star.

The prince looked pitiful, so helpless, nothing like his cocky self. "What now?" Ever asked, breaking the tense silence.

"Rouse him with your viola." Rav clapped his hands and Anna grabbed a brand-new viola from inside the gazebo, its wood-stained cherry red. Too beautiful. Too perfect. Too new. All it did was remind her of how Rav had broken her old one. Not meaning to, her expression slipped. Anna caught it before Ever masked it, but the vampire didn't say a word, only handed her the viola and bow.

"The prince has been enjoying 'Waltz Of The Flowers,' so let's give him what he wants." Rav grinned, his teeth bared wickedly in delight.

Focus, Ever. A little longer. But for how long? She didn't know what the hell would come after this. Her fingers trembled, yet she did what she knew how to do—she played, letting the notes flow from the strings, low and gentle, growing bolder, stronger, filling her heart, her blood, her soul. With everything in her, she tried to play it differently, so it wouldn't remind Chess of what he'd experienced while hearing it.

She didn't know how many times she'd played the song before Chess's eyes peeled open, his gaze meeting hers, no one else's. A smile tugged at his lips, then it fell away as he must've remembered where he was and everything that had happened to him. She didn't know all Rav had done…

The prince lifted his arms and they fell back into place. Even through his weakness, his usual smirk made an appearance. "What's wrong? Not ready to say goodbye to me yet?"

"You deserved everything you've gotten, you piece of shit," Rav spat, taking a leather holster of daggers from one of the guards and stepping beside Ever. "I was going to have my sister start with cutting off your legs, but I'm growing bored of your voice so we'll have her carve out your vocal cords instead." He paused. "Perhaps this first though."

A dagger tore toward Chess, whistling with the wind, before striking straight through his left thigh. The prince sucked in a sharp breath, then released a grunt as another pierced his right leg. Blood bloomed to the surface as two more cut through the air, each landing in one of his arms.

"Fuck you!" Chess snarled, his eyes igniting a fire of their own.

"Is that any way to talk to your king?" Rav taunted. "Your father loved you, you know. But he was naïve as fuck and believed your mother loved him. She was only ever with him because she conceived his child before marriage."

Chess didn't take the bait, only drew up his lips in a small smile.

Rav halted before throwing another blade. "I suppose I won't throw a dagger at your cock, but if you give me another one of your pathetic smirks, I'll rip it right off, Prince."

Ever had to think fast and think now. If she tried to kill her brother at that precise moment, the vampires would end her life before she could set Chess free.

"Now, forget the vocal cords, cut out the bastard's heart, Ever." Rav handed her the same dagger from his boot that she'd used on the prince earlier. "Once that's done, we'll drain his blood so I can use it in my lab."

Ever wanted to dig her nails into her brother, rip off his flesh piece by piece and use *that* for an experiment. Her lungs were thirsty for more air—she felt as if she couldn't breathe, but she kept it as steady as she could and nodded. She set down the viola, then padded toward Chess, avoiding his brilliant eyes so she could think, calculate.

Taking a breath, she stopped in front of him, finally peering up at his eyes. He watched her, several emotions burning there. Disbelief. Hate. Melancholy. But something else, something bright, strong, something like … love.

Trust me, she mouthed and stabbed him in the chest, the soft squish echoing. She slowly carved in a circular motion, tears filling her eyes while he groaned. A horrid thought washed over her because the next step was ripping out the heart. This was going farther than she could've ever imagined and time had run out—she couldn't think of a way to save him. Even though Wonderland depended on her, even though the vampires of Ivory and Scarlet did too, she wouldn't push herself to do the next step of this. Maddie, Mouse, Noah, and Ferris could continue what she'd started. If something happened to her, they could finish Rav.

Perhaps she was a coward.

Perhaps there were better vampires who could've been queen.

But she was who she was and that was what she'd come to accept.

Whirling around, Ever hurled the dagger, and just as it was about to penetrate her brother's heart, the vampire with dreadlocks jumped in front of him, blocking the blow.

That was her one chance, and she knew it had been a long shot. Ever lunged forward, fangs bared, but her brother was stronger, faster, knocking her to the ground on her back. A groan escaped her as pain radiated up her spine from the impact.

"You weren't supposed to do that, sister," Rav growled. "Perhaps you're just as obsessed with the traitorous prince as he is with you."

"No!" Chess croaked. "Don't hurt her!"

Rav slammed his hands on the sides of Ever's head, a pain shooting through her from his crushing. Then when her neck started to crack, a sharp cry ripping from her throat as she writhed, his body slumped on top of hers. Her brother's hands fell from her, and the world spun, but she didn't hesitate to shove the bastard's body off her. Ever pushed to her feet, ignoring the spasms in her neck as she stumbled, her wild gaze connecting with Anna's. The vampire's hand cradled Rav's bloody heart, a neutral expression on her face.

A slender female guard lunged forward, tearing Anna's throat out with her fangs, blood spraying across the already red roses. She tossed Anna's body to the ground, then spun to face the White Queen. But it was too late, Ever had the vampire's head between her hands, kicking her foot against the female's chest, and ripped it from the shoulders.

"Don't you dare touch the White Queen!" Chess spat to the rest of the vampires who stood there, watching, his eyes wide while Ever waited to see who she would need to murder next. "I'm your true king and I swear on all of Wonderland that you *will* obey me."

"Why would we obey someone who killed our queen?" a dark-haired male shouted.

"Bloody hell! For the last time, I didn't kill my fucking mother. The vampire who did it is dead and I didn't give her a pretty death either. Rav was a delusional piece of shit who lied to you. Things need to change around here and the White Queen and I will be part of that change," he panted. "Well, once she gets me down anyway." With how badly he needed to feed, Ever was surprised he'd been able to get all those words out and not faint.

The guards stood there, silent, questions swirling in their gazes, but they didn't make a move toward them.

"Get him some blood. Now!" Ever shouted, unsure if anyone would listen.

But then the male with dreadlocks stormed in the palace's direction, while Ever went toward Chess, not turning her back on the vampires as she removed each of his chains.

"I thought you betrayed me, Queenie," Chess whispered.

"I'm a pretty good deceiver, aren't I, Princeling?"

"Ah, I'm not sure you can call me that anymore since I'm king now." A smirk crossed his face, then his body slumped as she unfastened the last chain. She easily caught Chess, letting him lean on her as she brought them both to their knees, his chest heaving against her.

Ever wished she could've thanked Anna—she didn't know her at all, but perhaps she was tired of what Imogen and Rav had been doing too. Or perhaps it was something as simple as she hadn't wanted to dress as Imogen in Rav's bed. Whatever it was, she'd helped save Wonderland.

The guards continued to watch, their lips parted as they must've come to the realization that there was more between Ever and Chess than Scarlet and Ivory working together. And in that moment, she realized what it was too, what she'd been feeling.

Love.

"Ivory and Scarlet united," Ever called out to all who were listening as she held tightly onto Chess, protecting him fiercely.

"United," the guards said in return, sinking to their knees before them, their heads bowed.

It was a true start.

A new beginning.

In more ways than one.

CHAPTER TWENTY-FIVE

CHESS

The carriage clattered over the cobbled streets as it made its way out of Scarlet and onto the bumpy dirt roads that would take Chess and Ever to Ivory. It was not the fastest route nor the most comfortable, but it made a statement. Bringing out the royal carriage said they were in no rush. Just a couple of royals, traversing their lands in style, all while the grind of the wheels announced their presence and made it clear they weren't afraid of shit.

Two days after defeating Rav, both the King of Scarlet and Queen of Ivory needed all of Wonderland to know they were untouchable. Thankfully, Anna had been the one to kill the fucking bastard in front of witnesses, but Chess would never be free of suspicion over his mother's death—there would always be *someone* who believed the lies. He wasn't foolish enough to pretend that couldn't lead to problems in the future. And then there was Ever, who had hidden herself away for four years. Her reputation would be rebuilt, but it would take time and effort.

They had stayed in Scarlet long enough to send the enslaved mortals home and see Rav's body burn in a royal funeral, though he hadn't deserved it. Even Ever had appeared conflicted over the honor. The vampires in Scarlet seemed appeased enough afterward that Chess felt comfortable leaving guards in charge so he could escort Ever back to Ivory. As rightful heir to the throne, he didn't think anyone would try to steal it already, but he wouldn't risk an ambush as Ever left his territory. If he didn't see her safely back to her doorstep, he wouldn't be able to focus on a damned thing.

"We should've sent the carriage to Ivory without us in it," Ever grumbled as it bounced violently over a rock in their path.

Chess rubbed the side of his head where it had slammed into the carriage window. "I think we've earned a little rest."

After all, he had been starved, repeatedly murdered, and stabbed in the chest by the female he loved. As for Ever, she'd been a moment away from having her head ripped off by her brother, a moment where Chess had nearly broken apart. She'd played Rav as well as she played her instruments, and that brief time when he believed she'd joined her brother was almost as painful as the torture. The helplessness he felt toward the end, before Anna saved the day, still lingered. He imagined it would for a while yet, but he couldn't bring himself to admit that out loud.

Ever grabbed his chin playfully. "This is not restful, Your Majesty."

He chuckled and wrapped his hand around her wrist, drawing her closer. Their lips nearly touched as he nudged her nose with his. "I know more exciting ways to make the carriage rock."

"I thought you wanted rest?" she pointed out, arching a brow.

More than rest, he needed to get closer to her. To forget everything and focus entirely on the one good thing in his long, wretched life. Chess grinned and hoisted her onto his lap in one fluid movement. A beautiful laugh escaped her shapely lips, her deep brown eyes latched onto his. The skirt of her white lace dress rode up to her hips as she straddled him, her heat settling against his growing length. Fuck if he cared whether the coachman heard them or not.

"I do," he agreed and kissed her neck. His hands slid up her thighs and around to grip her arse. "But why rest when there is fun to be had?"

Ever tilted her head aside to give him better access to her neck. His lips roamed over her skin. One hand left her arse to tangle in her neatly pinned hair and the other tugged the top of her dress down her shoulder. He rained kisses across her collarbone, savoring her, and felt her center moisten against the fabric of his trousers. A low growl left him as he shifted to unbutton himself.

The carriage jolted again, sending Ever's chest straight into Chess's face. He looked up at her and smirked. "I rather like the carriage, actually."

"Hmm, you would," she whispered. "Though I must admit, it might have its benefits."

Her hands went between them to help pull his cock free. When her soft fingers wrapped around his length, he closed his eyes with a grunt. She pumped him slowly, sliding her thumb over his slick tip. Her touch was unlike anything he'd experienced before. She seemed to know exactly how to move, how fast, how hard, as if she were made for him. Perhaps she was.

"Damn, Queenie." He pulled her hand away gently when he felt his release start to build. As much as he would've loved to come, he had every intention of bringing her pleasure first. Quickly, he slid her panties to the side. Their eyes met and a sense of *rightness* flooded through him, making his pulse race.

"Chess," she pleaded.

"Go on then," he dared.

Ever drew in a sharp breath and lined his hard length up with her folds. Sinking down slowly, she shared her heat with him. When she'd taken him fully, Chess gripped her hips tightly to hold himself back. His body wanted to move, to please, but he gave her every ounce of control instead. Ever ground against him, shifting her hips in small circles. The most exquisite moan slipped from her mouth, and he growled in response.

"*Chess*," she breathed, this time against his lips just before she kissed him. Their mouths collided, their tongues dancing together. Ever wrapped her hands around the back of his neck and rocked her hips. Chess felt every inch of her as she moved languidly on him, making him practically vibrate with pleasure.

As the carriage continued to bump and jostle, Ever's pace grew faster, harder. Chess shifted his hips up to meet her, his heart accelerating with the friction. His breath turned ragged and he broke the kiss, trailing to her neck once more.

Fuck. He would never get over how perfect she was. How perfect she felt. Tasted. His fangs dropped at the memory of her sweet blood. She shivered against him as he dragged them along her neck, then moaned when he sunk them into her tender flesh. Her blood flooded his mouth and stars flashed behind his eyes while she slammed down on him again and again. When he pulled away with a deep breath, Ever smiled at him, her fangs on display.

Chess tilted his head to the side in invitation and held his breath in anticipation. The moment her fangs broke into his neck, he knew he wouldn't last. She drank deeply. Fucked beautifully. His heart nearly exploded with the combination of love, happiness, and utter bliss.

"Ever," Chess roared as his climax rushed through him. Ever cried out when she met her own pleasure, fluttering around his cock.

"Fuck," he breathed. "I love you, Queenie."

Ever settled her head into the crook of his neck, still drawing deep breaths. "I love you, King of Scarlet."

Hearing those words from her mouth was what he'd been waiting for his whole damn life, and he hadn't known it. "I told you that I know *many* ways to make this trip more exciting," he said, smirking against her ear.

She laughed. "Hmm, you may have to show me in order for me to believe you, *Your Majesty*."

"Naturally." He chuckled, and spun her around so her back was flush with his chest. Guiding her legs together, he widened his own. "Hold onto something."

The carriage slowed to a stop and Chess flicked aside the deep red curtains. The Ivory Palace loomed outside with its spires and parapets. Chess released a silent sigh. He wasn't ready to bid the White Queen goodbye yet—not ever. They would reunite, of course, but that didn't make leaving any easier.

"You're home," he sang, letting the curtain fall again.

"Already?" Ever shifted on the bench and patted at her mussed hair.

Chess chuckled. "You're a mess, my queen."

"I suppose I should thank you for that." She gave him a wink.

"No thank you necessary." He leaned over and nibbled playfully at her creamy neck. "I'm willing to repeat the process any time you wish."

She turned in her seat to face him fully and took his cheeks in her hands. "Soon."

Chess studied her face and found something he couldn't recognize there. He saw her affection for him, her love, but there was something else. Something he didn't like—not one bit. "What is it?"

"Nothing," she whispered.

"Liar." He nipped at her lips. "Tell me."

"It's nothing. Things just feel like they'll be different now." She rubbed her thumbs along his cheekbones. "So I suppose I'm soaking up the moment."

"I'm not leaving you," he insisted. "Things will be different, but that was the point of all of this, wasn't it?"

Ever nodded. "You're right."

Chess understood then that she was mourning her brother. Now that the danger had passed, now that she was back home, the reality was descending. Anna had murdered her brother and, while they both had needed the bastard dead, she had loved him once. There was no shame in it. He wasn't exactly looking forward to going back to Scarlet and picking up the pieces his mother and Rav had left. And to do it alone… At least Ever had friends by her side.

"Come on," he said gently. "Let's get you settled inside."

After a lingering kiss, he opened the door and held his hand out to help her down. She placed her hand into his palm and stepped onto the grass, sparing a nod to the carriage coachman Chess had commandeered from the garden at the Ruby Heart Palace. The main doors banged open and Maddie raced across the drawbridge with a wide smile, leaping at her friend in a flurry of purple fabric. Ever slid one foot back to take the impact. The two females wrapped their arms around each other and laughed. Chess turned away to give them their moment and found Noah, Ferris, and Mouse hurrying toward them.

"Ever!" Mouse said with a smile. "We were so worried."

"It's done," the White Queen assured them. "Rav is dead."

The group descended into conversation. Or more like an interrogation, as far as Chess was concerned. A thousand questions swirled through the air about what happened. Ever barely got the answers out before a new one was asked.

Chess made an exaggerated sigh and pushed his way back

to Ever's side to save her from an endless bombardment. "Enough with the questions," he said, rolling his eyes. "Play inquisition later after we've had a bath."

"Ignore his insufferable manners," Ever said, "but I do need a bath. We'll get into all the details tomorrow, Maddie."

"We'll have a tea party." Maddie grinned.

Ever laughed, then threw a wink at the foursome before heading toward the castle with Chess. "They just want to know what happened."

"And *I* just want to clean up in the bath, preferably with you." He kissed the top of her head. "Call me selfish, but there will be plenty of time to fill them in after I leave."

"Oh, you are certainly selfish." Her lips tugged upward at the corners. "But I'll forgive you this time."

"You better."

It wasn't until Ever was fast asleep after a bath, fucking twice more, and another, longer, relaxing bath, that Chess slipped from her bedroom. They had both needed to distract themselves with each other's bodies, but reality couldn't be avoided forever. Before he left to start things anew in Scarlet, he wanted to make the first step toward a life partially in Ivory.

"Prince," Maddie drawled when he poked his head into one of the drawing rooms. Her brow arched at the sight of him and Noah tensed beside her on a small settee. In front of them, a fire crackled, casting the room in a warm glow. "Where's Ever?"

"I'm a king now. And she's sleeping." He smirked, stepped into the room, and folded his arms across his chest. "I actually wanted to speak to you, Hatter."

She wrinkled her nose. "Why?"

"I was hoping we could have a civil conversation." He glanced at Noah. "Alone."

"Fuck no," Noah said.

At the same time Maddie let out a suspicious, "Ooo-kay."

"Maddie, I'm not leaving you alone with him," Noah whispered urgently.

"I'm *right* here," Chess scoffed.

"It's fine," Maddie assured him, although she still eyed Chess. "Could you please give us a moment?"

Noah hesitated, glancing between them, before stalking toward the door. "I'm waiting right outside. If I hear anything—"

Chess groaned his annoyance. "Yes, yes. If she screams, please do rush back in."

"You really shouldn't goad him." Maddie cocked her head. "It's very unnecessary."

"Many things are *unnecessary.*" He shuffled farther into the room and lifted a dusty book from the mantelpiece. "Yet, they are still done."

She leaned against the back of the settee and blinked, staring at him as though trying to read him. "What do you want?"

"To make peace. For Ever's sake," he added. He didn't give a shit otherwise. "It looks like we'll be around each other often, even if we both hate it. So, I figured, it might be beneficial to have more than a tentative agreement not to murder one another."

She shrugged, her fingers skimming the brim of her hat. "If it weren't for Ever, I would gladly use your skin as a pincushion."

He offered half a smile. "And I would strangle you with the ribbon from your own hat."

"That settles it then," she sang, a small grin on her lips. "You may leave."

He laughed, then quickly sobered. "I…" It was so easy to

admit this to Ever, but in this moment, he was exposing himself to someone he should hate. "I love Ever."

This time when she blinked, it was rapid. But then a huge grin took up her whole face. "The heartless prince somehow found a heart."

"Well, let's not go getting crazy now," he said with a raised brow. "I'm leaving for Scarlet soon, so I wanted to ask you to stay with her. I know you've likely got your own life to start now that my mother isn't holding Mouse hostage and—"

"I'm not going anywhere," she interrupted. "This was my home long before my cottage was, though I'm keeping that too."

Chess set the book down and held his hands up. "No one will touch it."

"Good. I had to leave behind many hats."

"I'm sure." He chuckled. "Ever is lucky to have you. All of you."

"We are lucky to have each other." Maddie waved a hand in the air and studied him. "Fine, *King*. You've talked me into it. We'll be friends."

"We'll be … friendly," he amended. Though he hadn't asked for friendship from her, he found he didn't entirely hate the idea.

She stood and offered her hand. "Ah, once you've had my special tea, you'll change your mind. Friends, it will be."

Tea sounded horrible, if he was being honest. It had never tasted good to him, but especially as a vampire. Still, he smiled and shook her hand. "Make sure your male gets the memo, yeah?"

"I'll pass it along, but I make no promises." She pulled her hand back and adjusted her hat. "Now if you don't mind, we were having a bit of a romantic evening."

Chess spun on his heel and slinked away. *There.* That was settled. He grinned at Noah on his way out of the room. "Do continue, lover boy."

A featherlight touch along Chess's nose woke him. He grinned, knowing without opening his eyes that it was Ever. "You should do that a bit lower," he breathed.

"Hush you." She laughed and playfully smacked his shoulder. "It's morning."

"And I must leave," he said, voicing the unspoken part of her sentence. He opened his eyes and stared up into hers. His reluctance to leave her was mirrored in her expression. "Though I'd much rather stay right here."

Ever smiled. "I'll keep the sheets warm for your return."

Chess rolled on top of her and kissed her fiercely. He really did need to get back to Scarlet but the longer their lips touched, the harder it was to pull away. In all honesty, he shouldn't have left immediately after Anna murdered Rav, and it was imperative he get back to stake his claim. Weed out traitors. Set new laws. He was exhausted just thinking of it all.

"I'll miss you," he mumbled against her lips. "But not for long."

She sucked in a breath.

"Because I'll be back before the sheets even have time to cool." He pressed a quick kiss to her forehead and slid from the bed before he could talk himself into staying a *little* longer.

"We'll both be kept quite busy," she offered. "Which means we'll be preoccupied."

Chess buttoned his trousers and swiped his vest off the floor. "Not preoccupied enough."

He put one knee on the bed and leaned over for one last kiss. Their lips touched, lingered, caressed, for only a moment, but Chess committed the entire feeling to memory. "You taste sweet," he said as he leaned back. "Stay here and rest. Don't see me out or I might change my mind about going."

Ever settled back into the soft pillows, only a sheet covering her naked body, and studied him. With her white hair tumbling over her shoulder, she looked every bit the goddess she was. "Be safe and hurry back."

"One week," he vowed. That was as long as he thought he could manage without laying eyes on her again. "Even if it's for one night, I'll be back next week."

Ever's eyes lit up. "If not, I may have to take another journey to the Ruby Heart Palace."

EPILOGUE

EVER

Ever paced back and forth in her lily garden, the trees around her blooming with bright silver and white flowers, as she glided her bow across the viola's strings. This time, she chose to play a modern song she'd heard in the mortal world at a club once, letting the bow kiss and meld against the strings, the deep notes surrounding her while she got lost in the melody's richness. She smiled at the way she was changing it to fit her own classical edge.

Two weeks had passed since a Scarlet vampire had ripped out her brother's heart, two weeks since Ever had realized she loved Chess, two weeks since they'd last brought each other to bliss, two weeks since he'd left the Ivory Palace, and two weeks that she'd missed the damn princeling with every aching fiber in her… Kingling just didn't have the same ring to it, so he would just have to get used to the nickname.

Some days Ever thought that perhaps, since they were kingdoms apart, Chess had concluded that he'd only wanted her because she'd been convenient. They'd needed each other to succeed before and now that they'd both gotten their kingdoms back, she didn't know if he'd changed his mind since he was late. Then she peered at the instrument as she continued to bring it to life through her movements, the song. The viola was a gift sent to her, an instrument that had belonged to the famous musician Carl Stamitz. It had been accompanied by a short note that still made her heart full.

Queenie,

I went to a lot of trouble stealing this from a museum. This may not be your first instrument, and I wish dearly that I could've mended the other one for you, but I hope this will please you.

Your Princeling

Ever glanced back at the palace, where Ferris was inside training the new guards she'd collected from the city. Ever still had to learn to trust the new staff, but they seemed relieved she was back in Ivory, that Rav no longer had control. Even the air had slowly started smelling sweeter as it once had, not stale and cold. The vampires of Ivory had been welcoming, bringing gifts to the palace, but she still feared they would always wonder if she would abandon them again.

Ever wouldn't. And she would continue proving it.

The song ended and she played another, this time "Clair de Lune," a slower classical piece that would never get old. Though her brother had to die, she still missed the damn bastard at times. Then she would think about what he'd done to Chess, as well as the harm she'd caused to the prince, and it made her heart plummet to her stomach.

But Wonderland would now become better because of all they'd faced, all that had happened. A piercing roar wailed in the distance, shaking the trees—the Jabberwocky. Fear crawled through her at the sound, and she stumbled over a chord. The beast had already been in Ivory before—what would stop it from returning? She prayed it wouldn't, but she would need to prepare in case it did.

Two arms circled her waist and Ever gasped, then she inhaled Chess's lovely scent. She returned to her song, creating music while he nuzzled her neck and pressed tender kisses just below her ear.

"You're late," she said, leaning into him.

"It seems Scarlet needed more help than I'd anticipated. Don't stop playing," he whispered in her ear, pulling her even closer so she was molded perfectly against him. Her breathing increased, her heart pounding in desperation for him, yet she finished the song for them both.

With a smile, she set the instrument down, then whirled around and backed him against a tree trunk. He looked like himself, his hair hanging freely around his chin and neck, his dark vest tight against his chest, showcasing each of his sculpted abs. It made her smile that he wasn't in hiding any longer, that she wasn't either. "It's strange, isn't it?"

"What is?" He brushed his nose against hers, his gaze hooded with burning desire that mirrored hers.

"You once failed to take my heart." She cradled his cheeks, a wary expression crossing his face as if he were worried she would break his. "Yet you ended up claiming it anyway. It's yours, Princeling."

Chess's body relaxed, then he grasped her by the waist and drew her to him, gently caressing her hip bone. "And mine is fucking yours." He smirked, his fingers deliciously skimming down her thighs.

"I'm tired of our homes being separate already. I wish you didn't have to leave." Ever turned in his arms and unbuttoned the first two buttons of his vest as he stroked her over her panties, sending tingles through her.

"You have no fucking idea how much I've missed you," he rasped.

Ever had thought about something else over the past two weeks, something that needed to happen. "My brother did have one thing right."

Chess stopped his movements and arched a brow, blinking as he waited for her answer. She knew he believed Rav had done nothing right, but there was a small seed he'd planted that had potential.

"To unite the territories." She unfastened another button of his vest, her lips tilting up at the edges. "I was thinking perhaps you and I could build a palace in the center of Wonderland?"

Chess chuckled, his familiar grin growing wide. "Queenie, are you asking me to be your king?"

She rolled her eyes. "You will forever be infuriating, but yes, I am. We can look after Wonderland together."

"I'm more interested in looking after you at the moment, but I agree." Chess hoisted her up, her legs wrapping around his hips. He took them to the ground, sitting with his back against the tree.

"Good." Ever pressed her forehead to Chess's, her gaze locked on his as they studied each other, taking in this moment, *them.*

As she skimmed her fingers down his chest, a strong metallic scent filled the air. *Blood.* Ever leapt from Chess and whirled around, her fangs exposed.

A small form walked through the garden, her dark dress billowing in the wind—bright crimson painted nearly her whole body. Even her pink hair was mostly red.

Ever took a deep swallow. "Mouse?"

"Are you all right?" Chess asked, his voice concerned as he moved to stand beside Ever.

Mouse's lips were drawn into a tight line while she held her caterpillar close. "I did a very bad thing. Don't tell Maddie."

Did you enjoy Chess?

Authors always appreciate reviews, whether long or short.

Want more Vampires in Wonderland? Check out Book Three, Knave, in the Vampires in Wonderland series!

He's tortured. She's broken. Together they must face the most legendary beast of all.

Ferris didn't hesitate to leave behind his mortal life as a drummer. Not when it meant rescuing the alluring, pink-haired vampire who saved his life years ago. But now that they're both free from the Queen of Hearts, an unexpected emotion is surfacing—lust.

Mouse fled the mortal world centuries ago after a heinous event nearly destroyed her. She would never have guessed that her new life would take a monstrous turn once away from the Ruby Heart Palace. But now her thirst for blood is all-consuming.

Seeking a way to destroy the Jabberwocky seems like a good way for Ferris and Mouse to focus their energy, but the danger only heightens their mounting sexual desire.

A desire that needs to be sated.

TURN THE PAGE TO READ THE FIRST CHAPTER OF KNAVE!

CHAPTER ONE

FERRIS
BEFORE

Do something enough times and the body remembers. Brushing teeth, putting on a shirt, tying a shoe—all of it was accomplished without thought. For Ferris, that list included playing drums.

One. Two. Three. And four.

He counted beats in his head, even though he didn't need to. It was just something to fill his thoughts as his arms moved across the drum set in front of him. Sweat dripped down the back of his neck, and flashing lights illuminated the bar. Dozens of people crowded the stage, rocking out to the loud music. The heavy drumbeats, the quick guitar notes, the screaming vocals.

One. Two. Three. And four.

The heart-pounding song poured from him in sync with the

rest of the band, Death Remedy. Perfect. Well-practiced. All body memory and no conscious thought. Without his arms knowing the movements, the beats, he wouldn't be able to play anymore. His mind was numb. Empty. Except for the counting…

One. And two. Three. And four.

Ferris's lifeless eyes followed the studs on the back of the lead singer's jacket as he moved energetically across the stage, riling up the crowd. The man had to be sweating his nuts off since Ferris was in a tank with torn-off sleeves and still dripping. Dark hair fell across Ferris's slick forehead and stuck, whereas Oliver kept his short, so at least he had that going for him.

That and the lack of anxiety over getting another hit. Oliver had been suspicious that something was up with Ferris and had searched his stick bag earlier, discovering the dwindling coke stash. Ferris had hidden it in there before the show, deciding to wait until after the gig to take more and relying on hard liquor to get him through the performance. There would be a fight later. Another one. Which only made Ferris need the high all the more. Needed it so he could fucking forget. Forget *everything*.

What the fuck did Oliver care anyway? Ferris had his addiction completely under control. It was *fine*. He just needed something to take the edge off the pain. His bandmates didn't understand—*couldn't* understand. And they were no saints either. They'd all experimented at some point and he'd never given them shit.

One. Two. And three. And four.

Shit. That was wrong. Lucas, their bassist, shot him a sideways look as Ferris stumbled to catch up with them. Maybe he needed to stop counting and just let his body do all the work. Let his mind shut down.

Ferris squeezed his eyes closed. If only it were that easy. Thoughts circled through his brain endlessly, reminding him, blaming him. That was what the drugs were for: *forgetting*. The cymbal *crashed* against his stick and he flinched.

Images of *that* night came between flickers of the strobe light. Metal crunching. Tires squealing. Flashing blue police lights. Blood. Everywhere … blood. The heat of it streaming down his forehead, into the corner of his right eye. And—

The drumsticks fell from his hands. "Fuck!"

"You okay, mate?" Lucas asked as his fingers kept plucking the string of his bass. Oliver's singing never faltered and Johnny didn't miss a chord on his guitar.

Ferris could barely hear the question over the music. Or perhaps it was the ringing in his ears. The phantom *whoop whoop whoop* of the ambulance as it took away everything important to him. He turned his head just in time to avoid puking all over his snare.

Lucas jumped back as the vomit splattered the stage next to the bassist's custom rainbow-checkered Vans. "Ferris! The fuck?"

Ferris shoved up from his stool and tripped, falling forward. He crashed into the drums, sending them flying, and slammed face first on the old wood floor. The song screeched to a halt. Every eye in the godforsaken room landed on the drummer, the silence deafening, as he struggled to get back on his feet. Embarrassment flushed his face. *Just fucking perfect.* Oliver met his gaze, his eyes hard. Ferris winced.

"Fuuuck," Ferris groaned when he was finally standing again, swaying. He reached for something to steady himself, but found his crash cymbal. The moment he put weight on it, the metal tilted, dumping him back to the floor again.

"Shit," Johnny said as he hurried to catch him.

And failed.

Ferris rolled onto his back and closed his eyes with a disgruntled *hmph*. He could hear his friends now—*loser!* And his family—*such a disgrace!* First, he'd gotten Ellie pregnant before marriage, and now he couldn't function without shooting up. He couldn't function *with* the fucking drugs either. He was too far down the rabbit hole and there was no climbing out. He didn't *want* to climb out. But this… He closed his eyes against the shame and let himself pass the fuck out.

Whomp, whomp, whomp. Ferris groaned, clutching his head as his pulse thrummed in his ears, echoed in his mind. The sounds of the bar boomed, muted, through the walls of… Where was he? Squinting, he took in the off-white metal interior of the van plastered with different band stickers. The band name *The Swingers* carved into a pineapple, a red snake circling a skull, an angry, zombified teddy bear, and on and on. Collected from all the bands that Death Remedy had played with over the years. Some from concerts he and his friends had been to before they'd became popular. And, now that they were popular, the band was phasing Ferris out.

"Fuckers," he wheezed. His band members had dumped him in the back of their van and… He listened harder. And went back to playing? The twats. "See how good you are without a drummer, arseholes," he shouted to the stickered ceiling.

Rubbing his face, Ferris forced himself to sit up, kicking empty beer cans away. His palms were sweaty, hands shaking, and he ground his teeth against the urge to scratch his face. He needed his fix *now*. Oliver could go fuck himself. Except… *Damn.* His stick bag was inside with the rest of the equipment.

He stared at the stickers above him and focused on the one of a penguin holding an iced coffee. Stars rested in its overly large eyes and a smile lingered on its beak. *Ellie.* His girlfriend had been just as excited, just as happy, as that stupid bird.

About nearly everything. It was what made Ferris fall in love with her when they were sixteen and stay in love with her for the last four years. Her optimism was contagious, her smile more addictive than the drugs his body now craved. If he could, he would trade anything to hear her laugh again. Give up his damn soul to bring her back.

But he couldn't.

No one could.

Because she was dead. And their unborn daughter had been ripped from the earth along with her.

Ferris and Ellie had danced in the rain on their fourth date, then cuddled in the van when lightning struck at the park. She'd seen the band's paltry sticker collection at the time and fished out the penguin from her purse. When he'd asked her why she was carrying it around, she said she'd bought it on a whim that morning. Where she randomly found it was a mystery and he regretted not asking her, not that it really mattered. He was sorry he hadn't asked a million things over their three-year-long relationship. Little things he would never know now, things that anyone else would call irrelevant. But when someone died, *everything* was relevant about them—it was just too late to realize it.

Pressing the heels of his hands against his eyes, Ferris willed away the building tears. It had been eleven months since the accident. The one where *he* had been driving. Where *he* hadn't swerved in time to avoid the car driving down the wrong side of the road. Eleven months and thirteen days.

Every day since had been a complete and total spiral into hell.

"Damn," he croaked.

He needed to get high before his thoughts went any further. Like to the list of baby names in Ellie's handwriting that he still carried in his wallet even though they'd eventually decided on Luna, or to the plant she'd kept in their shoddy flat that was now withering because he was apparently shit at keeping anything alive.

No. He scrambled to unlatch the back door and flung it open, practically falling to the pavement. Drugs were exactly what he needed to forget *them.* The fact that they were gone. He needed—

"Ferris!" a deep masculine voice called.

He squinted down the alleyway, catching sight of someone he'd painted houses with a couple years ago. Roger? Or Richard? Something like that. He looked the same as he did back when he was sacked for showing up to a job while tripping. Ferris grinned.

"Hey, man." He stood up straight and smiled. *Raymond!* That was it. "How you been?"

"Good, good," Raymond said. "Looks like you're having a rough night, though. Did you hit your head up on stage?"

A wave of shame washed over Ferris but vanished as quickly as it had come. "Nothing a little pick-me-up wouldn't fix."

Raymond smiled knowingly. "I thought as much. You got cash?"

Ferris stumbled up to him, hands shaking with need, and cast a quick glance over his shoulder to make sure they were alone. Pulling his wallet from his back pocket, he drew two fifties out—his last banknotes—and handed them over. "What will this get me?"

"What's your poison? Pills? Powder?"

"Coke." Ferris licked his lips, aching for a hit.

"For a hundred?" he asked, brow raised.

"Come on. As you said, it's been a rough night." First Oliver finding his stash, then the stress of the impending fight, and the whole falling over his own drums…

Raymond studied him for a moment. "I've got something new tonight. Not sure what it's cut with, but it should do the trick."

"I'll take it," Ferris blurted. As long as it made his mind

shut the fuck up.

His old acquaintance dipped his fingers into his pocket, taking his sweet time as Ferris's heart beat anxiously, then reached out to shake hands. "Have fun, mate."

Ferris glanced down at the bag of white powder. His needles were in the stick bag, but that was fine. Tapping a messy line out on the back of his hand, he quickly snorted it, then repeated the process. The burning inside his nostrils faded to numbness. Ferris sighed, eager for the full effects of the high to kick in, and stumbled through the backdoor of the bar.

The world spun for a moment. Florescent lights in the hallway became starbursts and it felt as if the ground tilted beneath him. Ferris collapsed to the dingy floor with just enough time to realize how badly he'd fucked up.

Soft lyrical voices drifted around him. Dreaming. Dying. Images of Ellie floated across the back of his eyelids. Her long blonde hair danced around her oval face, her dark eyes glittering as she smiled. She cradled the baby bump that grew beneath her shirt and held her hand out to him. He stretched to grasp it…

Pain lanced his arm and he tried to pull back, but couldn't. His fingers twitched, unable to reach Ellie with his free hand or move the other away. A scream built in the back of his throat, trapped, captured by his unconsciousness. Then the pain faded. Pleasure replaced it.

Every inch of his body hummed with life. His skin tingled, a warming sensation spreading through him, through every cell, just right. He imagined himself floating. Up, up, up. Toward something better. Something sublime.

The smile fell from Ellie's face and the image of her blurred. Faded. Disappeared. He fought to pry himself away from the pleasure clouding his thoughts, anchoring him. To follow Ellie and their daughter.

Let me go, he pleaded.

Let him join them, wherever they may be. He wanted the

pain to stop, to end it all. Overdosing like this had been an accident, but maybe it was for the better. Then he wouldn't be such a burden to everyone around him. He wouldn't have to suffer this loneliness anymore…

Come back, he begged Ellie. *Don't leave me here without you.*

"Is it working?" asked a woman.

An intense pressure came against his arm as someone sucked. He gasped and his eyes fluttered open. The pale-yellow walls were bright, too bright, around him. The tiles too hard. His arm lowered on its own.

No. Not on its own. Someone gently placed it on his stomach and patted him. "There now, you're all right."

Ferris forced his eyes to focus. A woman leaned over him, her head haloed by the ceiling light, her face in shadows. He dragged in a ragged breath. The woman shifted to where her face was visible. Delicate features with a spattering of freckles across her nose and cheeks. Violet eyes and soft lips. A pink plait draped over one shoulder. He'd never seen anyone so beautiful before … so *inhuman.* Perhaps he was dead after all.

"Are you an angel?" he rasped.

The young woman blinked, a smile slowly spreading across her cheeks. "Me? Gracious, no."

Ferris sat up slowly, his head throbbing, body shaking. Another figure with purple curls and a bowler hat atop her head moved behind his angel. The second woman looked similar, except her features were a bit sharper. A sister, maybe. "Looks as if this is your lucky night," she sang, grinning as she adjusted her hat.

Sure, if bad luck counted as luck… Ferris thought for a moment, letting what had happened sink in. He'd had a horrible reaction to whatever Raymond sold him, had been dying, had *wanted* to die for a moment. Because Ellie was… He swallowed hard. Somehow, he was awake now. Not only awake but clear headed.

"I…" His body ached with a soreness that ran bone-deep. "I think we have different definitions of *lucky*."

"He looks like a newly-hatched baby bird." The purple-haired one poked his arm.

"At least he's sober now," the angel replied.

Sober. When was the last time he'd been that way? *Eleven months and fourteen days ago.* "I don't understand." Ferris lifted his arm, his gaze locking onto two puncture wounds with a trickle of blood running from each. What kind of strange ass shit were these two into? "The fuck?"

"I drank the poison from you," the angel said softly.

Did she say *drank*? As in pierced him with something, then drank his *blood* to sober him up?

"Good thing, too. You'd be dead if Mouse hadn't found you." The purple-haired woman waved her hand in the air.

Dead. Yes, he'd been dying, but hearing someone else speak the word was jarring. Ellie and their daughter were gone, but he wasn't ready to join them. Not really. Not yet.

The angel—Mouse—knelt beside him, a comforting gardenia scent drifting around him. What sort of name was Mouse, anyway? As she leaned in to whisper, Ferris forgot the question. "You look as though you need a friend. And perhaps I can help you, if you help us. If not, I can make you forget."

Ferris arched a brow. He wouldn't easily forget this night, no matter how much coke he snorted in the future. "What do you mean exactly?" The ache in his temples throbbed harder, distracting him from gathering proper thoughts.

A faint smile twitched at Mouse's lips as she drew closer, caressing his ear with her voice, her warm breath brushing his skin. "You want a high and we want to feed. So would you like to make a deal with a vampire?"

ALSO FROM CANDACE ROBINSON

Wicked Souls Duology
Vault of Glass
Bride of Glass

Marked by Magic
The Bone Valley
Merciless Stars

Cruel Curses Trilogy
Clouded By Envy
Veiled By Desire
Shadowed By Despair

Faeries of Oz Series
Lion (Short Story Prequel)
Tin
Crow
Ozma
Tik-Tok

Demons of Frosteria
Frost Mate (Prequel Novella)
Frost Claim

Cursed Hearts Duology
Lyrics & Curses
Music & Mirrors

Immortal Letters Duology
Dearest Clementine: Dark and Romantic Monstrous Tales
Dearest Dorin: A Romantic Ghostly Tale

These Vicious Thorns: Tales of the Lovely Grim
Campfire Fantasy Tales Series
Between the Quiet
Hearts Are Like Balloons

ALSO FROM AMBER R. DUELL

The Dark Dreamer Trilogy
Dream Keeper
Dark Consort
Night Warden

Forgotten Gods
Fragile Chaos

Faeries of Oz Series
Lion (Short Story Prequel)
Tin
Crow
Ozma
Tik-Tok

Darkness Series: Temptation
Darkness Whispered

The Prince's Wing
When Stars Are Bright

Vampires in Wonderland Series
Rav (Short Story Prequel)
Maddie
Chess
Knave

Once Upon A Wicked Villain
Spindle of Sin

ALSO FROM AMBER R. DUELL

The Dark Dreamer Trilogy
Dream Keeper
Dark Consort
Night Warden

Forgotten Gods
Fragile Chaos

Faeries of Oz Series
Lion (Short Story Prequel)
Tin
Crow
Ozma
Tik-Tok

Darkness Series: Temptation
Darkness Whispered

The Prince's Wing
When Stars Are Bright

Vampires in Wonderland Series
Rav (Short Story Prequel)
Maddie
Chess
Knave

Once Upon A Wicked Villain
Spindle of Sin

Acknowledgments

Thank you so much for journeying with us through Wonderland once again! Chess gives you a smirk while Ever plays her viola.

This vampire world has been a blast for us to write! And there are so many amazing people that helped shape this story! Thank you to the editor, Brandy, for making this story even better!

To Amber Hodges, who has been incredibly wonderful to us! Jerica, for always supporting us! Elle, for helping us through another series! Hayley, for your superb British wording! Ann, Vic, and Lindsay, who scavenged quick fixes for us!

Our families who continue to support us through this emotional writing journey, you rock! And now, are you ready to read Ferris and Mouse's friends to lovers story next?

About the Authors

Candace Robinson spends her days consumed by words and hoping to one day find her own DeLorean time machine. Her life consists of avoiding migraines, admiring Bonsai trees, watching classic movies, and living with her husband and daughter in Texas—where it can be forty degrees one day and eighty the next.

Amber R. Duell was born and raised in a small town in Central New York. While it will always be home, she's constantly moving with her husband and two sons as a military wife. She does her best writing in the middle of the night, surviving the daylight hours with massive amounts of caffeine. When not reading or writing, she enjoys snowboarding, embroidering, and snuggling with her cats.

www.ingramcontent.com/pod-product-compliance
Lightning Source LLC
Chambersburg PA
CBHW021316190726
48288CB00003B/859